KARIN BIGGS

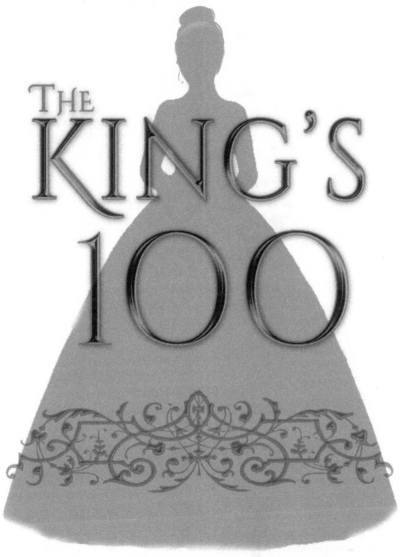

THE KING'S 100

Immortal Works LLC
1505 Glenrose Drive
Salt Lake City, Utah 84104
Tel: (385) 202-0116

Cover Art by Ashley Literski
http://strangedevotion.wixsite.com/strangedesigns

ISBN 978-1-7349046-5-9 (Paperback)
ASIN B08BJQ18XG (Kindle Edition)

For Tony

CHAPTER
1

I handled my relationship with my sister the same way I handled a glass microscope slide—with as few fingerprints as possible and an irrational fear that one misstep could shatter everything. As I neared her office door, I found the hall of our compound to be void of patrol officers. A friendly voice served as the only sound, talking to me from speakers embedded inside my ears. "Princess, it's time for you to review your match details. The queen sent me an alert to remind you."

"Thanks, Chip. I just have to show her something first."

A blue glow emanated from the underside of my left wrist as Chip processed my words and communicated with my sister's own Bio-System. "Dottie informs me that Queen Evelyn is currently busy."

I sighed. "Chip, she's always busy." My fist tightened around a folded card that confirmed a hypothesis I'd held since our parents' deaths. I hoped it was the evidence Evelyn needed to finally initiate the formal investigation I had been requesting for years.

"Princess, your heart rate has accelerated and you're not participating in aerobic activity. I suggest you return to your room to review your—"

"Chip, do me a favor and go silent for the next twenty minutes or so, okay?"

"Yes, Princess."

The metal door slid open as a service droid exited Evelyn's office. I took a deep breath and stepped through the threshold before it closed again. "Your Majesty," I said to my sister, tilting my chin to my chest.

"What do you want, Piper?" she asked. Her office smelled like copper and mint. Two large computer monitors lit her pale face and white-blonde hair, while she sipped on her afternoon cup of peppermint tea. The zipper of her grey vest touched the tip of her chin, although the cooler autumn temperatures had yet to arrive in our kingdom.

I straightened my back. "I thought your points last night about the new drone technology were exceptionally valid, considering the ambassador's counter."

"You're interrupting me for a compliment? In case you haven't noticed, your queen is quite busy. On top of needing to finalize this contract deal for the ambassador of Brumitas, I was informed that one of our security gates is down for the next twenty-four hours." Evelyn glared at something on her monitor as her fingers punched the keyboard.

I rubbed my thumb over the edge of the folded card. "Oh...which gate?"

"That's confidential."

"Yes, Your Majesty. And I'm sorry to disrupt you, it's just...well, this." I held out the white card and waited a few more keystrokes till she took it out of my hand.

She squinted as she read the hand-written message. "'Your mother is alive and living inside the Mondarian king's Mansion.'" She huffed and handed the card back to me. "It's a sick joke."

"I considered the possibility of it being a fallacy, but what if—"

Evelyn groaned. "I thought you were past this, Piper. It's probably just another taunt from your *incident*."

My *incident* happened three years prior when I lost control of my emotions and sobbed at my parents' End of Life Ceremony. The repercussions of the unacceptable behavior followed me through the years in the form of medication with unsettling symptoms and handwritten notes, stating my inability to represent Capalon as royalty. Most of the writers chose to stay anonymous, while others had no qualms signing their name and ward.

But the note in my hand was oddly specific, as opposed to a generic insult of my weak mind. The previous evening, I had prepared myself for another long sales meeting with our kingdom's top innovators and foreign representatives, when I noticed the card tucked under my dinner plate. "I just thought we could have a chemist in the Science Ward look at the paper and ink. Maybe they could confirm the origin of the paper and—"

"Piper," said my sister with a steady tone, "If Mother or Father were alive, I would be elated because I'd be free to complete my research on solar photovoltaic technology without any concern for the state of our kingdom's budget or trade relations with our allies." She pushed the keyboard under her monitors and lifted the steaming teacup to her chest. "You're the princess of Capalon and you're about to be matched to a boy who will be the prince. As royalty, we're supposed to be perfect role models of innovation and concentration. But our citizens already know about your infamous meltdown, they've caught on to your wild notion that mother is still alive and there have even been rumors about your...*singing*." She said the last word in a whisper as if our Bio-Systems broadcasted our conversation about my shameful activity across the kingdom.

I bit the inside of my cheek to fight off the embarrassment creeping up my neck. I thought I had been doing a good job of hiding my disgraceful affinity for singing. But once again, I was wrong. I was always wrong and Evelyn was always right. There was a reason she was queen, and I was Capalon's royal failure. Capalon wasn't the greatest kingdom in The Lands because of singing and crying, but because of our citizens' ability to cut out distractions from their lives and concentrate fully on innovation in their respective Science, Technology, Engineering and Mathematics Wards.

Evelyn sipped her tea, then shook her head. "What kind of example are you setting if you continue this kind of behavior? You need to pay attention to the things that matter, like your match details."

Unlike most kingdoms, Capalon didn't fall victim to the distracting illusion of love. We knew the truth—that love was just a word given to the release of various chemicals in the brain which could easily be ignored with dedicated practice. Instead of forming unions based on love, Capalon pairings occurred through matches of intellectual test scores. And as the Capalon princess, I had the honor of being matched with the highest-scoring male in my age group to continue the family lineage of the smartest minds in the kingdom. No other matches could take place in the kingdom until the completion of my match ceremony on my seventeenth birthday.

I nodded. "You're right, sister. I'll open my match details as soon as I'm back in my room. I apologize for disturbing you." In need of something to calm my tense muscles, I took a couple small steps to the corner of her desk, where my sister kept a vial of my mother's scented oil. It was strange for any Capalon to hold on to a keepsake from a deceased family member, but I knew Evelyn only held on to it for me. She pretended to get a call or read a memo on her computer screen so I could inhale the remaining mix of peppermint, lavender and lemon, before she chose to continue or end our conversation. The indigo vial was the only reminder I had of a person who slipped farther away from me with the passing of each day.

"Are we finished?" asked Evelyn, signaling the end of our unspoken ritual. "I need to complete this contract before I leave tonight."

"Yes, Your Majesty." I tilted my chin down, then exited her office.

Once in my room, I fell backward onto my bed, preferring to stare at the white tiles of the ceiling as opposed to my windowless, grey walls.

Why did I think Evelyn would see any truth in the note?

It had been nearly three years since our parents' speedcraft crashed along the northern tip of Mondaria. The day after the crash, Evelyn became queen and a month later, her match became the new king. For Evelyn, my parents' deaths sent her into an unwavering sense of duty and power. For me, their deaths released all the unacceptable emotions and actions I had been taught to suppress, hide, and ignore since birth.

As Capalons, we believed firmly in facts and the fact remained that patrol officers recovered my father's body from the speedcraft accident, but not my mother's. Evelyn trusted the accident report stating Mother's body had been destroyed in the flames, while I trusted my anecdotal gut feeling that she was alive.

I shut my eyes and pressed open palms against my eyelids, hoping to dissolve the morbid image of my parents' demise from my mind, but like normal, it refused to budge until I found something to take its place. "Chip, open my match's...on second thought, don't do anything."

I reached under my bed for an indestructible black box intended for protecting physical copies of research reports. But rather than filling the box with important documents, I used its protection to hide Mondarian artifacts I had collected over the years from the creek near our Compound. If anyone ever discovered my abhorrent collection, the accusatory notes of my inept mind would triple in volume.

As a child, I would have been punished through the Capalon tradition of Focus—marathon sessions of seclusion in my windowless room to learn self-discipline through breathing. I should have been awarded a Token of Achievement for the amount of time I had been forced to endure in Focus for things like singing, tapping my leg or lagging behind on test scores. We were taught to be thankful for any opportunity to improve our minds, but my gratitude was routinely suppressed by the heavy weight of isolation. My only reprieve from the unsettling loneliness of Focus came at age nine in the form of my Bio-System, giving me a forever companion within my own body.

After the installation of Chip, the torturous threat of seclusion in Focus eased with the option to play math games, listen to archived research studies or guess my health-stats.

But even with the companionship of Chip, nothing compared to time with my Mother and sister. When my father was away, my mother led us down to the creek and allowed my sister and me to perform any unacceptable behavior we pleased—spurred by her belief in a healthy cleanse of the mind. My mother's scent mixed with the smell of creek water, the sound of Evie's laughter and the feel of my facial muscles pulling my mouth into a wide smile. If I had been gifted the option to choose my location for Focus, it would have been in the creek where my fingertips grazed not cold, windowless grey walls, but soft, mossy earth under a ceiling of treetops and never-ending sky.

I unlocked the box's heavy lid and removed a few of my favorite artifacts, which included a purple polka-dotted sock, a green and red jeweled pin in the shape of a tree and a cracked plate with an artistic depiction of a boy playing in snow.

My fingers moved on to my most recent find—a red card with Mondarian citizen information for a girl my age named Paris Marigold. I wished I could communicate to the girl in the picture to ask her if she knew anything about my mother and why she was smiling.

I set down the girl's card and picked up my favorite item—an antique voice recorder with only one recording I had left untouched for nearly three years. Taking a deep breath, I pressed the 'play' button.

"Say something," said my happier, younger self.

"That's an object of our enemies, Piper! You should toss it back over the gate so it can be destroyed."

"Oh, come on, Evie! Say something. Anything."

"Fine. Piper Parish...is an ignoramus!"

The recording stopped in the middle of our howling laughter. I found the recorder a few weeks before our parents died, during a time when I could already feel us becoming two completely different people. Where Evelyn stayed short, I grew tall. Her hair kept to a wavy white-blonde, where mine darkened to a stick-straight dark-blonde. She took pride in winning research debates and I celebrated a day without being punished for humming in the labs. The precious stolen moments with our mother in the creek decreased as we grew older, loosening the thread that held us together. The day my parents died, Evelyn unraveled, and I was no longer viewed as the little sister she could laugh with in secret, but as her greatest source of disappointment.

I dropped the recorder and chewed on my thumbnail.

Evelyn deserved a sister who could be the princess the kingdom needed—a girl who reviewed her match details without hesitation, ignored any and all distractions and hid her unnecessary emotions.

Evelyn deserved better.

And I was so tired of being seen as Capalon's problem princess.

I can do better.

Hairs raised on the back of my neck as my adrenaline spiked. Maybe our relationship needed my behavior to improve to bring back our days of laughing in the creek. And if I put my wild ideas about my mother behind me, maybe I could finally move on and make my sister proud.

Excited with my new burst of determination, I hopped up from my bed and marched back to my sister's office, passing a waste-droid in the hall. "Chip, ask Evelyn for permission to enter."

The door opened and Evelyn greeted me with an eye roll. "What now, Piper?"

I held my head high and spoke with conviction. "Your Majesty, I just wanted to say I'm sorry about the note and about everything—the singing and my erratic emotions included. You're right. If I'm going to be matched soon, I need to take my role as princess seriously and..." My eyes settled on a newly empty corner of Evelyn's desk.

Following my eyes, Evelyn cleared her throat. "I just deposited Mother's vial into the incineration chamber of the waste-droid. I can't help but feel it's been partially my fault for allowing you to have unnecessary emotional attachment. But if you're serious about your previous statement, then you'll agree that this is the best move for you and for Capalon."

My throat swelled and my heart rate increased.

Terrified of the truth behind my sister's eyes, I took a step back toward the door. "Yes," I choked out. "I want to do what's best for Capalon."

Evelyn continued to speak, but I sank into an emotional pool of water, hearing only muffled sound and losing my source of oxygen.

I nodded to my sister's inaudible words, then exited her office without a formal goodbye. I needed a private space to hide before the unacceptable emotions took over. The thought of my windowless room constricted my lungs, so I headed to the skybridge and took the elevator down to ground level.

"Princess Piper, you're heading outdoors," Chip said. "Would you like me to clear all citizens from your path so you can enjoy the benefits of a brisk walk without interruption?"

"No." Citizens in my vicinity didn't need to be alerted that the princess would pass them at a dead sprint.

"May I call a hover pod for you?"

"I just...need to get...to the creek," I said between heavy breaths as I pushed my way through a sea of grey-clad citizens and my feet pounded against a cushioned walkway. The ground switched to the leveled grasslands of the Field, where a group of primary level citizens gathered around surveying equipment. A young girl spotted me and pointed. "Innovator Harris, isn't that Princess Piper?"

I didn't wait to hear Innovator Harris's response and entered a dense line of trees, then hopped down the bank of the shallow creek. When my feet met sand, I bent over and rested my palms above my knees. "Chip...talk me down."

Blue light emitted from my wrist. "Princess, inhale on one, two, three four and exhale on one, two, three, four."

Breathe. Focus. Breathe.

With Chip's assistance, my breathing calmed but the anger in my chest roared with an untamable fire. I picked up any small rocks I could get my hands on and hurled them as hard as I could down the creek. I blamed my mother for causing me to be a poor excuse for a Capalon princess.

She was the one who embraced us and touched our cheeks when mothers were instructed not to show physical affection to their children. She was the one who sang to us in the creek and encouraged us to search for Mondarian artifacts when Father was away. And she was the one who told me I had a gift through my voice and to never stop using it.

My mother, the queen of Capalon, was defective, and I wished I could eliminate her from my mind as easily as Evelyn had. But it had taken me nearly three years to finally admit to myself that I would *never* move on until I knew for sure that my mother was dead.

The tears won their battle against my eyelids as I picked up my fifth rock. I hurled it at a tree branch, scaring a bird into a wild flight for safety. I blinked through my clouded eyes as I watched the bird land on a flat surface behind the tree. It puffed its vivid-red chest and ruffled its ink-black wings as it sent out an angry call. Normally my eyes would have been transfixed by the bird's bright color, but they fell to its new resting place—one of the gates in our security wall.

Birds avoided the security wall and its scorching invisible forcefield that ran along the top, which meant—

The broken gate.

The boulders in the creek served as a crossing path as I bounded up the creek bank to get a closer look. After the bird flew away with a frantic call, I tossed a rock over the top of the gate to test my observation. A nervous jolt shot through me when it landed softly on the other side. The neurons in my brain jumped together to form a lightning-powered idea.

I could do it.

I could leave Capalon over the dead gate and search for my mother in Mondaria.

The idea scared me, sending me back into a tree. I picked at the bark with my fingertips as I processed the possibility and inhaled the scent of dry, autumn leaves. For years I had pestered Evelyn with my hypothesis that Mother was alive, only to be consistently turned away. I never considered the option to take the investigation into my own hands.

The security wall served the purpose of keeping our citizens inside the perimeter of our kingdom in addition to keeping our enemies out. Capalons were never permitted to leave the kingdom, aside from the queen and king and invited innovators. The world beyond our walls was too dangerous and filled with distractions, germs and evil people who wanted our innovative secrets. One kingdom even held a mandate for the right to kill Capalons if found on their land—that kingdom was the only place in The Lands where it snowed, the least technologically advanced, home to the king who could be holding my mother captive and most importantly, our one and only true enemy.

I removed the note from my pocket.

Your mother is alive and living inside the Mondarian king's Mansion.

Maybe whoever left me the note knew I was the only one who would be willing to leave Capalon to search for her. I had Paris Marigold's identification card and the dead gate. I just needed to make a few alterations to the card and scale the gate before it was fixed within the next twenty-four hours.

"Princess Piper, your sister will be visiting you in your bedroom in fifteen minutes. Would you like me to call you a hover pod to make it back to the Compound in time?"

I wiped my shirt sleeve across my cheeks. "Yes."

Chip's voice reminded me I would need to find a way to go offline if I didn't want my every step traced by Patrol, landing me back in Capalon before I could even set one foot in Mondaria.

But how? The only way to operate offline was with voice permission from the king or queen to switch to manual-operation. And there was no way Evelyn would ever give me permission.

The hover pod returned me to the Compound in half the time it took me to run to the creek, so I examined Paris Marigold's identification card, which sat on my bed with the other Mondarian artifacts. I would need to find a photo to replace her brown eyes, brown skin and brown spiral hair.

My metal bedroom door slid into the wall before I placed all the forbidden items back into the box. I sat rigid on the bed, blocking the items from view behind my back when Evelyn stepped into my room.

"Piper, about mother's vial—"

"It's okay," I said with a forced cheerful tone. "I need to move on and eliminating the vial was the proper thing to do."

She nodded and stepped deeper into my room. "I also wanted to confirm you've reviewed your match's details before I leave the kingdom."

"No, I'm sorry. I haven't—"

"Haven't what, Piper? Had the time? You've been too busy sneaking away to the creek to practice your forbidden singing?" She crossed her arms and leaned against my worktable. "Honestly, Piper, I don't know how to get you to—"

"What I meant was...I haven't received your formal permission." My dry throat attempted to swallow as my thumb slid over the voice recorder behind my back.

"Formal permission?" Evelyn scoffed. "You don't need my formal permission. I've been asking you to do this for days! But if that's what it takes to get you to follow my request, then so be it. Permission granted by Queen Evelyn Elaine Parish of Capalon," she said with punctuating movements of her hands. "Happy?"

"Yes. Thank you, sister. It's just...I think that's what Father would have done."

Evelyn rubbed the bridge of her nose and closed her eyes. "Piper,

I think it's time to talk to the pharmaceutical lab again. Maybe they can give you something stronger."

I nodded. "I'm willing to do what's best for Capalon."

Her eyes focused on mine and for a moment, I thought she might close the distance between us and offer me an embrace, but she pushed herself off my worktable and headed to the door. "I have to go. I'll be back tomorrow night. Send me a memo when you've reviewed your match and I'll set up a time for the three of us to meet."

"Yes, Your Majesty. Safe travels."

The door closed behind her and I hit 'stop,' then 'rewind' on the recorder. Evelyn's voice emitted from the small speaker. *"Permission granted by Queen Evelyn Elaine Parish of Capalon."*

Maybe I was suffering from mental weakness. Maybe my sister was right that I needed a more powerful medication to avoid the temptation of singing and crying. And maybe I was crazy, most of all, for believing that what was best for Capalon and my relationship with my sister, was to risk death in the kingdom of our enemies to find my mother.

CHAPTER
2

I set the voice recorder aside and moved to my worktable, opening every drawer to dig around for the proper tools to alter Paris Marigold's identification card. Clearing my table of the last microscope I used, I donned a headband magnifier then commenced my project. After removing the plastic laminate on the card, I changed the eye color text from BROWN to GREEN, choosing to leave her birthday and height untouched. The bigger challenge was finding a photograph of myself to fill the small square since our kingdom didn't support the use of videography or photography for personal use.

I swiped through a few images Chip found for me above my wrist and settled on a still taken at my parents' End of Life ceremony. My right thumb and index finger zoomed in on my face to reveal I had unknowingly been staring directly at the camera's lens. My face was completely drained of life as if I was the one being locked in a vault that day. I slid the photo to the right to see my sister wearing a similar expression. Only, she sat tall in her chair and her eyes focused on our father's urn, as if she could bring my parents back to life with her mind.

Chip sent the photo to the printer down the hall in the auxiliary room. After retrieving the photo from the printer, I was about to pass the king's room when one of my sister's advisors emerged. His cheeks reddened when our eyes met, but he addressed me as if nothing were out of the ordinary before passing me in the hall.

I felt a connection to King Xavier ever since I caught on to his visits with other men. Though we never discussed it, I found comfort in knowing that we were both flawed, even though his need for intimacy was kept a secret while my emotionally unstable mind was well known.

Capalons didn't believe in romantic love, so something like sexual preference wouldn't have swayed my sister's decision when she accepted Xavier as her match—his intellectual genes were needed for the future king or queen of Capalon.

When I returned to my room, Chip informed me that my protein levels were low and I needed a nourishment break, but I ignored his warnings. Tension crept up through my neck and across my shoulders, but I worked through the pain until Chip interrupted my concentration once again.

"Princess, you have a call from King Xavier."

I dropped the identification card. "Accept."

"I'm pretty lonely in the dining room without you," said Xavier with his sing-song voice he only used with me.

I cleared my throat. "Sorry, I must have gotten carried away with...a new *experiment* I've been working on. I'll be right there." More time was needed to dry the new laminate, switch Chip to manual drive and pack a bag of supplies, but it would all have to wait until after dinner. I carefully placed the card inside a drawer of the worktable and headed to the dining room to meet Xavier.

Our conversation was lighter as if Evelyn's absence lifted a weight off the dinner table. Xavier described the colors he had witnessed in the sunrise that morning and I told him about a time I witnessed a nursery droid having to remove a toddler girl from kissing a toddler boy. We didn't talk about the latest Innovator Report or underperforming citizens in the labs as we normally did with my sister.

"So, what's your secret experiment?" asked Xavier at the end of our meal of kale and barley cubes.

I choked on my water. "Nothing."

"Nothing?" He laughed. "I'm offended, Piper. You know I won't steal your research, unless it relates to sustainable alternative jet fuels —then I would have Patrol raid your room for every shred of information."

My brain failed to produce a believable lie as blood drained from my face.

"Piper, I was just—"

"Accept call from Patrol, King Xavier?" Gill asked through Xavier's wrist.

"Sorry," Xavier said. "I've been fighting a terrible headache all day, so I switched Gill to speaker mode." Xavier rubbed his dark brow and commanded Gill to accept the call.

"The Technology Ward has informed us that the dead gate will be reactivated in thirty minutes," said a deep voice from his wrist.

"That was fast. Thanks for the update, Patrol."

The call ended with a twist of my stomach. I only had thirty minutes to get over the dead gate before the forcefield came back online.

Xavier stood up from his chair and his action required me to do the same. "Well, I'm headed to my lab. I'm experimenting with a new hover pod model. Oh, and Evelyn wanted me to remind you to review your match details. I'm sure she's sent Chip a whole bunch of reminders, but I'm the *human* reminder for you."

I tilted my head. "Yes, Your Majesty."

Xavier winked, which curled my lip up into a smile. Where Evelyn was hard and dismissive, Xavier was soft and patient. I even overheard him whistling from time to time in his office.

"Xavier?"

"Yes, Princess?"

I cleared my throat and spoke a little too loud. "After reviewing my match's details, I plan to go to the Field to test the Technology

Ward's new micro-telescope. I'll need to be away from the light of the Compound for conclusive results, so I'll be out after dusk. I just... wanted to tell you, so you're not alarmed by my absence."

Xavier smiled as if he knew he was secretly offering me his blessing to partake in a forbidden activity. "Chip, keep an eye on the princess."

Chip responded on speaker mode through my wrist. "Yes, Your Majesty."

Knowing that I wouldn't be seeing Xavier for the next few days or potentially weeks, I felt the urge to step around the table and pull him into a tight embrace. Instead, I offered the standard phrase for a Capalon heading to a lab session. "Innovation First, Xavier."

"Innovation First." Xavier tilted his head and exited the dining room.

As soon as the door closed behind him, I sprinted back to my room and pulled a backpack out of my closet. I filled it with the supplies from my emergency cabinet; packaged food, water, flashlight, knife, blanket and extra clothes.

Clothes.

What did Mondarian teenagers wear?

"Chip, lift query restrictions on the subject of Mondaria."

"Restriction override requires permission from—"

"Permission granted by Queen Evelyn Elaine Parish of Capalon."

I clutched the voice recorder and held my breath as I watched my wrist pulse with a blue glow. If Evelyn's recording didn't work on the query restriction, then it wouldn't work on my offline request, which would mean my whole plan would have to be scrapped.

It had never taken so long for Chip to process anything.

It wasn't going to work. I would have to move on with my match and take the medication that Evelyn—

"Restriction override approved."

I dropped the recorder as my hands flew to my mouth. But I didn't have time to revel in my success. "Chip, how do Mondarian teenagers dress?"

"In autumn, Mondarian teenagers often wear articles of clothing like blue jeans, sweaters, flannel shirts, and boots."

I opened my closet to a monochromatic grey scale of clothing. Luckily, Capalons wore sweaters too, but I had never heard of blue jeans or flannel shirts. I swiped through the photo samples Chip provided until I found a picture I could match—a girl in tight pants with a loose sweater and boots. I tied my hair up into a hairband, unsure of exactly how to replicate the girl's tight ball of hair on top of her head. I would need to purchase Mondarian clothing to blend in with the other citizens once I arrived in the kingdom.

"Chip, how do visitors pay for items in Mondaria?"

"Mondaria has exchange offices throughout the kingdom for visitors to trade in their own kingdom's currency to make purchases."

I tossed a box of Capalon coins into the bag, then pulled it over my shoulders. Paris Marigold's identification card was still a bit tacky, but I was out of time so I shoved it into my pocket.

I picked up the voice recorder and took a deep breath. "Chip, switch me to manual-operation."

"Switch to manual-operation requires—"

I played Evelyn's voice one final time.

"Princess Piper, you are now on manual-operation."

My finger held down the record button. "I meant it when I said I wanted to do what's best for Capalon, Evie. I'll be back with or without her in time for my match ceremony. Thank you for your permission." I hit the stop button, then placed the recorder on my bed next to the anonymous note. After a final mental checklist, I left my room and headed to the skybridge.

I waited for Chip to tell me to calm my breathing and steady my heart rate, but he remained silent. A hover pod brought me to the Field and after it hummed back to the main thoroughfare near the Compound, I was left in complete darkness. I plunged my hand into my backpack and pulled out the flashlight. But even with the light, I winced as low tree branches poked against my face and shrieked when I slipped on a rock in the creek, sending my foot into ankle-deep cold water. I selected the gate I thought to be dead and was about to heave myself up with the help of a nearby boulder when I thought a test would benefit my life first. I tossed the flashlight over the gate, only to watch a burst of orange incinerate it into oblivion.

I panted in shock. I was at the wrong gate and I had just sacrificed my only flashlight, leaving my eyes to be guided by the dim light of the moon. I moved two gates to the left and felt for a rock on the ground. Tossing the rock over the top of the new gate, I was relieved to hear it come to a soft landing on the other side. I hoisted myself up with the support of a bent tree trunk, then flung my legs over the top, resting my bottom on the thin row of brick. A tree branch extended to the middle of the gate, so I shimmied my body toward it with the push of my palms and ankles. I reached for the tree branch when an overpowering heat pushed me forward, knocking me to the earth.

I was immobile against a mix of leaves, moss and dirt. Having fallen at least seven feet, I was sure something was broken. But as I slowly moved each limb, the only pain I felt was soreness. I tore my backpack off to find half of it burned, along with the majority of its contents. My food, blanket, and a pair of pants were destroyed. The knife must have been blasted out to the other side of the fence or was hidden under the leaves. But I had to exit the forest before a perimeter camera picked up my movement. I hugged my bag to my chest and pushed my way through the dark forest, not stopping until my feet hit asphalt.

Lifting my eyes off my muddy shoes, I took in my surroundings. Behind me was a black, dense forest that hid the only home I knew. The road I stood on had to be the Lands Vehicular Roadway or LVR. In front of me, sharp mountain peaks pierced a round, silver moon.

I shivered from exhaustion and a wet foot, but I craved water. I set my bag down on the edge of the LVR to take a drink. The heaviness of night settled around me like a thin jacket with the reality of my situation. Evelyn would be livid once she discovered my note the next day. Xavier would be concerned for my safety. But they would both be elated and dumbfounded when I returned with my mother, alive. Then and only then would life feel right again. Evelyn would be happy to not have to be queen anymore and I would be happy to no longer be seen as a disappointment to the kingdom and my sister. I had already managed to escape the most protected kingdom in The Lands, so entering the kingdom of our dull-minded enemies would have to be easy in comparison.

I took one final drink of water, then picked up my bag. "Chip, take me to Mondaria."

CHAPTER
3

Pain seared the soles of my feet as I walked along the LVR. Finally, to my relief, I approached a public auto-taxi rest stop. For the late hour of the night, I didn't see any patrons inside the food and bathroom facilities but I chose to remain outside in the safety of dark shadows. A couple exited the building just as I neared the call-station, causing me to take a few steps back and nearly trip over a low shrub. The woman waived a card over the door handle of an antique four-wheeled vehicle, then slid into the back seat of the vehicle with her partner. After the car left the station, I mimicked the woman's actions with Paris Marigold's identification card on the door handle of the only remaining vehicle.

"This auto-taxi has been reserved. Please visit the call-kiosk to reserve an available vehicle for your travel," said a feminine voice from the door handle.

My head swiveled to find an upright rectangular structure with a speaker box and a glowing white button.

After pressing the round button, a voice identical to the one from the door handle spoke to me. "An auto-taxi is approximately...*four miles* away. Would you like me to call it for you?"

"Yes."

"Okay. Your auto-taxi is traveling at a current speed of...fifty miles an hour and will arrive in...five minutes."

I huffed. "Four minutes and forty-eight seconds is not five minutes."

The door to the building opened to reveal two girls who looked to be about my sister's age. Ducking behind a structural beam, I held my breath.

"You are so drunk, Claire!" shouted a voice.

"Am not! I'm just...a little uncoordinated."

"Uh-huh. And your incoordination landed you in the middle of nowhere at an auto-taxi station. What was that?"

The box of Capalon coins slipped out of the burnt portion of my bag and thudded against the top of my boot. The sound of my heart beating through my ears was deafening as I waited for my brain to decide to stay or run.

"Is someone there?" asked one of the girls.

"Yeah, Prince Corbin, is that you?"

The other girl's inquiry sent the two into a fit of laughter as they finally entered their vehicle. I didn't exhale or reach for my box of coins until they were out of sight. The bright beams of an approaching vehicle made me wince. Nobody else exited the building to claim the car, so I waived my card over the handle.

To my relief, the door unlocked, and I plunked myself down on the back seat.

"Which kingdom serves as your destination?" asked the center console of the taxi.

"Mondaria."

"Please scan your...*Mondarian* citizen ID or guest pass."

I waved Paris Marigold's identification card in front of a scanner.

"Hello, *Paris Marigold* of...*Green Heights*. What is your final destination in...*Mondaria?*"

"Take me to the king's Mansion."

"Do you mean...*the Royal Grounds of Mount Greystone?*"

"Um, sure."

"I'm sorry, you do not have clearance to...*the Royal Grounds of Mount Greystone.* Would you like me to take you to your hometown of...*Green Heights?*"

"No."

"Would you like me to take you to the neighboring town of...*Badger River?*"

I hit the scanner with my palm. "Take me to the king's Mansion!"

"Okay. I'll take you to...*Badger River.* Please sit back and enjoy the ride."

I groaned. "Ancient tech."

The autonomous vehicle bumped over the terrain as I tied the pieces of remaining fabric together on my backpack and pulled the leaves and twigs from my sweater and hair. The vehicle slowed as we approached a red gate that sat across the LVR.

My fingernails dug into my thighs, wishing I hadn't lost the knife in the forest. I waited for Mondarian guards to swarm the vehicle, but to my delight the gate slowly opened, allowing me passage into the kingdom.

"Welcome to Mondaria," said the vehicle.

My sore muscles relaxed. "We made it, Chip." I leaned my head back and closed my eyes.

A SERVICE DROID TAPPED on my door. "Chip, tell that droid to come back in an hour," I said, not bothering to open my eyes.

"There are no droids in range, Princess."

The tapping turned to pounding and my eyes flashed open to see an elderly man with long silver facial hair. "I've requested this taxi!" he shouted. "Get out or I'll call the Guard on you, squatter!"

I screamed and jumped back from the window. What kind of nightmare was my brain projecting?

But then I remembered the auto-taxi's misdirection—Badger

River, Mondaria. I was in the kingdom of my enemies and one of them threatened me from the other side of an auto-taxi window.

I grabbed my bag and opened the door, catching an overpowering foul odor as I stepped past the man. He grumbled something to himself as he slid into the auto-taxi, leaving me in the middle of a cement walkway. Golden sun burned away the lingering traces of night, making me visible to the people of Mondaria. I watched a man with a bloated belly waddle by, wearing a bright green shirt. The sight was unlike anything I would have ever seen in Capalon, where our citizens were trim due to our controlled diets and issued clothing in only shades of grey.

I clutched my bag to my chest. "Chip, I'm in Mondaria. What do I do?" I whispered, unmoved from my spot on the walkway.

"Princess, you are forbidden to—"

"Chip," I said through a clenched jaw, "what should visitors in Mondaria do upon arrival?"

"Visitors in Mondaria may visit exchange offices to exchange their kingdom's currency."

"Exchange office. Right." I was happy to have a new goal to focus on, rather than the shock of my surroundings. I pulled my bag over my shoulders and picked a direction. The walkway sat beside a long stretch of red brick buildings, divided by varying storefronts with colored fabric awnings. I paused to stare at a large photograph that sat in the window of one of the stores, depicting a man and woman embraced in a passionate kiss. Both were completely naked, except for their private body parts, which were carefully covered by a sheet that looked as if it billowed in the wind.

"Are you a Drake and Daniella fan?" asked a woman emerging from the building. She set out a sign that said SALE TODAY AT MOUNTAINS OF BOOKS!

Unable to close my mouth, I shook my head.

"Not a romance reader, eh? Don't blame you. It's mostly smut, anyway. Anything I can help you find instead?"

My jaw twitched back to life. "Yes. The nearest currency exchange office."

"Nearest one is eight miles south of here in Wisteria."

"Do they accept Capalon currency at that office?"

Her eyes narrowed. "You serious? Everyone knows Mondaria doesn't exchange Capalon currency."

Everyone but Capalon princesses. "Oh. Right."

I walked away before I revealed another ignorant comment to the woman. "Chip, why did you fail to mention that Capalon currency wasn't exchangeable in Mondaria?"

"Princess Piper, I have no record of being asked if Capalon currency was exchangeable in Mondaria."

Angry at Chip and myself for vagueness on the subject of monetary support, I sped up my pace, passing a man in soiled clothes begging for money. I also passed two women holding hands, a mother planting kisses on her smiling baby's face and a restaurant emitting one of the most delicious sweet smells I had ever inhaled.

My stomach growled, but I only carried Capalon currency. I weaved in and out of the passersby, scanning every woman's face for one that resembled my mother's, but then my eyes landed on two uniformed Mondarian guards heading my direction.

Had the woman from the book shop called the guards on me?

I ducked behind a large board of brightly colored papers and held my breath. When I heard their boots pass, I exhaled and leaned my head against the board.

What was I doing?

I didn't belong in Mondaria. The threat of death followed me with every step in a kingdom I knew nothing about. How was I supposed to gain clearance to the king's Mansion? And how was I supposed to survive with no money? Would I be reduced to begging for it on the street like the man I had just witnessed?

The smart choice was to go back home and apologize to Evelyn for my brief lapse of logic, take the time to review my match's details and be the princess that Capalon deserved—not a silly girl who thought she could resurrect her dead mother from the enemy kingdom.

I started to walk away and call for an auto-taxi when bold scarlet letters on a cream-colored paper pinned to the board caught my attention:

Ever dreamed of living in the king's Mansion?
Audition to be a court member of the King's 100!

I pulled the paper off the board. "Chip, define 'audition.'" My sleeves covered my glowing wrist, but I tucked it under my other arm just in case.

"Performing a talent in front of one or more people who judge the act based on skill."

"Chip, what—"

I screamed as a canine barked and snapped at my ankles. My identity had been revealed and the Mondarian Guard sent ferocious animals to attack me. I would die at the jaws of an angry four-legged ball of fur. I backed up as a woman shouted, "Petunia, hush!" and pulled its neck with a jeweled rope. I turned to escape the terrifying situation when I collided with something soft and hard, feeling a warm liquid splash across my chest and arms.

Anger welled in my empty belly. "What did you do, you... ignoramus!" I shouted both at myself and my assailant. My eyes refused to look at anything other than my arms, soaked in brown liquid. I felt the familiar forbidden emotion creeping into my throat and stinging my eyeballs. Not only was I a failure, I was a failure drenched in some sort of Mondarian beverage.

"I'm so sorry! Um, here's a napkin," said a boy's voice. I felt a palm touch the back of my hand and place a napkin across my fingers.

Touch. When was the last time I had been touched by another human?

I looked up at the boy just inches in front of me. He was slightly taller with brown eyes and black shaggy hair that reached his thick brows. He wore what I recently learned to be blue jeans and a long-sleeve red and black flannel shirt. He looked like a Mondarian male teenager who would have appeared above my wrist in my fashion search, only a bit more disheveled. My eyes trailed to a dent in the corner of his lip and a warm sensation other than the liquid crept up the back of my neck. The fear of having an emotional outburst subsided as I accepted his napkin and dabbed it over my arms.

I caught his eyes examining my chest and his mouth straighten into a line. My face flushed. Had I missed something about physical appearance in an area where I wasn't necessarily considered voluptuous like the poster of Daniella?

"Wow, it's really...*on* you," said the boy. "I'm so sorry. Let me buy you something from the cafe to make up for it."

I looked down to see brown splotches across my sweater. "No, it's okay. I'm fine." I pressed the napkin against my sweater, but the brown stains rested in the fibers of their new home, refusing to budge.

"Please, I feel really bad about the whole thing. I deserved to be called a what was it—an ignoramus? Come on, they just pulled some cinnamon rolls out of the oven down at Dan's. They're best when they're hot. And I need a new hot chocolate anyway since mine is..." He tipped his cup upside down and shrugged.

My stomach rumbled at the boy's offer. I didn't have money, after all. And I needed to get my mind off hunger if I wanted to form a plan for my next steps—even if those steps were to walk to an auto-taxi station and leave Mondaria. "Okay."

I followed the boy into a small cafe about the size of my room at the Compound. He placed an order with a woman behind a counter before handing me more napkins. "Are you auditioning?" he asked, pointing at the paper in my dry hand.

"I don't know."

He cocked his head to the side. "You might as well give it a try. The worst they can do is say no. I'm not really the type of guy to *want* to wear a tuxedo every night for the next four seasons, but with the monthly stipend, I can save up enough money for carpentry school. And I guess playing drums and living in the king's house isn't a bad perk. What's your court talent? Oh, let me guess...magic?"

Not sure of how to respond, I stared at the boy's face. I had looked at Capalon boys' faces before out of necessity, but had I taken the time to notice the symmetry of their cheekbones? Or the edge of their lightly stubbled jaws?

"Singing?"

There was a beat between us until the boy asked again, "Are you a singer?"

I pulled my eyes from the gentle crease between his eyebrows and cleared my throat. I *could* technically sing. I was just forbidden to do it in my own kingdom. And if having a 'court talent' was a vital trait among Mondarians, then I needed to look like I belonged. "Yes," I said. "I'm a singer."

"Cool," he said with a smile that deepened the dent in his lip. I looked at him in awe. I had never felt whatever it was I was feeling just from seeing the boy smile. He was like a joyful sun, pulling me into his orbit.

"Ari, your order's ready," said the woman at the counter. He turned to take his food, then his fingertips lightly brushed mine as he handed me a drink and a rolled piece of bread, sending the return of warmth to the back of my neck.

"The cinnamon rolls are great but the hot chocolate is the best in Mondaria. One taste and you'll be hooked," he said with another bright smile, and I couldn't help but be drawn to the curve of his lips.

I had never wondered how another person's lips tasted until that moment. "I look forward to tasting them. I mean *it*—the hot chocolate, that is. Thank you," I said, feeling flames dance across my cheeks.

"It's the least I could do for giving you a hot chocolate bath." His eyes traveled to my sweater again and then he unbuttoned his flannel shirt, revealing a white t-shirt underneath.

I nearly dropped my cup of hot chocolate. "Wha...what are you doing?"

He placed the flannel shirt over my shoulder, then shrugged. "I owe you a shirt for ruining yours. Wait, can I see that?"

He reached for the paper about the audition and his eyes widened. "Ah, crap on the king! The boys' bus leaves this morning. I got it mixed up with the girls' time. I gotta go. It was nice meeting you."

My fake name hit my tongue like a foreign taste. "Paris."

"Paris," he said with a nod.

The taste settled a bit after hearing the name from his mouth. "Ari, was it?"

"That's me. See you around. And sorry again." He waved goodbye and exited the cafe.

After letting out a long exhale, I took a seat at a tiny table near the cafe window and set down the contents from my hands before removing Ari's shirt from my shoulder. It was too colorful to ever be an approved article of clothing in Capalon. I ran my fingers across the soft fabric, then inhaled a new smell that was more delicious than the scent of the baked goods in the cafe—a mix of pine, wood and soap. The liquid from the spilled drink had cooled against my skin, so the thought of slipping into Ari's warm, dry shirt was too tempting of an idea to ignore.

After changing in the cafe's bathroom, I sat back down at the table and stared at the hot chocolate and cinnamon roll. Citizens of Capalon ate a restricted diet to keep our brains at the highest functioning capacity. Nothing too salty, sweet, or fatty ever crossed our table. Alcohol, caffeine and tobacco were illegal, while peppermint tea was the most popular beverage of choice for keeping an alert mind.

I consumed sugar once when my mother gave Evelyn and me some candies from a foreign dignitary. I remembered the jolt of wild energy, followed by a sobering crash of fatigue, learning firsthand why such concentrated sugar was illegal in our kingdom.

But I needed to eat *something* for my survival in Mondaria.

I sipped the hot chocolate, feeling an intense burst of flavor coat my tongue. I cursed myself for loving the evil sugary drink. Sugar made concise thinking blurry and impossible.

But hadn't I already committed to something blurry and impossible by being in the kingdom of my enemy and wearing one of their citizens' shirts?

Ari was right about being hooked with one taste. I couldn't set the cardboard cup back on the table for more than a few seconds before my tongue craved another sip. I read the audition paper as I continued to shamefully enjoy the forbidden drink.

Ever dreamed of living in the king's Mansion?
Audition to be a court member of the King's 100!

Comprised of talented young singers, drummers and magicians, the King's 100 is an elite performance court that serves as hospitable hosts for the king and queen's welcomed guests. Court members earn a monthly stipend and live in dormitories attached to the Mansion. Length of stay is four seasons but is contingent upon a season-to-season Showcase for His Majesty, King Orson Anders. Must be seventeen years old by December 31 to audition.

The bottom of the paper listed the details for auditioning, with the girls' bus leaving from Badger River in the late afternoon. I moved on to the cinnamon roll and licked a drop of frosting off my finger as I considered my options—I could forget my whole plan to find my mother and go back home, I could beg for Mondarian money on the street or...I could audition for the King's 100.

I wasn't seventeen, but Paris Marigold would be by December 31.

The sugar increased my heart rate. I wanted Chip to speak up in my ear and tell me to stop—tell me I was consuming an evil food and its powers had infiltrated my frontal lobe, but my manual setting kept him quiet.

The final drop of hot chocolate hit my tongue and though my stomach craved more, my brain craved an answer to a hypothesis. And finding the answer to that hypothesis wasn't possible without access to the king's Mansion.

Research.

Auditioning would be part of the research needed to conduct the experiment. And besides, it wouldn't be me, Piper Parish, Princess of Capalon auditioning to be a singer for the King's 100—it would be Paris Marigold. And Paris Marigold had nothing to lose.

CHAPTER
4

Conducting an experiment required planning and preparation. If I wanted to convince a panel of judges I was worthy of performing on the King's 100, I had to prepare an audition piece. I mimicked the other customers inside Dan's and cleared my table, then retreated to the bathroom and locked the door. I asked Chip to play songs typically sung for a Mondarian audition, but they were all too powerful for my ability. "Chip, play a song that works for my voice."

"Are you an alto or soprano?"

After Chip's definitions of the two words, I felt I was better suited as a soprano.

"Princess Piper, I believe the Mondarian Anthem is a comfortable fit for your voice range."

"Praise to Mondaria, the superior kingdom
Under a ruler we shall never abandon.
The snow-covered mountains—magical and unique.
Our love and togetherness make strong what is weak
We stand for a kingdom so great and so free
Oh Mondaria, we sing for you with glee!"

I laughed out loud. The superior kingdom? Capalon had been the superior kingdom since winning the War of the Ancient Data centuries ago. Mondaria wanted the Ancient Data destroyed since they considered it to be the root cause of the demise of the old world. But the people of Capalon knew the precious information was necessary for human advancement. The Mondarian queen forfeited the Ancient Data after a Capalon citizen executed the unarmed Mondarian king. She famously stated that even the most sophisticated technology would never mend her broken heart, then issued a mandate deeming Capalon as Mondaria's eternal enemy. She forbade her kingdom to buy or use Capalon products created from the Ancient Data and ordered her people to kill any Capalon citizen that entered her land. Her grief was viewed as a foolish weakness by Capalon and served as a cautionary tale for Capalon children about the repercussions of emotional delusion.

It would be impossible for me to sing the words of the Mondarian anthem and mean them, but finding my mother would also be impossible without setting foot inside the king's Mansion. I let out a defeated sigh. "Fine. Play on repeat till I have the thing memorized."

After an unknown amount of time, pounding on the restroom door ended my singing. "Get a move on, honey. My restroom is not a rehearsal studio," said a woman's voice from the other side.

I pulled my bag over my shoulder and opened the door to see an elderly woman wearing a dirty apron.

"I apologize for my unacceptable behavior," I said, hoping to diffuse any cause to call the guard.

She blinked her wrinkled eyes. "Oh...well, it's alright, honey. I just need the bathroom for my other customers. We go through a lot of coffee here, if you know what I mean," she said with a smile.

I nodded even though I had no idea what she meant.

After walking the main street of Badger River for a couple of hours, practicing in available bathrooms and alleyways, it was time to head to the bus stop. I checked the audition paper to make sure I was in the right location and waiting at the right time since I was the only person at the stop. Then a rectangular-shaped vehicle pulled up, and the driver opened the vertical doors with a lever. "Headed to the king's Mansion for court auditions?"

I nodded.

"Come on up."

I climbed the steps into the vehicle, spotting a carpeted aisle that divided five rows of brown leather seats. Two girls sat together in one seat in the middle of the bus and both pairs of eyes followed my every move.

"I just need to check your ID and make a call to verify your record before you sit down," said the bus driver, holding his hand out to me.

An identification check?

My heart leapt into my throat and I suddenly wanted to exit the vehicle, sprint down the mountains and back to my kingdom. What if my altered version of Paris Marigold's ID didn't pass the inspection? Would I be killed instantly on the spot in front of the inquisitive girls?

I handed the man my identification card as blood pounded in my ears.

He held a black box to his mouth with a spiral cord connected to the console beside him. "Yeah, I got Paris Marigold of...Green Heights?"

"Standby," said the voice on the other end.

I felt the eyes of two other girls burn into the side of my face as we all waited for a response.

"She's clean," said the voice.

The driver smiled and handed me back the ID. "You're good to go. Have a seat."

I was flooded with relief, but also apprehension as I walked the carpeted aisle. What if other Mondarian teenagers were more attuned to the characteristics of a Capalon princess than Ari?

"Sit by us," said the girl on the aisle seat with long, auburn hair. "I'm Genevieve." She extended her hand.

"I'm Paris." I reciprocated the social gesture I had witnessed outside the restroom of an outdoor recreation shop, then took a seat across the aisle from the two girls.

Genevieve's eyes widened. "Your name is Paris? I love that name! I want to be a chef someday and Paris used to be the culinary capital of the world!"

"And the city of love," said the girl beside her with light blonde hair and crystal-blue eyes.

"Oh, this is Heather," Genevieve said. "We've been best friends since we were eight."

I waived to Heather as the bus lurched forward, then leaned back as it descended a slope of the mountain.

"Isn't this the nicest bus you've ever been in?" asked Genevieve.

It was the largest ancient multi-passenger ground-vehicle I had ever been in. "Yeah," I said.

"What part of Badger River do you live in?" asked Genevieve. "I have an uncle who lives up by the Christmas tree farm."

"Oh, I'm actually from Green Heights," I said, remembering my new facts about my fake life.

Heather's blonde head poked around Genevieve's shoulder. "Why did you get on at the Badger River stop?"

"Um...I wanted to get a cinnamon roll and hot chocolate."

"From Dan's? They have the best in Mondaria," Genevieve said. "But of course, one day I'll have a restaurant with the best of everything in Mondaria," she said with a smile. "So, let me guess— you're a singer?"

I nodded.

"Me too!" Heather said.

Genevieve pushed her red hair behind her shoulders and straightened her back. "I'm a magician." She then looked me up and down. "Paris, is that what you're wearing for your audition?"

Compared to Genevieve and Heather's made-up faces, flower-printed dresses and tangible confidence, I looked like an antique commercial airline on a tarmac of Capalon speedcrafts in Ari's baggy flannel shirt and grey Capalon pants. "Yes?" I answered.

Genevieve shook her head. "They won't let you on the Mansion lawn with that look. Didn't your Junior Court advisor tell you about the audition process? Wait, I don't remember seeing you on Green Heights' Junior Court. Are you homeschooled?"

I didn't know what a Junior Court or homeschooled was, but in lacking facts about what seemed to be a well-known activity, I hoped the obvious term would cover me. "Yes, I'm homeschooled."

"That explains it!" She bent down and pulled something out of her bag. "Here, you can use my spare dress. I packed an extra one in case something happened."

I accepted the white dress with a radiant-pink flower pattern and the two girls stared at me. "You want me to put it on now?"

"Yes! We're only two towns away from the Mansion. And we can help you with your make-up and hair, too...if you want," Genevieve said.

I could tell from her tone that she was trying to be polite, but I was clearly in need of improvement. Having never changed clothes in front of anyone other than droids, I nervously unbuttoned Ari's shirt while trying to use the dress as a shield. I managed to slip the dress over my head and remove Ari's shirt in a swift motion. As Genevieve zipped me up, my eyes drank in the dress as a welcome differential—clothing with *color*. But with its string-like straps and exposure of the top of my back and chest, I felt nearly naked.

The bus slowed to a stop and its doors opened for a girl wearing black pants and a dark-blue, fitted shirt. She had to be at least a head shorter than me with toned arms, shoulder length dark brown hair and olive skin. I was instantly jealous of the coverage of her outfit and after the bus driver cleared her ID, she took the seat behind me.

Genevieve started to introduce herself, but the girl cut her off. "I just want to make something clear," she said, pausing Genevieve's words with her hands. "I'll learn your name, but I won't be your friend until after the audition and we're official court members."

Genevieve's brows lifted and her mouth puckered. "Ok...well, I'm Genevieve, this is Heather, and that's Paris."

"Layla," said the girl with a nod.

"So, *Layla*, are you a drummer?" asked Genevieve.

Layla shook her head. "Singer. Nice try using stereotypical judgment, though. What is it again? Drummers are the strong, brainless ones. Magicians are nerdy and socially awkward. And singers are the beautiful whores, even the guys." Layla leaned forward to Genevieve. "Let me guess, you're one of the beautiful whores, aren't you?"

Genevieve scoffed. "I'm a *magician*. Heather and Paris are singers. You won't last a day at the Mansion with that attitude."

The girl flashed her middle finger, then slouched back in her seat. The gesture was new to me, but from the look on Genevieve's face, it was meant to be insulting.

Heather piped up from behind Genevieve. "Let's talk about something else, like the court men!"

Quiet laughter bubbled in the seat behind me.

"We can talk about boys without being *whores*," Heather said with narrowed eyes. Then she lowered her voice as if she were sharing classified information. "We'll be with the most sophisticated, talented boys in all of Mondaria!"

Ari's face flashed into view and I blinked to erase the image. Mondarian boys had to be the absolute last thing on my mind. And it would be a miracle if I was even offered a spot on the court, having only learned my audition song that morning.

"I have a boyfriend," Genevieve said. "He's apprenticing for my father's plumbing business."

Layla grunted. "We'll see how long that lasts."

Genevieve dug her nails into the leather seat. "Why are you so rude?"

"Why are you so dense?" Layla spat back. "If we make the court, we'll live and breathe Mansion life and nothing else. No time for fun and especially no time for weekend getaways to see hometown boyfriends. Better end it as soon as you make it or should I say *if* you make it."

"You're terrible."

"You're an ignorant bi—"

"You guys!" Heather shouted. "Shut up and look out the window."

We passed a brick road lined with alternating red, green, blue and yellow wood-paneled storefronts with lacey-white trim beneath slanted roofs.

"I can't wait to shop at the ritziest stores in all of Mondaria," Heather said with her nose pressed against the window.

A wrought-iron arch displayed the name of the sight as "The Village."

I had to blink my eyes a few times for my brain to register not only the burst of alternating colors, but the massive mountain that served as the backdrop to the shops. The four of us stared out the windows in silence and after The Village left our sight, the bus lurched up another slope to reveal my target—the Mondarian king's Mansion. Surrounded by pine trees and constructed of layered tan, slate and copper stones, I felt as if I was staring at my beloved creek's interpretation of a human dwelling, beckoning me to enter.

The bus paused for a security check at a gate before rolling onto the grounds, passing a semi-circular drop-off etched into an expansive green lawn and parking in a side lot. About seven other parked busses opened their doors to exiting teenage girls—all in dresses, curled hair and make-up. The peaceful awe I held for the Mansion dissolved at the sight of my other competitors.

"Crap on the king, I forgot to do your hair and make-up, Paris," Genevieve said.

I scratched behind my ear. "Oh, it's not important."

"It is if you want to impress the judges," she said pulling some things out of her bag.

It was ludicrous to think that a hairstyle and an enhanced face were critical factors in judgment based on talent but I was no longer in Capalon, the land of logic.

Layla sighed. "Maybe Paris doesn't want your help and she's too polite to say anything, *Gen*."

"Maybe Paris was homeschooled and needs my help, *Layla*," Genevieve hissed.

Layla turned to face me. "Well, what'll it be?"

The two girls stared me down, and I became the subject of the quickest battle ever conceived. I concluded that Layla wasn't one to upset but I couldn't refuse an offer to complete my Mondarian transformation. "I could use some help."

Layla let out a "psh" sound and Genevieve bounced into my seat. She redid my ponytail, making it high and tight and poked something into the band that pinched my scalp.

I winced with each insertion. "What are those?"

"Hairpins," Genevieve said. "Now turn."

Genevieve held my chin in her hand, glided a pink stick over my lips then handed me a mirror. "I would have done more, but it'll have to do since we have to get off the bus now."

The small hand-mirror reflected a tight ball on top of my head and fluorescent-pink lips. Evelyn would have died from a fatal occurrence of coronary thrombosis at the sight of me.

We stepped off the bus and followed the crowd to meet a tall girl with curly tawny hair and a sharp nose. "Ladies," she shouted over our heads, "please follow me and refrain from talking."

My fists held onto the straps of my backpack in a death-grip as I moved forward with twenty other girls, climbing the stone steps into the Mansion of my enemy king.

CHAPTER
5

The threat of sudden death sent a chill down my spine as the girl led us into an entryway with a low arched ceiling and a round brass chandelier, casting a low light across the stone walls, red area rug and wooden high-backed chair. Our eyes naturally fell to a wide staircase, leading to an undiscovered new world.

The tawny-haired girl instructed us to find a seat or a spot on the floor as she handed us papers on clipboards. "My name is Agnes Airendale. I'm a Fourth Season singer and Manager of the Ladies of the Court. Please fill out your applications and then we'll begin the auditions in the Polaris Auditorium."

I found a spot on the area rug next to Layla and after writing down my fake name, fake hometown and fake birthday, my mind drew a blank for the remaining questions.

"How come you're not writing anything down?" whispered Layla.

"I...don't know what to say."

"Ah, the homeschooled princess needs help. Allow me," she said, taking the application out of my hands.

I almost asked Layla how she knew I was a princess, but then remembered the use of endearing terms I overheard in Badger River. 'Honey' and 'baby' did not, in fact, address a bee's sugary creation or an infant. As she scribbled away, my eyes searched for clues about my mother—signs that pointed to a hidden prison, a painting of the king holding a knife to her chest or note taped to the wall with my name on it.

Agnes interrupted my thoughts to collect our applications. "I'll take these up to Maestro Leto, and when I come back, I'll bring you in one by one in alphabetical order to perform. When you're done, the maestro will tell me which room he's selected for you. After everyone has auditioned, you'll find out if you're in the room for those who've made it or the one for those who will be sent home."

Agnes disappeared up the staircase, sending the small lobby into a burst of sounds as the girls practiced their audition pieces. I witnessed dropped cards in the middle of a magic trick, loud vocal exercises with strange words like mee, may, mah, and moo and tapping drumsticks against wooden armrests and exposed surface of the stone floor. I resisted the urge to command Chip to play the latest Innovator Report on full volume in my ears to drown out the incessant noise.

Agnes's presence in the lobby served as the only reprieve from the cacophony as she took girls one at a time up the stairs for their audition. Genevieve Littleton was the first of the four of us from our bus to perform for the elusive maestro. I echoed Heather's sentiment of "good luck" while Layla retreated to a dark corner to shut her eyes and mumble the lyrics of her song.

I hummed the tune of the Mondarian Anthem as I processed an explosion of concerns. Was my talent worthy of the king's performance court? I could technically sing, but what did I know about talent compared to *real* Mondarian girls? What exactly did Layla write down on my application? If I was revealed to be the Capalon princess, would Evelyn mourn my death? Or would she easily discard me from her life as she had done with Mother's vial? And would the Mondarians kill me on the spot or torture me until I begged them to end my life?

I hugged my knees to my chest as the thoughts sent a wave of terror through my body.

Layla emerged from her corner. "You okay, Paris? Do you have stage fright or something?"

I stared at a small stain on the rug. "There's no such thing as stage fright, only the autonomic nervous system's reaction to a stimulus which sends the body into a fight-or-flight response."

"Um, what?" asked Layla with a laugh.

I blinked over dry eyeballs.

Layla unwrapped a small oval and dropped it in her mouth. "The only thing I gathered from that explanation was that there's no such thing as stage fright, which I don't believe for a second. I mean, I don't have it, but I've seen plenty of people who do."

The lobby went silent.

"Paris Marigold, you're up," Agnes said.

Layla curled her fingers into fists and extended her thumbs. "There's no such thing as stage fright! Good luck!"

Heather told me to shatter an appendage and displayed a wide smile which I found to be a confusing combination of words and facial expression. I carried my backpack at my side and followed behind Agnes, climbing the set of stairs to a long hallway dotted with brass chandeliers. We rounded a corner and Agnes opened a set of doors leading into a massive, dark auditorium.

The auditorium emanated a buzzing energy the moment I stepped inside, as if the molecules in the air welcomed me with an invisible vibration. I followed Agnes down an aisle-way between rows of plush, deep-red seats as I took in the details of the intricate, twisting woodwork set in the shadows of the walls. A single guiding light directed us to a center spot on a wide, wooden stage, reflecting the name of the auditorium—Polaris, or North Star. We climbed a small staircase to the top of the stage, passing a drum on a stand and a black-draped table. Then Agnes removed my bag from my hand and directed me to stand in the middle of the stage under the light. I turned to say something about the loose strands of fabric on my bag to Agnes, but she had already disappeared into the blackness.

"Begin," said a male voice from behind the wall of light and somewhere above my head.

My mouth refused to open and my lungs forgot how to pull in oxygen.

If I open my mouth, they'll know who I am. They'll all know I'm an imposter and I'll be killed on the spot under these hot lights.

"If you're too scared to sing, can you please get off my stage?" asked the man.

Too scared to sing? Yes, I was scared of dying, but singing? I wished Layla's assumption was right that I had stage fright. Stage fright wasn't real and could be controlled by—

"No," I responded into the void. "I'm ready to sing."

I closed my eyes and reached into the part of my brain that knew how to focus from so many years of self-discipline.

Breathe. Focus. Breathe.

I will not die on this stage.

I'm a Capalon and I control my emotions.

I opened my eyes and sang the Mondarian Anthem. I used my hands, feeling the sound waves fall all around me and enjoyed the sensation of singing without barriers, without fear and without consequences. I had just one more line of the song when I was interrupted.

"Blue Room," said the voice from behind the light.

Agnes reappeared on stage and nodded for me to follow her to the right.

"Wait," said the voice once more.

Agnes paused and led me back to the center of the stage. She glanced up at something to our upper right and through the blinding light, I could make out the silhouette of a dark head sitting in a curved box.

"Paris Marigold...you've sung for hospice patients, created a ministry choir at your local chapel and sold baked goods at Junior

Court competitions as a way to raise money for your homeschool projects, and you watch the performances."

I swallowed, unprepared to hear the lies Layla put on my application.

"So, why are you here?" asked the man.

A new jolt of nerves shot through my body. Did he know? I swallowed down a lump in my throat. "I...I'm sorry?"

The man shifted in his seat. "Paris Marigold, homeschooled girl from Green Heights. Why are you *really* here? Is it the stipend? The lavish dinners? What is it for you?"

I was there to find my mother and nothing more. But espionage wouldn't be a valid reason for the Mondarian man behind the light. "I..." I started to speak without an end in mind, but I recalled the smile of the boy from Badger River. "I'm here because I'm attracted to joy, and...I feel joy when I sing—it's when I feel the most like myself."

The lights hummed in the period of silence that followed. Finally, the man spoke. "Green Room."

Agnes led me off the other side of the stage and into a small room with light-green walls, a low ceiling and large tan sofas. When the door clicked behind her, Genevieve jumped in front of me—her face streaked with wet, black lines. "How was your audition? Did he like you? What did he say?"

"Um, I don't know."

"What do you mean you 'don't know'?" Her hands gripped my shoulders. "Did he applaud? Laugh at you? What was it?"

"I don't know, Genevieve. There was no response that would indicate negative or positive emotion from the man behind the light."

Genevieve released her grip and wrapped her arms around her abdomen. "I sucked so bad. My queen went flying in my queen of hearts trick and I had to play it off with a side slip to the queen of diamonds."

I nodded as if I understood what she was talking about.

She shook her head. "I'm not going to make it. There's no way."

"All we can do now is wait," I said, reaching for comfort in the facts. I sat down on one of the plush sofas while Genevieve paced the length of the room. For the next hour, the door opened, a girl entered, she was interrogated by a room full of nervous girls and the process repeated.

Genevieve didn't believe Layla's response that she 'killed her audition,' but was pleased to see Heather. "You guys, I think we made it! Heather is a great singer!"

Heather shook her head. "I forgot the lyrics to the last line of my song, so I sang it as 'ahs.'"

"Oh. That's okay. That's.... Oh, Heather, why did you have to mess up on your court audition of all things?"

Genevieve's comment sent Heather into her own tearful tirade, sending Layla to the furthest corner of the room.

Left to my own thoughts, I scanned our room—Layla Tanvi, Heather Romaine and Genevieve Littleton sat among myself and nine other girls, making us a room of thirteen. If the auditions were over, that put twelve girls in the other room. Were we the ones who would make it? Or because the program was so selective, were we the ones to be sent home with the extra body? I considered my talent compared to the rest of the girls and I convinced myself we were the room to be sent home.

And without money, signs of my mother or a feasible backup plan, I would go back to Capalon. Hopefully, Evelyn's fury about my departure would be short-lived and I would go on to meet my match, whoever he was, and be joined to him for life in a ceremony on my birthday—all for the sole purpose of keeping the royal lineage of the utmost intelligent minds of our kingdom.

I sighed and leaned my head against the wall. At least I had the opportunity to sing. *Really* sing. I picked my bag up off the floor and my fingers grazed the flannel shirt through the torn fabric.

Aside from being granted the opportunity to perform, I discovered there was something about the combination of black hair, brown eyes and a radiant smile that spurred a positive emotion within me. Maybe my failed trip was worth the briefest taste of joy. And perhaps I'd be matched with a boy who shared a similar genetic make-up as Ari, the kind Mondarian boy from Badger River, and—

"Congratulations!" shouted Agnes as she opened the door. "You're all now court ladies of the King's 100!"

CHAPTER
6

The room erupted with high decibel screaming that I feared would rupture my eardrums. Shortly thereafter, we were fed 'pizza,' which looked disgusting, but tasted wonderful. When we were finally escorted to the court dormitories, I looked for clues of my mother while Genevieve and Heather clung to each of my arms. The physical contact made me uncomfortable, but I had positioned myself in a new world that was *entirely* uncomfortable.

We reached a set of glass doors that opened to a large domed room, framed with heavy wood beams. A tall silver stone fireplace served as the room's centerpiece and matched the hexagonal outline of the room. It displayed six hearths framed by six sets of scarlet plush chairs and wood tables. Bookshelves and additional seating sat on the perimeter of the room and three windows cut down the back wall from floor to ceiling.

"Where are all the other court members?" asked Genevieve.

"It's end of season break, so they all went home," Agnes said with a hint of frustration. "But they'll be back tomorrow night." Agnes read our roommate assignments off of a list, which came down to four girls—myself, Heather, Layla and a girl with short brown hair and a freckle-covered face.

"Heather Romaine and Nicole Jordan," Agnes said. "That leaves Paris Marigold with Layla Tanvi."

Genevieve offered me a sympathetic look. "I'm so sorry, Paris."

Agnes held her hands behind her back. "Absolutely no boys in the Ladies' Dorms at any time. If I see a boy in the hall or in your room, it can result in immediate dismissal of both of you from Maestro Leto."

"No late-night booty-calls, Genevieve," Layla said a little too loud.

Genevieve's face turned bright red. "She's joking," she said to Agnes. "I have a boyfriend back home. We've been together for ten months."

Agnes raised her brows. "We also have a special mascot living with us—a cat named Little Bernie. He lives in the manager's dorm room but he likes to visit everyone. If he enters your room, just make sure to put him out before you close your door."

The other girls responded with 'aws' but my skin crawled at the thought of a feline laying on my bed. The only animals I had ever come into close contact with were research specimens, as domesticated animals were strictly forbidden.

Agnes dealt out instructions of when and where to meet the next morning, followed by a list of activities. "From this point forward, you will all be referred to as New Ladies and you'll be meeting the New Men tomorrow. Anytime you're addressed or asked a question, you're expected to reply with 'yes, sir' or 'yes, ma'am.' Do you understand?" Agnes lifted a hand.

"Yes, ma'am," murmured the girls around me.

A shiver of uneasiness ran up my spine. Had I joined a performance group or a militia?

We followed Agnes up a stairwell behind a locked door. "Your keys are on your desks inside your rooms, along with your court handbooks. Get some rest, ladies. You have a big day tomorrow."

A few girls said the appropriate response of 'yes, ma'am,' but most of us headed to our assigned rooms. I found two large paper music notes with "Paris" and "Layla" written in swirly handwriting four doors down on the right side of the hallway. I opened the unlocked door to find a small room with two beds head-to-head in an L shape, two dressers, two desks and two closets with full length hanging mirrors. My eyes fell to the most wonderful thing I had ever seen in a room—a window.

Layla stepped inside behind me. "So, I get to spend the next four seasons with the homeschooled princess," she said, tossing her bag onto her desk. "With my track record, you'll either love me or hate my guts by the end of it all."

For being my enemy, I already had a fair amount of disdain for her intestines but as a Capalon undercover, I had to ease any source of tension. "I have hopes that we'll maintain a cordial relationship." I ran my fingers along the edge of the window and took in the view of the edge of the roof and a sliver of a mountain peak. It didn't compare to the scenery I witnessed from the bus window, but all that mattered was that I would be sleeping in a room with a window for the first time in my life.

Layla laughed. "You're weird, princess. And that's why I like you." She yawned. "I'd love to continue to chat but I really hate girl talk and I'm tired. No offense."

The girl's dislike for conversation worked in my favor. "Okay. I'm going to take a walk."

Layla groaned. "If you're going boy-hunting, just don't forget your key so I don't have to get out of bed."

"Boy-hunting?"

She snorted. "Why else would you risk breaking curfew on your very first night in the Mansion?"

Because I'm looking for my mother, the former queen of Capalon.

"You have superior intuition."

"Whatever." Layla plopped onto her bed and opened a book with an identical cover of the poster I saw in the window of *Mountains of Books*.

I grabbed the key off my desk and made my way down the

stairwell, through the empty Lounge and out the glass doors. "Chip, do you have schematics of the Mondarian king's Mansion?"

"No, Princess. Those schematics are not available."

"Of course. That would have been too easy."

Then I jumped at the sound of a rough voice behind me. "You're breaking curfew."

I turned to see a short, stout man, who looked as if he had just sprinted the length of Mondaria.

My heart hammered against my chest. "Yes, sir. I apologize, officer."

"*Captain.*" He looked past me. "Where's your friend?"

I tucked my wrist behind my back. "I'm alone."

He shook his head. "I heard you talking to someone else."

"Just to myself. I do that sometimes."

He ran the back of his hand across his sweaty forehead. "You need to return to your dormitory immediately. You don't want to be kicked off the court before you had the chance to wear a pretty dress."

"Yes, sir," I glanced at his nameplate, "Captain Murphy. Goodnight." I brushed past him, keeping my wrist hidden from his view. I stomped across the patterned carpet floor of the Lounge with balled fists. I lacked a solid plan for how to track down my mother but wearing a pretty dress was the absolute lowest priority.

❧

Beeping woke me from a restless sleep. "Chip, silence alarm."

"Who's Chip?" asked a girl's voice.

My eyes flashed open and a series of images flooded my mind like a dream—switching Chip to manual-drive, taking an auto-taxi to Badger River, meeting a black-haired boy with lips I considered tasting and becoming a singer on the King's 100. But I wasn't dreaming and my new roommate waited for me to respond to her question. "My dog," I finally said.

"You ask your dog to 'silence your alarm' for you?" she asked.

The only dog I had ever come in contact with was the one that barked at me in Badger River. I would have loved to tell my sister about the Mondarians' obsession with animals and how they—

My sister.

She would have returned to the Compound at the same time I was having my run-in with Captain Murphy.

I was tempted to go to the bathroom and ask Chip to play any received audios, but I couldn't allow my sister's threatening messages to influence me to leave before I even had a chance to search the Mansion for my mother.

Layla snapped her fingers. "You're clearly not a morning person."

"Hm?"

"I've you asked the same question three times now," she said as she put on our court attire for the day—tan pants, white shirt and a navy blazer with the Mondarian crest embroidered on the left breast pocket in silver thread. Each article of clothing hung too long and too wide on her. "Ugh, I can't wait till we get our tailored uniforms. I feel like I'm wearing my dad's clothes. At least we get to wear our own stuff when we're not rehearsing or performing. You packed light, by the way." She gestured to my partially destroyed backpack. "Must not have believed you would make it, huh?"

Instead of giving Layla a fake excuse for why I had limited clothing, I tucked the backpack under my bed and pulled on my own assigned uniform.

"No fair," Layla said. "You look like the perfect court lady."

I didn't know how a Mondarian would respond to her comment, so I moved to the dresser mirror to pull my hair back with a band.

"But looks can be deceiving, can't they?" she asked.

An icy chill crept up my spine. Had she figured out who I was while I was asleep? I turned to face her.

She clicked her tongue. "I bet you're one of those homeschooled girls who's going to turn wild now that you're away from Mommy and Daddy."

I shook my head. "That won't happen. And—" I was going to say 'my parents had been dead for almost three years,' but that fact felt too revealing. "And I have a job to do as a singer for the King's 100 so I must present myself with elegance at all times."

Layla placed her index finger in her mouth and stuck her tongue out, making a retching sound. "I'm going to work on you, princess. By the end of the season, you'll have more bite than *me*." She curled her fingers like claws, exposed her teeth and growled. Anyone in my kingdom would have called her behavior shameful, but the muscles around my mouth couldn't help but tighten into a smile.

We headed downstairs to meet Agnes in the Lounge with the other New Ladies.

"Are we eating breakfast with the boys this morning?" asked Heather.

Agnes nodded. "Yes, you'll be dining with the New Men."

Giggling rippled through the group of girls and something trembled within me at the thought of seeing Ari's face again.

"Except for two of you," Agnes said. "Staci Ringer and Paris Marigold—you'll have breakfast in the salon since your new looks will require more time."

Staci Ringer was a drummer who didn't look strong at first glance. She was long and lean with her hair cut to her ears and dyed pink. I understood why her hair would require more time in the salon but what had I done to earn the extra attention? Was there something about my look that came off too Capalon?

Agnes directed the girls toward a large dining hall before taking Staci and me into a salon inside the Mansion. We were greeted by a short woman with round purple glasses and a matching purple apron. After asking our names, she handed Staci off to a man, then took a step closer to me. "Well congrats to you, Miss Marigold," she said, looking up at me over her purple frames. "You won the random brunette drawing. Too many blondes this season." She smiled but my face was frozen, unable to return the sentiment.

I couldn't have my hair altered. What if my mother didn't recognize me with brown hair? And what kind of wrath would rain down on me from my sister when I returned home with a new hair color? "I really don't want my hair altered."

She clicked her tongue. "Sorry, sweetie. It's part of being a court member. Your hair no longer belongs to you—it belongs to the king, or Bernie for that matter. I swear there's not much of a difference between those two. Anyway, if you don't want it done, you'll be dismissed from the court."

"Are you serious?"

She nodded with an unusually joyful smile. "So, are you going to follow me to my chair now?"

THE PROCESS of changing my hair color may have been painfully long, but I enjoyed munching on an endless amount of sugary breads and reading Mondarian magazines. They were full of color and articles that I found fascinating—*Fall Trends this Season*, *Delectable Apple Desserts* and *What His Kiss Style Means*. To think I spent my entire life learning code, memorizing the periodic table and crunching numbers for structural engineering exams when the citizens of Mondaria were studying seven different ways to coat apples with sugar was perplexing.

Other New Members came in and out of the salon for hair trims as I waited for each round of my coloring process. I kept an eye out for a black-haired boy to enter the salon but he never showed. At one point I had to leave to be measured by the Mansion's tailor and when I returned, Staci had left, leaving me as the lone court member to finish up in the salon.

When the color change was finally completed, I entered the Mansion's enormous ballroom. My mouth dropped at the sight of the sparkling crystal chandeliers covering the ceiling and the vastness of the room which was comparable in size to a small aviation hangar. A wide wooden stage sat in front of me, on what I determined to be the east wall based on the amount of sunlight pouring in through a tall arched window. And the walls on either side copied the same shape of windows, but smaller. So many windows. So much light. So opposite of any room in Capalon.

"Oh Paris, I love your hair!" Genevieve's fingers ran through my new brown locks, pulling my eyes off of the windows.

Layla shot me a quick glance. "I hate it."

"You're so rude, Layla!" Genevieve said.

Layla shrugged. "I'm just being honest. She looked better as herself, not as a creation of the maestro's obsession with hair balance."

"Don't listen to her, Paris. You look great." Genevieve smiled at me before dipping her head down to whisper something to Heather.

"Look at this place, princess," Layla said looking up at the sparkling ceiling. "It's not like home is it?"

"Far from it." I was about to mention the amount of electricity it had taken to light up the whole room when Layla fell backward onto the polished wood floor of the ballroom, landing on her rear-end.

A tall boy with light brown hair reached down to help her up but Layla brushed his hand away. "Thanks, but I can get myself up."

The boy's face twisted. "Just thought I'd help since it was my foot you tripped over."

Layla pushed herself off the floor. "So, you tripped me with your big feet? Thanks."

"No, *you* tripped over my *normal* sized feet."

"Ladies and gentlemen!" shouted a boy from the stage.

Our group responded with 'yes, sir' and moved to the foot of the stage.

"I'm Eric Blackwell, Manager of the Court Men. Welcome to the Stardust Ballroom." Agnes introduced herself too, then instructed us to find partners to learn the steps to a dance.

The tall brown-haired boy turned to face Layla. "Let me prove to you that I'm not the clumsy one."

Layla sighed. "Fine."

I felt a tap on my shoulder and turned to see a dark-skinned boy with black-framed glasses. "May I have the pleasure of serving as your dance partner?"

"Yeah," I said. "Oh, I mean yes, sir."

Agnes and Eric demonstrated how to introduce ourselves to our guests.

My dance partner smiled and bowed. "Hello miss, my name is Darden McCray."

I curtsied. "It's a pleasure to meet you, Mr. McCray. My name is Paris Marigold." I felt like a complete and utter fool but it was the price I had to pay for residence inside the king's Mansion.

The managers led us through the steps of the Mondarian Waltz which was harder for me to learn than Darden.

"Wait, what was that last count?" I asked.

"You really should just pay attention to what our managers are saying."

"I'm trying, I just can't get a hang of—"

"Shh," he said, pushing me in the right direction.

Eric paused the music. "You'll need to learn the dance well enough that you're not thinking of the steps, and instead, focusing on the guest. When we start the music again, start from the top with your introductions, then try holding a conversation while dancing."

We repeated our introductions and Darden was the first to ask a question. "So, were you on Junior Court in Green Heights?"

"No. I was homeschooled. But I saw some competitions," I said, matching the lies Layla wrote on my application.

"Were you at the Valley Spring Spectacular?"

I nodded as my eyes focused on the sunny windows behind his head.

"What did you think about the drama with the director from White Wood?"

"Um..."

Darden stared me down as we danced in a circle.

Was he catching on to me?

I had to say something—anything generic to move him off the subject. "He was out of line."

His face twisted. "He? The director from White Wood is a woman. The judge slapped her in the face!"

What was it I had heard the Mondarians say? *Crap on the king.* I sucked in a breath. "Oh yeah, I remember. I was just really sick, so my memory is fuzzy."

"Well you certainly remember who won?"

"Yeah, of course."

"My school should have won, but I'm obviously biased."

"No, Green Heights should have won. But of course, I'm biased too," I said, proud of my answer.

He laughed. "You're funny, Miss Marigold. You must have been really sick if you don't remember that your town *did* win!"

"Oh, yeah." I bit my lip, hoping not to let anymore false statements fall out of my mouth.

"Well then, I'm guessing you don't remember seeing me accept the award for Best Individual Performance by a Magician? I'm the only one to get it three years in a row."

"You must be a good magician."

"The *best* magician, actually."

Darden chuckled and I forced a laugh out, unsure if he was conceited or just awkward with humor.

"Okay, switch!" shouted Agnes.

Darden passed me off to the next New Man—a singer named Bradley Wafer who stepped on my toes multiple times.

"Switch!"

The dance partners following Bradley proved to be more coordinated, and I found myself smiling, enjoying the ease of the steps, no longer worrying about the counts or what to say to my partner. I even closed my eyes when my last partner spun me on to the next. But my heart stopped when I opened them to see a familiar pair of brown eyes the color of hot chocolate.

CHAPTER
7

The boy from Badger River bowed. "Hello miss, my name is Ari Novak."

I was supposed to curtsy and say my name but my whole body experienced a sudden bout of paralysis.

"May I have this dance?" he asked, exposing an open palm.

Somehow my hand knew to accept his, warming instantly at our connection. When Ari's other hand dropped to my waist, my skin came alive under his touch—a sensation that had been absent with my other dance partners.

"Are you enjoying your time in the King's 100?" he asked.

Did he not recognize me with my new brown hair?

I forced words through a swollen throat. "Yes. It's been intriguing to say the least."

We spun around the same path we had been following the entirety of the lesson, but I felt like I was performing the dance for the first time.

He smiled and bent his mouth down to meet my ear, his warm breath caressing my skin. "And have you called anyone else an ignoramus?" He pulled his head back to reveal the sun-bursting smile I remembered from Badger River. "Didn't think I'd recognize you?"

"I...wasn't sure," I said with a nervous laugh.

"It's okay. I was worried you wouldn't recognize *me* without my standard flannel. These jackets are super scratchy."

I smiled and was about to tell Ari I intended to return his shirt when I caught him observing me with an intense gaze. "Don't take this the wrong way, but I like the real you better."

My lungs constricted. The real me? Piper Renée Parish, Princess of Capalon—me?

"I mean, they did a nice job and all but I just have you in my head as a blonde."

I exhaled a sigh of relief. "Oh, you're talking about my hair."

"Yeah, what else would I be talking about?"

"Nothing, I...I like your hair too. I think it brings out your eyes." I tucked my chin down to conceal my flushing cheeks.

"You like it? My girlfriend's been begging me to get a haircut for a while now. I hope she likes it when she's here for Grape Stomp."

The other people in the Stardust Ballroom reappeared in my periphery. Ari was matched to another girl by choice. "What's a Grape Stomp?" I asked to take my mind off his relationship-by-choice with another girl.

"Some event we have to have dates for. My roommate was telling me about it. He seems to be the Court's number one fan. And possibly the best magician I've ever met."

"Is your roommate Darden Mc—"

"Switch!" shouted Eric.

Ari stepped back to open the space between us. "I'm glad you decided to audition, Paris." He squeezed my hands before dropping them and I spun on to the next boy.

As I listened to my new partner talk about his family's goat farm, I considered Ari's matched status to be a positive observation for my data collection. As a Mondarian, he belonged with a Mondarian girl and as the Capalon princess, I belonged with the future prince of Capalon. Ari proved to be a surprising distraction, but I possessed the mental tools for preventing my mind to stray into unacceptable territory. Finding my mother was the goal, and I wasn't about to let

Ari's kindness or brown eyes prevent me from proving a long-believed hypothesis.

When our dance instruction ended, the magicians were called to a sectional with the maestro and the drummers followed Eric into another room for etiquette training. I left the Stardust Ballroom with the other singers for a tour of the Mansion. We revisited the Polaris Auditorium and climbed a narrow staircase behind the stage which led to a set of dressing rooms. Each table in the court ladies' dressing room provided cushioned stools and mirrors framed in large bulbs for six girls. Our seats were assigned by roommate pairings but when Layla found her name, she switched the cards.

"Layla, what are you doing?" I asked as Agnes talked to some girls on the other side of the table mirrors.

She shushed me. "Will you keep it down? I'm just doing some rearranging. I won't survive the season if I have to sit next to Genevieve. Blondie will want to be next to her BFF, anyway." Layla's new order started with Heather on the far-left end of the table, followed by Genevieve, myself, Layla, Staci Ringer and Nicole Jordan. Layla's change went unnoticed as we all filed out of the room to the next location.

I expected Agnes to give a detailed history of the Mansion's architecture but she only rattled off information about the King's 100 during the rest of our tour. Performance time would be divided between the ballroom and the auditorium. Ballroom performances coincided with a seasonal or holiday event intended for invited guests only and required the court to host tables, dance with guests and perform our talent as predetermined by the maestro. Auditorium shows symbolized the strength, beauty and wisdom of the Mondarian people and were available to anyone willing to pay a steep price for a ticket. A King's 100 season ended with a private Showcase for the king who offered feedback of changes for the following season, sometimes resulting in court member eliminations. I didn't listen too closely to the details of the Winter Showcase for our season since I was determined to be back in Capalon with my mother and sister long before then.

As we walked one of the wide hallways to our final location on the tour, Layla strode up beside me. "Of course, Reese Olsen is a singer—one of the beautiful whores."

"Is he the boy who tripped you?"

"Yeah. He kept leading me through the steps like I couldn't figure it out on my own."

"Maybe he was just trying to be helpful," I said.

"No way, look at him."

I looked up ahead, where Heather and two other girls giggled at something Reese said.

Layla groaned. "He's so full of himself. And he says he plays guitar and writes his own music which is just so stereotypical."

Agnes led us into an arched room called the Hall of Memories where photos of the king and the royal family covered the walls. There were also numerous photos of the king with all rulers of The Lands, with one deliberate exclusion.

I paused on a recent framed picture of the Royal Family—King Orson Anders with Queen Marisol and their two sons, Corbin and Taran.

"Oh, the princes," Heather said behind me. "Are the rumors true? Is Prince Corbin really a playboy?" she asked Agnes. But Agnes ignored her question to point out some historical event in one of the photos.

"I'd take the playboy over Prince Taran," said another New Lady in our group of singers. "I heard Corbin's got a talent for magic in addition to being the future king." The girl squinted her eyes as she examined the photo. "Taran always looks so serious and...boring."

Heather laughed. "But Taran's our age. Maybe one of us will marry him and become a princess."

Layla approached the photo. "Why settle for princess when you could be queen and finally tie down the playboy?"

Reese appeared beside Layla. "Is that your type? The playboys?" he asked with a cunning smile.

"No," Layla said, turning to face Reese. "The playboys are still *boys* and I need a *man*."

Reese and Layla argued about the definition of a 'boy' so I wandered back to the entrance of the room, lost in the photos of a royal family that lived a life so opposite from my own upbringing— attending lavish dinners, partaking in sporting events, dancing with—

"Do you have any questions?" asked a guard at the door. He looked to be in his early twenties but had early signs of hair loss down the middle of his head.

"No thank you," I said, hoping to rid him of his strange stare. But I paused. "Actually, I do. I know this might be an odd question, but is there any sort of prison in the Mansion?"

He smiled. "No prison. But if you're into Mansion secrets, they're all documented in the Records Room."

"And court members have access to the Records Room?"

"No miss, you don't. Gotta be royal or a guard to get in." A twisted smile appeared across his pocked skin. "But now you know a guard," he said jingling a key in front of my face. "Maybe you and I could...make an arrangement?"

"Like what?" Excitement brewed in my belly. Maybe the Records Room was the key to locating my mother.

"Get lost, creep," Layla said from behind me.

The guard's face paled, and he moved away from the door.

I clenched my fists. "Why did you have to interrupt, Layla? He was going to offer me an arrangement for...an additional tour of the Mansion."

"Yeah, but whatever *you* think he meant by 'arrangement' is absolutely *not* what he was thinking."

"Time for etiquette!" shouted Agnes.

"Then what *was* he thinking?" I asked Layla, trying to calm the anger in my voice.

Layla patted my shoulder. "Time for etiquette, princess."

CHAPTER
8

After an agonizing hour of etiquette training, we headed to the court dining hall to eat lunch with the other New Men and Ladies. Two guards passed us in the hallway, escorting a tearful girl who I recognized to be Heather's roommate, Nicole Jordan.

"The maestro is a tyrant!" she shouted. "Anyone who's willing to follow him is insane!" We watched the scene until the guards pulled her around the corner and her incoherent shouting ceased.

When Heather saw Staci at the doorway of the dining hall, Heather latched onto her arm. "What happened to Nicole?"

Staci played with the ends of her new ink-black extensions. "Maestro kicked Nicole out at the end of our sectional."

Heather's hands flew to her mouth.

Staci's small eyes widened. "He just zeroed in on Nicole and wouldn't let up. He told her that if she couldn't keep up with his tempo, that she...she must not be good at anything in life. Nicole fired back at him so Maestro called the guards on her." Staci bit her lip. "I was warned about the maestro from some people back home, but I had no idea he would be this bad."

The surrounding girls offered comments of shock.

"Did Nicole truly fail to meet the maestro's expectations?" I asked Staci.

She shrugged. "Yeah, I guess."

I stepped forward with the movement of the food line. "Then perhaps he was right to eliminate her from the court."

The girls in front of me cast sideways glances. The line lurched forward but Layla tugged me back. "And I thought I was the mean New Lady."

I shook my head. "I don't understand your reference."

"Paris, I know you've missed out on the whole girl-code thing since you've been homeschooled your whole life, so I'll offer you one small tip." She crossed her arms and took a step closer, causing me to tilt my chin down to meet her eyes. "You need to be more sensitive around these girls. I know that's ironic coming from me, but *you* actually care about what people think about you, right?"

No. I didn't care how the other court members perceived me but I needed to keep my true intentions hidden under the guise of my Mondarian cover. "Yeah, I do care," I said, taking a step closer to the food table to grab a plate. "Thank you for the tip." I filled my plate with forbidden food and sat next to Layla.

The other court members at our table listened to Genevieve recount an incident with the maestro. "He said messing up your social tricks is like offering somebody a beautiful blueberry muffin for free. Your guest is so excited you gave them a free muffin, but when they bite into it, instead of sinking their teeth into sweet berries," Genevieve paused and winced, "they bite the heads off of fat slimy maggots."

Layla dropped her fork. "I knew I picked the wrong table."

I looked past Genevieve to see Ari at the next table, bobbing his black-haired head as he spoke to the drummer beside him.

He caught my eyes and smiled.

Heat rushed to my face, so I bent my head down to finish my lunch. After Nicole's dismissal and Genevieve's story, the singers at my table expressed their dread for our sectional with the maestro. But for once in my life, I eagerly welcomed a distraction.

THE REHEARSAL ROOM lacked the familiar arched ceiling present in the majority of the Mansion. A tall, narrow ceiling rose into layers of smaller tiers trimmed in old copper. The final piece of square ceiling featured a deteriorating painting of angels singing in the heavens. Large fabric rectangles were bolted into the walls, a semicircle of risers filled half the room and a grey-haired man sat at a long black piano. He smiled as we entered and directed us to stand on the risers by voice part. My nerves about meeting the so-called evil maestro calmed when I took my spot on the riser.

But then I saw *him*.

Leaning against the wall behind the door, the maestro stood over six feet tall with sleek chestnut-brown hair, a square jaw and a pointed brow that sat higher on his forehead than its partner. He rested the back of his head against the wall, as if he too dreaded the sectional. He appeared to be in his forties and in contrast to the other Mansion staff we met, the maestro dressed as if he needed to be ready for a formal event with the king at a moment's notice.

After the last singer took her spot on the riser, he closed the door and moved to a music stand beside the piano. "I'm Maestro Bernard Leto and this is Francis Bleu," he said, tilting his head toward the old man at the piano. "You may call me Maestro and Francis is Francis." He looked down at his music stand and raised his hands in the air. "The Mondarian Hymn."

The sopranos next to me scrambled to pull the appropriate sheet music out of their assigned folders so I followed suit. I had no idea what the notes on the pages meant, so I only read the words and tried to match my voice to what I heard around me. Thankfully, Heather stood to my left and seemed to know exactly what to sing and when.

My eyes were buried in my music when the piano stopped.

"Ladies and gentlemen," said the maestro.

"Yes, sir."

The maestro leaned his elbows on the music stand. "Good, you all know who you are; ladies and gentlemen. Do you know what that means? That means you are no longer girls and boys. I'd like to invite you all to have a meeting with yourself and ask, 'what can I do to kill every ounce of girl or boy within me?'" He instructed us to close our eyes and picture our juvenile selves. "Now pick up a long, sharp knife and...RIP THEM TO SHREDS!"

The volume of the maestro's voice sent a mix of yelps and laughter across the risers.

"Let their blood flow over your arms, pierce the blade into their chest, for the kill. Twist it if you have to, to ensure the heart is destroyed. KILL, KILL, KILL!"

I opened an eye to peek at the maestro. His smile stretched across the width of his tan face, curling up into his cheeks. A piece of hair fled its captive spot on his head, resting in front of his right eye.

"Are they dead?" he asked. "For good? Well, go ahead and let me know."

"Yes, sir."

"Good! Let's keep it that way! Now that your inner boy or girl is dead, you don't ever *ever* have to sing or act like boys or girls again. You're welcome." The maestro smoothed his hair back into place, then clasped his hands behind his back. "And because I'm in a good mood, I'll let you in on a little secret. You may have heard that you're on this court till the end of the season, when our king decides who stays and who goes. But the truth is, *I* can dismiss you at any point. Nobody here is irreplaceable. *Everyone* can be replaced. Do you understand?"

"Yes, sir."

The maestro's hands flew back into the air. "From the top!"

I tried my best to sing like a lady rather than a girl and erase the image of a blood-soaked-younger-me from my mind. There were elements of the rehearsal I enjoyed—the exercises to mature our sound, the maestro's explanation of how our soft palettes affect pitch and the chills that danced across my skin when our sound blended as a harmonious group.

I wasn't too fond of the maestro's instruction to keep completely still when singing and to hold a smile at all times.

Heather whispered to me that her face felt like it was going to fall off and I nodded in response.

The maestro stopped mid-sentence while speaking to the basses. "Miss Romaine, I couldn't help but be distracted from my work to hear your comment. Is there something I missed?"

"No," Heather said. "I just said my face felt like it was going to slide off from smiling so much."

"Miss Romaine, do you *really* want to be on my Court?"

"Yeah."

"Then I suggest you rehearse everything you can—from responding to me with 'yes, sir' to exercising the tiny muscles in your face so that you don't find yourself *sliding off* my court."

Heather trembled beside me. "Okay. I mean, yes, sir."

The maestro cued Francis to pick up from our latest measure, only to cut us off in the middle of the sopranos' solo section. "Wow. Miss Marigold."

Me? What did I do?

I straightened my back. "Yes, sir."

His eyes zeroed in on me, with his one high-brow arched to capacity. "Where do you look when you're singing?"

"At you. Sir."

"Really? Because if you were watching me, you would have seen my cut-off."

I dug my nails into my thighs. "I was watching, I just didn't—"

"I don't need an explanation, Marigold. But...because you're *so* confident that must mean that you don't need me up here."

"No, that's not—"

"*My kings!* Do you ever stop talking?" The maestro tore his eyes off me to face the group. "Hey everyone, Miss Marigold loves the sound of her own voice *and* she doesn't need me to direct her." He stepped away from his music stand and gestured to me. "Come on down, Marigold."

My body threatened to freeze in place but I took a deep breath and forced myself forward. "Yes, sir."

The sopranos parted, creating an aisle down to the floor for me. The maestro placed his hands on my shoulders and positioned me behind his music stand.

"Everyone sit. Miss Marigold will sing her part for us and we'll listen."

The room spun and my heart failed to keep up with my rapid breathing. Singing in the creek was one thing—singing to a black auditorium was another, but singing in front of *people?*

I wanted to protest. Run away. Hide.

But I took another deep breath.

Breathe. Focus. Breathe.

I'm a Capalon and I control my emotions.

The piano player cued my intro, and I sang my part, refusing to make eye contact with any faces. I stared at an empty spot on the back wall as my body violently shook, adding an unnecessary vibrato to my singing.

The maestro paced behind the risers, listening intently to my performance. "Oh, you held that note way too long!" He shouted. "Plowed right through that half rest. Didn't come in on the downbeat." He continued to shout corrections about my singing until he reappeared from behind the risers with his arms crossed. "The big finish, ladies and gentlemen...can she do it?"

I hit a crescendo with my final note, trying to hold it as long as we had rehearsed, but my lungs abandoned me.

The maestro applauded. "Bravo, bravo. So many mistakes. Tell me, can you even read music, Miss Marigold? And please, *don't lie.*"

My eyes held onto the blank spot on the wall. "No, sir."

His hand flew to the side of his head. "She can't read music! How many of you can read music?" Maestro faced the singers with a raised hand and nearly all of them mirrored his gesture.

He shook his head and placed his hands on his hips. "If only she had a maestro. Miss Marigold, I think you've proved to everyone that you are *terrible* without a maestro. Do you all agree?"

The room stayed silent.

"Well?" he asked with force.

"*Yes, sir,*" said only about a third of the room.

"Well, there you have it, Marigold," he said standing directly in front of me. "They also think you're terrible."

I swallowed, a stinging sensation creeping over my eyeballs as my whole body trembled.

"But...if you had a maestro...what do you think?" He tapped his fingers on his chin. "Do you think you're terrible unless you have me as your maestro?"

I prohibited my eyes from blinking and took in deep breaths, trying desperately to steady my beating heart. "Yes, sir."

"That's it? You love explanations, so offer us all one right now. We've wasted enough time on you as it is."

I clenched my fists. "I'm...terrible and I need you as my maestro?"

"Are you asking me a question?"

"No, sir."

He kicked a chair, sending it into the wall. "Enough with the games, Marigold! Just spit out what you're trying to say."

Anger brewed deep in my gut but I breathed through the fire burning at my insides. I wouldn't allow a Mondarian the pleasure of seeing me unravel.

Breathe. Focus. Breathe.

I'm a Capalon and I control my emotions.

I turned my head and looked him in the eye. "Maestro, I'm terrible unless I follow you for direction."

He bobbed his large head. "If that's how you truly feel...okay. Get back on the riser and sing your part again while watching me."

I climbed up the risers, happy to no longer be the center of attention.

The maestro retrieved the chair from the wall and walked back to his music stand. "Now that I'm your maestro again, here's a lesson for all of you." He turned the chair upside down, then rested its middle on top of his head with one hand, keeping his other free. "I'll direct you once through this whole song with a chair on my head so nobody will be tempted to look away. And from now on, whether you're singing in this rehearsal room, walking onto the stage in the auditorium or picking your nose in front of the king in the ballroom, your eyes should be on me, wherever I am, at all times. From the top!"

When I was five years old, I self-diagnosed a viral infection from examining my own blood sample under a microscope. During a particularly rainy summer, I built a central processing unit in one day. I was the product of a kingdom that believed in science, facts and rational thinking above all.

But if I wanted to find my mother, I had to throw rational thinking out the window and take direction from a deranged man with a chair on his head.

CHAPTER 9

Agnes ushered the singers into the Polaris Auditorium where we sat in a row of the plush chairs behind the other new court members. The chatter around me guessed at our purpose in the auditorium—possibly a group history lesson on the Mansion's architecture, another rousing visit from Maestro Leto or even a speech by the king himself.

Whatever it was, I was desperate for it to begin and end, so I could fast-forward to the end of the day's agenda and use our down time to continue my investigation.

The lights dimmed to black and the red-velvet stage curtain illuminated.

"Ladies and gentlemen," boomed a voice from the auditorium speakers. "Please enjoy a special performance by the returning members of the King's 100."

GENEVIEVE AND HEATHER couldn't contain their admiration for the returning members' show as we walked the hall back to the Lounge. I didn't offer any words of feedback but it didn't mean I wasn't impressed. I pounded my hands together in applause with the rest of the new members when the curtain closed, not *just* because it was the proper Mondarian gesture. It truly was an incredible display of music and magic, and I was amazed that I had somehow convinced a lunatic to put me on the same stage with Mondaria's best performers in the kingdom.

When we entered the Lounge, two large speakers boomed a heavy musical beat that reverberated against my rib cage. Layla, Heather and Genevieve's faces lit up at the sight of the eighty returning court members who filled every square inch of the circular Lounge.

I watched in shock and curiosity at the sight of bodies all around me and their movements, torsos pressed together as they danced in front of the fireplaces, hands on faces as they kissed one another on the sofas, and heads nearly touching in intimate huddles of conversations. Never in my life had I seen such a sight.

Shouting turned my head as a group of court members cheered over four bodies on the floor.

"Oh, a push-up contest!" yelled Layla. "Maybe the drummers will let a singer challenge them." She headed to the group of drummers and my fingers reached out for her, not ready to be alone among the mix of bodies.

"Maestro seems to be a complete ass, eh?" asked a voice over my shoulder.

I turned to see the mist-blue eyes of Reese Olsen looking down on me. I nodded to avoid shouting over the music.

He stepped closer, causing me to take a step back. "You probably didn't notice, but I kept my hand down when he asked who could read music. I can't read a single note, actually."

"Really?" I asked in a shout.

Reese nodded. "Yeah, I got on the court train pretty late in the game. Thought I had a shot on my own as a musician but it didn't work out."

Not having any knowledge of musicians in Mondaria aside from the court, I was at a loss for a response.

He extended his hand. "I'm Reese Olsen, by the way."

I nodded and accepted his hand, having already recognized him. "You danced with my roommate today. I'm Paris—"

"Marigold," he said with a grin and a light squeeze of my hand before dropping it. "Maestro said your name enough times for me to have it memorized."

"Right."

"I know it had to suck for you, but I'm glad we all got to hear you sing. You have a nice voice, Paris."

Heat rushed to my face. "Um, thanks," I said, tucking a strand of brown hair behind my ear.

"I'd like to sing with you sometime. Just the two of us."

A boy wanted me to do something with him alone? I had never been allowed to do anything alone with a boy in Capalon. The closest thing to being alone with a boy was if we were assigned lab partners of the opposite sex. We might have been at a table together, but we were in a room full of other people.

I wrapped my arms around my waist and took a step back. "I'm going to go look for my roommate now. Goodbye."

The group of drummers cheered on a new set of competitors in their push-up contest but Layla wasn't anywhere to be seen. I picked up a sandwich from a food table and scarfed it down as I walked a loop around the enormous stone fireplace, the makeshift dance floor and a serious group of magicians watching a girl dance a small metallic ball over her fingers. I finally spotted Layla behind the magicians with a group of boys.

"Paris!" she shouted to me from their table. "Come on over, we're playing Sink the Stiff,"

"Sink the what?" I shouted, as I stepped closer to their low table.

"The stiff," repeated Layla.

"What's a stiff?" I asked.

A boy with curly blonde hair narrowed his eyes on me. "Are you serious?"

"Homeschooled," Layla said, tilting her head to me. "A stiff is a Capalon, princess."

"Yeah, they're more robotic than human," said the boy. He moved his head and arms in rigid movements which elicited laughter from the other card players, including Layla.

"Oh," I said, forcing my eyes not to express the shock that stung in my gut.

The boy shuffled a deck of cards. "Anyway, somebody is randomly dealt the king of spades—that's the stiff."

"But Capalon is ruled by a queen," I interjected.

The boy shrugged. "When the game was created, it was a king. Anyway, you're trying to go after the person you think has the king of spades and if you guess right and take all their cards, you win. Wanna play?"

I shook my head, feeling suddenly nauseous.

A breeze hit my face, steering my attention to the back door. Feeling the need for fresh air, I dismissed myself from the card game and pushed my way through the mass of bodies. I opened the door and walked out into a cloud of smoke, sending me into a coughing fit.

"Hey, New Lady," said a returning court man with sun-kissed cheeks and a pale head of hair. Two other boys accompanied him, both wearing mischievous smiles. "Wanna smoke?" he asked.

"No," I choked out.

"What's your court talent?" asked the pale boy.

I said "singer" through another cough.

"Oh, well if you're a singer, you should probably stay away from us. Nicotine is damaging to your vocal cords," he said with a grin. "Doesn't matter for us, though." He waved his hand around the thin white object in his fingers and it disappeared, only to reappear in his other hand. "We're magicians."

The boys laughed, and I spotted a tall flame in the distance on the lawn. I pushed past them, crossed my arms and squeezed my fists in a march forward through the damp grass.

The Mondarians were a strange, disgusting breed of human.

Their behavior was repulsive, and they lived a life full of impure ideals. I sat on a log in front of the fire and picked up a thin stick, breaking off a piece at a time and tossing them into the flames.

"Needed some fresh air too?"

My heart jumped. "Ari," I said, spotting his face on the other side of the flames.

"I've seen a party or two in Badger River, but that's...well, I don't know what to call that," he said with a shake of his head. "Most of our parties are like this—around a bonfire, under the stars. It's the best way to party in my opinion."

I reached for another stick and tried to ignore the sting in my eyeballs—not from the smoke of the bonfire or the magicians at the door but from my own stupidity.

Why did I think being surrounded by my enemies would be easy?

"Hey, you okay?" asked Ari.

"Yeah," I said, holding back the tears that threatened to fall. "It's just...well, this is all so new to me and..."

And I was a fool to believe I could handle the shock of Mondarian culture.

"Are you homesick?"

Homesick? Ill of one's residence?

The fire popped in the break of my confused silence.

Ari shifted on his log. "Because it's okay if you are—this is an adjustment for sure."

I broke my stick in half. "Even for you?"

He nodded. "Yeah, of course. You think I'm used to all this hoopla? I'm the guy who's refused to have a haircut in over a year."

I laughed and sent the stick pieces to their death. "I assumed you loved all this, like everyone else."

He shook his head. "I love playing drums. And I need the money."

"For carpentry school, right?"

He scratched the back of his head. "Well, ideally, yes. But I plan to send my first season stipend money back to my dad. He, um...got himself into some trouble so I need to help him out."

"What did he do?"

"Lied."

I sensed there was more to the story but Ari didn't divulge any more details.

He tapped a stick against his palm. "Anyway, what's your plan?"

My plan? Surely, he didn't mean my plan to find my mother and reinstate her as the queen of Capalon. "What do you mean?"

"Say the king keeps you here for all four seasons. What are you going to do when you're done?"

"Nothing," I said, mesmerized by the reflection of the flames in his eyes. "I would go back home." I tore my gaze off his face and looked at the fire.

"And do what?" he asked.

As soon as I completed my match ceremony, I would be assigned to my area of focus in science, technology, engineering or math and take direction from the queen's requests for research. If my plan worked, I'd be taking direction from my mother and not my sister.

I sighed. "Whatever my mother needed me to do."

"Does she run a family business or something?"

I chewed the inside of my cheek. "Yes."

"Is that what you want to do?"

"I don't exactly have a choice."

The fire popped, sending a burst of embers into the air.

I had the urge to say more. To keep talking to a boy I didn't know —a *Mondarian* boy I didn't know—but I had already said too much. I tossed my last piece of stick into the fire. "I'm exhausted from the day. I'm heading to bed."

"Oh, are you sure? I—"

"Goodnight, Ari." I left the fire before hearing the rest of Ari's words, only to be stopped at the door to the Lounge by the same group of magicians.

The pale one looked me up and down. "Hey New Lady, wanna watch something else disappear? It's a two-person trick."

"No," I said, with no attempt to hide the disgust from my face. "Can you please step away from the door?"

The magician only smiled and took a step toward me. "But I think you're the perfect candidate for the trick."

I shuddered as he ran a finger under my jaw.

My sister and I each had a vial of pepper spray to deploy in emergency situations. All I had to do was hold my hand in front of the boy's face and give Chip the command.

I opened my palm against my thigh and my body stiffened.

"She asked you to move, Felix," Ari said behind me.

The pale boy's face twisted. "Oh, don't tell me you're hanging around Novak." His eyes narrowed on Ari. "Has your daddy gambled your mom away too? Because I wouldn't mind putting a bid in for her." The other boys laughed as new plumes of smoke rose from their mouths.

"Move, Felix," Ari said, taking a step closer to me.

Felix blew smoke in Ari's face before slowly stepping away from the door. Ari's fingertips touched my back, gently guiding me back inside the Lounge.

"He's the worst," Ari said, when we stepped inside. The loud music stopped, so he didn't have to shout. "He's from my hometown and I have no idea how the maestro has tolerated him this long."

Both our heads snapped to the sound of my name.

"Paris Marigold! There she is! Our last New Lady," Darden McCray said from atop one of the low tables. "Go ahead and show us your heart."

I looked at Ari first, then Darden. "My what?"

Genevieve's head popped up in front of me. "Darden did a card trick where all of his hearts vanished. And it turns out all the New Ladies have a heart! Check your pocket!"

I shook my head. "I don't have—" But when I reached my hands into my pockets, the fingers on my right hand grazed the edge of a card. I pulled out a two of hearts and held it above my head. The crowd in front of Darden burst into cheers.

"See, I told you all the New Ladies stole my heart," he said, placing a hand over his chest.

"Do one more!" shouted a voice from the crowd.

Darden's proud face nodded as he waved his hands in front of his face, then produced a notebook and a marker from the air. "Alright. But first I need a volunteer."

Hands shot up all around us.

"Paris Marigold," he said, meeting my eyes. "Since you were the last New Lady to steal my heart, how about you come up here?"

I tried to protest, but Genevieve tugged my arm, pushing me up to Darden's makeshift stage. Darden placed the notebook in my hands. "Paris will serve as my lovely assistant for this trick which I call Capalon McCray."

The crowd hissed, draining blood from my face.

"Death to Capalon!" shouted a voice from the crowd.

"Stinking stiffs!" shouted another.

I clutched Darden's notebook with stiff fingers.

Did he know who I was? And was this an elaborate Mondarian-magician way to have me killed?

"In this trick, I will prove that I have the same genius as our enemy. I need any five-digit number," Darden said, scanning the faces of his audience.

A number was shouted, and Darden wrote it down in thick black marker on the notebook in my hands. "Based on this number, I'll make a prediction."

Darden asked a girl in the front row to pick a card from a deck he pulled from his pocket. She showed it to the audience—the ace of clubs, then handed it back to Darden.

He rubbed his chin, wrote something on the card, folded it and placed it inside a small box on the fireplace mantle behind him.

"Okay," he said, "Now I will blindfold myself and turn around.

Miss Marigold, select two random people to write two more five-digit numbers below the first one."

I picked two girls from the front row who followed Darden's instructions.

"Got them?" he asked over his shoulder. "Good. Now, I'll add two of my own random numbers."

Still blindfolded, Darden asked for my guidance as he jotted down two more numbers, so that the page in the notebook looked like:

53898
67923
12602
32076
87397

Darden faced the audience. "I'd like somebody who thinks they are good at math to come up here and add this up. Not a drummer, of course."

The crowd responded with a mix of boos and laughter.

A returning member, claiming to be a magician himself, added up the numbers, displaying a total of 253,896.

"Miss Marigold, my lovely assistant, will you please take out my prediction and read it out loud?" asked Darden, smiling under his blindfold.

I retrieved the box and unfolded the ace of clubs. "Two hundred and fifty-three thousand eight hundred ninety-six." I flipped the card around to share the evidence with the audience which erupted in cheers and applause for the magician.

Darden tore off his blindfold and bowed to the audience.

Confident Darden was no longer trying to kill me, I leaned into him after his final bow. "It's clever."

"It's magic," he responded, half to me and half to the audience.

I laughed. "No, it's simple math."

Darden crossed his arms. "You think you know the secret to my genius?"

My mouth turned up into a half-smile. "The hearts—you must have placed them in our pockets during our dance training. And for the 'magic' number—it's just adding the nines and then—" But before I could finish, a wall of green smoke billowed around me.

"Hey, no smoke bombs in the Lounge!" somebody shouted.

When the smoke cleared, Genevieve and Heather stood in front of me and Darden had vanished.

"So, were you in on the trick?" asked Heather.

I stepped off the table. "No, I didn't know anything about it until—"

"Gen thinks you were in on it," Heather said.

"It's okay," Genevieve said. "You don't have to tell me, but that's my guess." Their heads turned at the sound of a guitar.

"Oh, that's Reese Olsen," Heather said. "The cute singer I was telling you about, Gen."

Genevieve grabbed my wrist and pulled me forward to follow Heather.

A small group of girls had already formed around Reese as he sang a song about summer love. The relaxed melody encouraged the girls to sway and bob their heads in time with the music. When Reese finished, all the girls clapped. "Play another one!" shouted Staci Ringer.

Layla strode up beside me. "Come on, Paris. Let me rescue you from this crappy music."

"Layla, don't be rude," Genevieve said. "Reese is an excellent musician."

Layla turned her back to Genevieve. "Are you coming or staying?" she asked me.

Reese started another song, and I needed a good excuse to try another venture out of the Lounge to look for my mother. "I'm going to stay and listen."

I received an eye roll from my roommate before she headed back to our room.

The other girls were too immersed in Reese's music to notice me easing away and heading out the Lounge door. I followed the sound of a slamming door but took a step back when a uniformed guard turned the corner. The guard exited a small room with large, clear windows. Peering around the corner, I saw multiple viewing screens with varying angles of the Mansion, plus cabinets and a large board covered with dozens of keys hanging from hooks. The door to the room opened again as one guard exited and another entered. One of the keys on the board had to unlock the Records Room. But I wasn't about to steal a key surrounded by a swarm of guards. I would have to find a way to track the schedules of the guards, learn their names and—

"Paris?"

I jumped with a shriek.

"What are you doing out here?" asked Reese, with a tilt of his head.

"Um..." What would a court lady be looking for? "Just looking for the rehearsal studios. I don't remember which hallway to take."

Reese smiled with his blue eyes. "That's where I'm headed. And lucky for you, I remember where they are."

I swallowed a lump of frustration down my throat. "I thought you were performing your songs for the Court Ladies."

He shrugged. "I'm done and wanted to work on some new stuff before I turn in."

I shot a final glance at the board of keys inside the guard's station. "Okay. Let's go to the rehearsal studios."

We entered a carpeted hallway lined with a series of transparent doors. Reese opened one and said, "Ladies first," waiting for me to take a step inside the tiny room.

I crossed the threshold, but kept my left palm available. "Can you keep the door open?" I asked. "I...don't like confined spaces."

"Okay." He took a seat on a piano bench. "So, I have this song that would be great with your harmony. Want to hear it?"

I was in a tiny room alone with a boy. I had already been disgusted by Felix's advance and was gaining an understanding of what the guard had meant by an 'arrangement' during our tour of the Hall of Memories. "Reese...just to clarify, is your only intention in this rehearsal studio to sing with me?"

He looked up from his guitar. "What else...wait, did you think I was going to—"

"I'm sorry, I don't know why I said that." I rubbed my forehead, wanting to disappear like Darden from embarrassment.

Reese opened his palms and shook his head. "No, it's fine. I get it, there's a bunch of guys you don't know and getting into a confined space with one could seem, well you know—like I have a hidden agenda, which I don't! I mean, not that there's anything wrong with you—you're a pretty girl, but I just want to sing with you—that's all, I swear."

Heat rushed to my face. I wasn't sure if it was because it was the first time a boy called me a 'pretty girl' or because I assumed he might attack me. "I'm not sure how good I'll be, but let's give it a try."

I found myself eventually relaxing, convinced that the only thing Reese Olsen wanted from me was my voice.

"How do you think that sounds?" he asked when we were finished.

"Nice. It's quite a talent to be able to compose songs in your head like that."

He nodded and puffed his cheeks. "Just takes more than talent to get noticed. And I haven't figured out what that is yet. But maybe harmonies are what I've been missing."

"Maybe."

Reese yawned. "Ready to head back?"

"No, I'm going to work on some scales," I lied. "In case I'm the focus of Maestro's sectional again tomorrow."

After Reese left, I headed back in the direction of the guard's station, when I saw the outline of the captain's silhouette turn my way. I exited the hallway through the first door I could find, leading me out into a dark courtyard. I hid behind a square-shaped bush when the sound of another door opened at the opposite end of the courtyard, followed by murmuring.

I poked my head around the bush to see Maestro Leto holding a woman, or perhaps a girl, in his arms. Their faces pressed together in a passionate kiss—the maestro's body and lack of light in the courtyard hiding any revealing clue to the identity of the maestro's partner. Then as quickly as they stepped into the courtyard, they turned to step back inside, flashing me the smallest hint of physical attributes of the girl.

And I could only think of one person who matched—Layla Tanvi.

CHAPTER
10

The next morning, one hundred court members filled the dining hall with their bodies and conversations. I followed behind Layla through the buffet line and stared at the back of her head between piling my plate with, according to their name plates, eggs, bacon and hash brown. I was thankful to have seen her in bed when I left the courtyard the night before, but she could have beat me back to the room through some unknown shortcut of the Mansion.

"Thanks again for last night, Paris," Reese said as he passed behind us. Then his eyes bounced to Layla's shocked expression. "What? She sang with me."

Layla turned her head over her shoulder to cast me a suspicious glance. "Sure, you did." She slammed a spoonful of gravy against her plate. "So, you've purchased a ticket to Reese Town. I thought you were one of the cool ones, Paris."

"I haven't purchased anything." I picked up a pastry which I had learned from the salon to be a *donut*. "Is Reese named after a city?"

Layla chuckled. "Nice try at a cute diversion, but you don't have to hide your infatuation for him."

Infatuation? Layla thought I had romantic feelings for Reese?

"Layla, my involvement with Reese Olsen last night only involved singing."

She nodded with a grin. "But that's how it always starts, right? First, it's singing, then it's talking and before you know it, you're writing Mrs. Reese Olsen on your sheet music."

I waited for Layla to pick a table but she tilted her head to the door. "I'm off to the rehearsal studios. I saw that they have a brand-new piano in there that's just begging me to play it."

I had plans to interrogate Layla over breakfast about her activities following the party in the Lounge. "I can eat while you play. I would love to listen."

"Sorry, princess. I don't play for other people. I only play for me. See you at rehearsal."

Unsure of where to sit, I picked an empty seat next to Staci Ringer and across from Darden McCray. "Hello, Darden. Where did you—" But he picked his tray up and left the table.

I had just taken a bite of a long cream-filled donut when Ari Novak took Darden's empty seat. "Good morning," he said, before digging into his eggs.

"Goo-muhr," I started, but took my time to swallow before speaking again. "Good morning."

"How are those?" His head tilted toward my donut in-hand.

"The white cream ones are better," I said, showing him the yellow custard innards of my pastry.

He nodded. "Good to know." He shoveled a heaping forkful of eggs into his mouth.

His silence made my shoulders tense, so I looked to Staci, who was caught up in a heated conversation about a Junior Court competition with Genevieve. Left to talk with Ari Novak on my own, I scanned my brain for questions appropriate for a drummer:

When did you decide you enjoyed hitting things with sticks?

Are you concerned about future hearing loss?

Do you buy everyone you meet hot chocolate or just me?

But to my relief, Ari was the first to ask a question. "Are you getting along with your roommate?"

I nodded. "She's very...strong-willed but has been a decent person for temporary cohabitation."

And is possibly our maestro's secret lover.

Ari smiled. "Cohabitation?"

"Oh, I mean—"

"No, I like it. I like you and your funny words."

Heat rushed to my face, so I stabbed my eggs.

Ari sipped on something from a white foam cup. "I thought Darden and I hit it off right away but he refused to talk to me last night. I'm not sure what I did to make him so upset."

Recalling my dissection of Darden's tricks and his deployment of a smoke bomb, I had a feeling Ari wasn't the cause of Darden's foul mood. "He's probably just...thinking of a new trick to perform."

"FELIX!" shouted a girl with a crooked-nose who stood to reveal a pair of smudged, intensely violet lips. "That lip balm you gave me last night was clear!"

Felix shrugged and didn't bother to rise out of his seat to speak with the girl. "Never trust a magician. And it looks like Sarah can't trust her boyfriend around you either."

I followed the turning heads in the dining hall to find a boy whose lips had turned the same vivid shade. The girl sitting next to him left the room crying, leaving the crooked-nose girl behind her shouting for both Sarah and the boy.

Felix and his cohorts roared with laughter. Nobody else in the dining hall seemed to find his trick as humorous.

I returned my attention back to my food. "Why is there animosity between you and Felix?"

Ari sighed. "That's a long story."

"I enjoy long stories."

Ari took another sip of his drink. "Tasha, my girlfriend, went on a ski trip last winter when I was helping my dad move into his apartment. One of her friends told me she kissed Felix, and we had this huge fight about how I hadn't been spending enough time with her. I was so focused on all the stuff with my dad, that I pushed her to the side I guess."

"So, did she really kiss Felix?"

He shrugged. "It doesn't matter if she did or didn't. We're better now."

"But why is Felix angry with *you*? It only makes sense that you should be angry with *him*."

"Wow, I haven't even finished my hot chocolate yet and you're asking the tough questions." Ari smiled, so I didn't feel like I was overstepping Mondarian bounds.

He rubbed the side of his nose. "My family used to own a tree farm that employed a bunch of people in Badger River. My dad managed the finances and told us we were doing well all the time, but then the bank showed up and kicked us out of our house. Turns out my dad wasn't gone for his sales meetings he told us about—he was gambling all our money away. Felix's dad worked for my dad, so when we lost our farm, Felix's dad lost his job."

I nodded and had a sudden appreciation for my kingdom. Capalons weren't allowed to gamble for reasons like Ari's dad. We were a productive people and gambling was far from productive. Still, I couldn't help but have sympathy for Ari. He lost his own home due to his father's poor decision-making.

Ari leaned his elbows on the table. "Anyway, how about some lighter conversation? What's your favorite color?"

I swallowed my last bit of donut. "All of them. Except for grey. Yours?"

"Red—the color of Christmas and my favorite flannels."

"Why the flannel obsession?"

"Why not?"

He smiled and my eyes lingered on his mouth. "How did you get the scar on your lip?"

"Fell while climbing a boulder when I was a kid. How did you get into singing?"

"My mother."

"She's a singer too?"

I nodded.

"And your dad—does he sing?"

"No. He's dead."

Ari's black brows softened. "Oh, I'm so sorry. Do you have any siblings?"

"One older sister."

"Has she taken over some of those parental responsibilities?"

"Yeah, kind of. Chip actually..."

What was I doing?

Ari waited patiently for me to continue, but I revealed far too much information to a boy who was also my enemy. A boy who could out me in front of a room full of Mondarians, resulting in sudden-death at the hands of Captain Murphy or anyone with a weapon.

"Chip? Who's that?" Ari finally asked.

I licked my lips. "Um...my dog. I actually need to go. Layla wanted me to meet her in the rehearsal studio, so..." I picked my tray up off the table.

"Oh, okay. Talk to you later?" asked Ari, his brown eyes waiting for my response.

Why did talking to Ari feel safe and dangerous at the same time? The Mondarian food had to be playing games with my neurons. "Yes," I said, cursing myself for the wrong response. "Talk to you later."

THROUGH THE TRANSPARENT glass of one of the rehearsal studios, I found Layla's head bobbing behind a piano. Then Darden walked past me toward a studio with a black opaque door. "Darden, can we talk?"

But he kept walking, so I followed.

"If you're going to bother me in here, could you at least close the door?" he asked.

Obeying his request, I closed the door, then turned around. "Why are you ignoring me and Ari? Is it because I solved your magic tricks? I won't tell anyone, I promise. I just think that it isn't fair to Ari that—"

"And tell me, Miss Marigold, how is it that you were able to solve a mathematical illusion in mere seconds?" He turned around and my feet carried me backward.

"Just...quick observation," I said with shortened breath.

"What's the name of the lake that sits in the middle of Green Heights?"

"Um..." My brain searched for an answer. "The locals all call it something different."

Darden crossed his arms and stepped toward me. "There is no lake in the middle of Green Heights."

"Oh...I know that. I was just—"

"I'm only going to ask you this once." Darden's face was so close to mine, I could taste his minty breath from his blue piece of chewing gum. "Are you from Capalon?"

I was cornered. I had nowhere to go. My pulse communicated the same message to my brain.

He knows.

My mouth opened for a second with no sound escaping other than my staccato breathing. "I'm not..."

Darden's eyes hardened on mine, my terrified face looking back at me through his black-framed lenses. I could almost hear the reverberation of my heart off his chest. His intense glare was such a foreign look for him, causing me to notice how he towered over me, how his forearm muscles wove between thick veins and his jawline cut at sharp, square edges.

He reached for something in his jacket and I panicked. "Chip, deploy pepper spray!" I shoved my palm in his face and turned my head.

Darden fell to the ground with a painful cry.

I jumped for the door.

"Wait!" Darden shouted through a violent cough and watering eyes. "I'm not going to tell anyone, I swear!"

I paused at the door as something fell at my feet. The thing Darden was reaching for was a notebook.

"Look through it. It's full of all my tricks and ideas. I could use your help—your scientific knowledge to make me an even better magician. Help me...and I'll keep your secret safe."

"And if I don't help you, you'll tell everyone who I am?"

Darden pulled a cloth from his pocket and wiped the mucus from his nose. "No. A magician never reveals the other magician in the room. But...I *could* make it easy for other people to make that discovery on their own. Who are you, anyway? Why are you here?"

I shook my head. "You know that I'm Capalon. That's bad enough."

He nodded. "Understood. A magician never shows all of his cards. So, it's a deal then?" He held out his hand, but I hesitated shaking it.

"What kind of trick do you need my help for?"

His eyes focused on the ceiling. "Something so spectacular it would make you fall in love with somebody you don't even know."

"You want to impress a girl?"

"Impress is too light of a word. I want her to be...*mystified.*"

I scratched the back of my head. "And you swear you won't tell anybody who I am?"

Darden's eyes returned to mine. "Miss Marigold, a magician's deepest secrets are the methods behind his tricks. This notebook contains everything. And I swear on this notebook—a paper-bound copy of my soul—that your secret is safe with me."

Could I trust a Mondarian magician with my secret? The door handle was inches from my hand. I could run out of the rehearsal studio and call for an auto-taxi outside the Mansion. I could go back to Capalon and forget that I ever set foot in Mondaria. I could forget about my mother, apologize to my sister and meet my match like a good Capalon princess.

But something about Darden's intensity felt familiar—it was the same ambition that controlled the citizens of Capalon—the same ambition that led me to Mondaria. "Deal," I said, shaking Darden's hand.

He turned my hand to look at the underside of my wrist which glowed blue. "Fascinating. Imagine the magic I could perform with this technology."

I reeled my hand away. "Who's the girl you're using illegal technology to impress?"

Through swollen eyes and a running nose, Darden smiled. "The queen of hearts."

OUR FIRST REHEARSAL as the collective King's 100 took place inside the Stardust Ballroom. Agnes and Eric walked us through placements on the ballroom floor before the maestro entered. His presence eliminated the quiet laughter and whispered conversation that took place during the managers' instruction. Maestro climbed the steps to a wooden stage at the front of the ballroom as Francis took a seat at a piano on the floor.

Maestro started to address us just as the main set of doors opened behind us. He lifted his head. "Mr. Adaire, are you *really* showing up late to my rehearsal?"

"Yes, sir, I apologize," Felix said as he fell into position with the other magicians.

The maestro crossed his arms. "How is it that you're in your fourth and final season on my court and you choose to show up late to rehearsal *now*?"

"No excuse, sir," responded Felix.

Maestro rubbed his square chin. "Okay. Get out."

"What?"

"You're off my court. I've only kept you this long because the king likes you, but I don't care anymore. You're done, Felix."

"That's not fair." Felix's voice wavered. "I need this last season stipend to pay off my new snowmobile."

The maestro's face twisted. "That's what you people spend your money on? Pathetic. Guards! Anybody out there? Come get this piece of trash out of my ballroom!"

Two guards appeared and escorted Felix to the doors.

"No! I'm not leaving! You can't do this to me! The king will find out and, and—" but the guards closed the doors before Felix could finish his threat.

Maestro pulled a music stand to the center of the stage. "Everyone can be replaced, people. Doesn't matter if you're a Fourth Season or a new member. Okay, places for the Blessing!"

My muscles instinctively tensed as I pulled out the sheet music for the Blessing Song. Would Maestro immediately target me once we started singing or would he wait till the end of the rehearsal? To my relief, I was gifted the comfort of singing through the entire song without interruption. My ears battled with the urge to listen to the surrounding voices or concentrate on my own notes. I loved the blend of the added voices from the returning members and how our sound filled the expansive ballroom. But my ears' warm bath in the bubbling blend of voices turned cold at the maestro's cut off on the last chorus.

"No! Tenors, what key is that? The key of lazy singing? You call yourselves singers?" He reached for something out of his pocket, then jumped off the stage. "Who needs a key? I have about, oh twenty on this keyring." He proceeded to peel brass and silver keys off his large key ring and hurl them at each tenor he passed.

I held my breath, fearing that one of the maestro's keys would impale a tenor's face.

And then the back of my neck prickled with excitement.

Keys.

Taking a key out of the guard's station might have been an

impossible task, but that was before my new friend, the magician, blackmailed me.

✦

AT LUNCH, I whispered to Darden to meet me in one of the rehearsal studios. I paced the floor of a doorless studio when he entered.

"This rehearsal studio doesn't have a door," he said.

I heard from one of the returning court ladies that Maestro hurled a chair into the door the season before out of anger at some singer. Thankfully, only the door was damaged. "All the other ones are taken. Just keep your voice down, we'll be fine."

Darden took another look behind him, then sat down on the piano bench while I continued to pace with my hands clasped behind my back. "There's something from the guards' room; a key."

"If you're planning to assassinate the king, I can't help you."

I shook my head. "No, it's nothing like that. It's the key to the Records Room." I took a step closer to him and lowered my voice. "I think one of our citizens might have escaped to Mondaria and I want to check the documentation."

"So, that's why you're here? You're looking for an escaped Capalon?"

I nodded.

He smiled. "Done. Stealing keys is no challenge for me."

"Thank you!"

"As long as you agree to be my date to Grape Stomp."

My throat went dry. "Why?"

"You know why. We'll be spending time together. Might as well make it look like there's a reason for it." I followed his eyes to the replacement acrylic glass panel that had been brought into the studio but not affixed to the doorframe. I hadn't even noticed it since it was so transparent. "I already have ideas," he said still staring at the glass pane. "And you're required to help me."

Grape Stomp was weeks away. I hoped I would be back in

Capalon with my mother by then, so I agreed to be Darden's date. "But I need the key first," I said.

He nodded. "Absolutely. A magician always follows through."

And he followed through with his task way faster than I expected. That night, I stood with the other new members inside a small dining room, where we were told we would dine with 'special guests.' Darden handed me a deck of cards as we awaited further instruction from Agnes and Eric. "You'll find what you asked for in here," he whispered.

I slipped the deck into my newly tailored blazer pocket. "That was fast."

"That's because I'm the best," he said with a smug grin.

I thanked Darden before heading over to Ari, who displayed a closed-smile on his face while rhythmically tapping his index fingers on an invisible drum. "Does your joyful temperament have anything to do with a certain magician getting kicked off the court today?" I asked, unable to fight a smile at the sight.

Ari stopped his air-drumming and shoved his hands in his pockets. "I don't like lying, so I'm not going to say no; that's *exactly* what it has to do with. Plus, my roommate decided to talk to me again."

"And the fact that we have no idea who we're dining with doesn't bother you?"

"Nope," he said rocking on the heels of his feet. "I just know it's nobody too important. They save the big events for the important ones—like the Harvest Ball tomorrow."

I nodded, finding comfort in Ari's logic.

Agnes finally told us all to find a seat, so I sat at a table with Ari, Darden, Layla and Staci. Four seats were still open at our table and my heart accelerated. Why wouldn't they tell us who we would dine with?

The room was silent except for Agnes, who shut the two large doors at the back of the room. She leaned against the door, as if waiting for some sort of signal.

Then three loud knocks from the other side of the doors turned our heads.

"New Ladies and Gentlemen of the King's 100," shouted Agnes.

"Yes, ma'am," we replied.

"Allow me to introduce you to our special guests this evening—" She grinned and opened the doors. "—the returning members of the King's 100."

CHAPTER
11

We stood to welcome our comrades as if they were real guests of the Mansion. Every returning courting member wore a ridiculous outfit—some elegant, most likely pulled from the back of the tailor's storage room. Others were homemade, like sheets held up with rope and hats made from toilet paper. Some boys were dressed as girls and some girls dressed as boys. Make-up was intentionally overdone and gaudy.

As the returning members chose their seats, Agnes hopped up on a chair. "Treat this dinner as you would a real one. Keep all the rules about court conversation in mind, no matter how...*challenging* your conversation may be. Okay, greet your guests!" Agnes pulled a large orange hat out of a bag and took a seat at a table.

Two boys and one girl approached our table. I greeted the boy to my right, who wore nothing but a purple velvet robe and had a black swirly mustache drawn under his nose. "Hello my dear, sweet court lady. I'm Mr. Sleeps-with-a-lot-of-women," he said in a low, dramatic voice.

The girl to my left introduced herself as a Lady Lovely and wore a bright red fitted dress that squeezed together an inappropriate amount of cleavage. Three feather boas wrapped around her shoulders and her make-up was a burst of color from her forehead down to the tops of her breasts. The scent of something sour wafted from her breath and her speech slurred. "It's a pleasure to meet you, Miss Mothercold."

After a few minutes, I discovered just *how* challenging the test was, given the fact that just about every statement or question out of the girl's mouth involved something vulgar or slanderous. But it forced me to use just about every conversation tactic in the court handbook:

Never apologize for a Mansion Guest's issues.

Refrain from answering personal questions.

Deflect from all topics pertaining to sex, politics and religion.

Even though the majority of the people in the room served as a colorful form of entertainment, my eyes continued to be drawn to a black-haired boy's laughter and smile.

I felt my stomach turn acidic from the amount of butter and fat from our meal, but I continued eating, savoring the flavor of every mouthful. I was about to shovel in another bite of food when a scream turned our heads.

Two court members wandered around the tables, scaring people by popping up behind their shoulders. I joined in with the laughter at the reactions, but when the two court members neared our table, I dropped my fork—their faces were painted to look like corpses, dressed all in grey and their exposed wrists were painted bright blue. Their name tags stated that they were THE EVIL KING GAVIN and THE EVIL QUEEN REBECCA or as I knew them, my father and mother.

I watched in horror as the fake king and queen danced around the room, scaring people with their touches and screams. The returning court members yelled things like "Get out of here, slimy glow worms!" and "Stiffs!" But the worst comment of all was when someone shouted, "Go die again, you ugly robots!"

I looked at Ari's face, hoping his would mirror the same image of disgust on mine but he laughed along with the rest of the room.

Why did I expect anything different from a Mondarian boy?

Acid churned in my stomach and traveled up my esophagus. I swallowed down the bitter taste, but it was too strong. I backed away from the table and headed to the nearest door, which took me outside to a small courtyard. I tried to breathe. Tried to settle the nausea but my stomach muscles cramped, forcing my torso forward and emptying the contents of my dinner onto the freshly cut grass.

I felt a cool hand on the back of my neck. "You alright there, princess?" asked Layla.

She handed me a napkin, and I wiped the corners of my mouth.

I wanted to tell her that my intestines were rejecting her kingdom's unhealthy cuisine. That I had forgotten for a moment I was Capalon. And her fellow court members had just made a mockery out of my dead parents. But I only nodded. "Yeah. Just ate too fast, I think."

She rubbed my back. "You shouldn't listen to them. They're morons."

I paused, considering the possibility she tried comforting me about the disturbing portrayal of my dead parents.

"Whatever Kelly Ortega is saying to you—it's all just to scare you. It's a joke. The dinner tomorrow will be nothing like this."

Kelly Ortega must have been Lady Lovely. "Thank you, Layla."

Thankfully, when we reentered the dining room, applause signaled the end to the evening, along with a dramatic exit of our 'special' guests. After some conversation tips from Agnes and Eric, I followed the other new members back to the Lounge.

Ari strode up beside me but I kept my eyes focused on the back of Reese's head in front of me. "Hey, are you okay, Paris? You disappeared from our table there at the end."

"I'm fine."

"Oh, good. Because I was thinking about taking a walk outside—I heard they have a statue of a giant moose on the lawn somewhere but no one can ever find it. You wanna join me for a moose hunt?"

I had allowed myself to believe that Ari was a nice boy, but I couldn't shake the image of him laughing at the pageantry of my dead parents. My fingers grazed the outline of the deck of cards inside my pocket. "No, Ari. I don't want to join you." I passed the Lounge and headed in the direction of the Records Room.

WHEN I ARRIVED at the Records Room, I looked both ways to make sure nobody was around before unlocking the door. I slipped inside and shut the door behind me, then made my way through the maze of filing cabinets and found it odd that the Mansion staff would go to the lengths of hanging framed photographs on the walls. I looked closer at the numerous pictures—each being only about the size of a square lunch plate and all of the same people—the rulers of The Lands and their spouses.

Why had the photos been hidden away in the Records Room and not put on display in the Hall of Memories? When I looked closer at one of the photos, I found my father's aggressive eyes looking back at me and small text in the bottom corner that read: *Annual Lands Rulers' Assembly.*

The Mondarian king doesn't display photos of his enemies.

The Mondarian king also didn't have the gall to throw photos of himself away, even if his enemies were in the picture. I scanned the photos, hoping to find my mother among the spouses but she never attended—I assumed because she embarrassed my father to such lengths that he forbade her from attending any outside events. Then, of course, the one year he took her, they died before my mother even had a chance to smell the centerpieces on the tables.

The photos progressed through the years as I walked toward the back to the room. I eventually landed on the last three, with my sister's hard, but nervous face replacing my father's. Only, in the last photo taken that summer, my sister's cheeks were reddened and her smile looked as if she were trying not to laugh—almost as if there were something she found so amusing, that she couldn't contain her composure in her one photo every year with the other leaders of The Lands.

In fact, I would have said she looked happy. I was instantly jealous of whatever had sparked her emotion, since I hadn't been able to pull an ounce of joy out of her since our parents' deaths. I scanned the other faces in the photo, unable to find King Orson and Queen Marisol. Was my sister happy that the Mondarian king and queen were absent from the event?

I gave up on the mystery of my sister's happiness and headed to the filing cabinets, starting with the cabinet of the coroner's reports. I flipped back to three years prior at the time of my mother's death and pulled all the files from that month. A Capalon speedcraft was the first to arrive on the scene, so there would be no reason for Mondaria to have any records of the incident, but I had to rule it viable evidence. I found only a laminated article, detailing the incident in a Mondarian newspaper.

KING AND QUEEN OF CAPALON DIE IN FIERY CRASH NEAR MONDARIAN BORDER

King Gavin and Queen Rebecca of Capalon were instantly killed in a fiery crash of their own high-tech plane. King Orson Anders celebrates their deaths as justice to Mondaria. Capalon will now be ruled by their sixteen-year-old daughter, who King Orson is calling "the upstart queen."

I stopped reading the article and placed it back inside the folder, then slammed the drawer closed before moving on to the file marked Capalon Royalty.

There was a folder assigned to each member of the royal family, dating back to the start of our kingdom. I flipped through to my family and pulled all four of our names. Both my mother's and father's folders were marked DECEASED. My sister's folder had her identification photo she had taken on the day of her coronation and listed the date she started serving as queen. And then there was mine —photoless and informationless other than my full name and birthdate.

The door opened. "Is anybody in here?" asked the captain. I hid beside the filing cabinet, out of view. His heavy boot steps traveled forward.

Clunk. Clunk. Clunk.

I held my breath. One more step and he would see me. They would arrest me and execute me shortly thereafter. My sister would probably start a war. Capalon would win and kill everyone in Mondaria, including a boy who I had recently turned down for a walk on the lawn.

Clunk.

"Captain Murphy, there you are, you ol' goon. Burning some calories again, buddy?"

The Captain turned away from me and I had never been so relieved to hear the sound of Maestro's voice.

"Bernie. Why are you here? This room is off limits to Mansion staff without the proper credentials."

"It's a *room*, Carson. Get off your high-horse. I want to know why I can't get access to the ballroom before noon tomorrow."

The captain sighed. "Bernie, we've been through this." The two men stepped away, carrying their conversation with them as the door shut.

I should have been able to calm my beating heart on my own. Take a few deep breaths and be okay. But I wasn't okay. I was gasping for air, unable to come back down from a potential death before I had any evidence to my claim for being in Mondaria. "Ch...Chip. Can you...talk me down please?"

Blue light filled the corner of the room. "Princess, inhale on one, two, three, four and exhale on one, two, three."

Chip's familiar voice helped me calm down and settle my breathing. I closed the cabinet door with my family's file and made a promise to myself out loud. "Chip, if I don't find any clues about Mother tomorrow, I'm leaving."

CHAPTER 12

The court ladies wore golden yellow lace gowns to represent the color of the turning larches, paired with matching lace masks that covered the bridge of our noses and eyes. The court men wore black tuxedos, which I was told was always their color no matter what the event, with black masks. Only their tie color would change with each performance—matched to the shade of our gowns.

As if handling a steaming-hot curling iron on my head wasn't torturous enough, we were also required to coat our faces with enhancements.

Layla had just finished helping me apply my make-up when she turned to scan herself in our dressing-table mirror. "This dress is an awful color."

"It's a color," I said in awe of the foreign shade against my skin.

"Too bad you're not still blonde. It might have actually looked good on you." She nodded toward Heather, who was complimenting herself with her eyes in the mirror. And in my opinion, she had every right to look infatuated with her appearance—the golden yellow against her pale skin and creamy-blonde hair made her look like a goddess of autumn.

Layla sighed. "At least these dresses have pockets."

Genevieve spoke from my left side. "All the dresses will have pockets for the magicians' cards."

"Then lucky for me, I have a place to hide my contraband." Layla flashed a smile to Genevieve, who turned her attention to Heather.

After Nicole Jordan's dismissal, Genevieve was given permission to move in with Heather as her new roommate, making them completely inseparable. Layla blamed Nicole for causing 'a disservice to us all.' But Nicole's dismissal only helped my whole 'blending in as a Mondarian' plan. Maestro issued an 'instant-dismissal' so Nicole was forced to leave her things behind. Heather took her pants, and I took everything else.

Agnes called us all to attention. "We'll be matching up with our walking partners downstairs in one minute. Oh, and drummers, make sure you don't miss your cue to leave the ballroom for the king's entrance. You'll need to give yourselves enough time to change out of your dresses and into your drumming uniform. And then you'll have an even faster change back into your dresses for dinner."

Staci groaned on the other side of Layla. "I didn't think I'd be changing clothes more than I'd be drumming for these events."

"And remember," continued Agnes, "this is a job. Your focus is to make our guests feel welcome, so no chatting with each other at any time."

"*Yes, ma'am.*"

We followed Agnes downstairs to match up with our section-assigned partners.

"You look lovely, Paris," Reese said as he held his arm out for me.

"Thanks." I took his arm.

Reese turned to look behind him with a huge grin on his face. "What is it?" I asked in a whisper as we lurched forward with the rest of the court and walked the twisting hallways to the Stardust Ballroom.

"Oh, nothing." But then Reese bent his head and spoke in a low voice. "It's just that Layla might actually convince someone she's a lady tonight."

Our double-line of court members paused as two Mansion staffers opened the large set of doors to the ballroom. The only thing I could see from my spot in the line was light pouring into the dim lobby where we stood. As we neared, a man's voice introduced the court over a loudspeaker, sending a wave of applause through the ballroom. When Reese and I finally crossed the threshold, the people had returned their focus to each other, giving me the opportunity to soak in the details of the Harvest Ball.

For having been a grey day in the mountains, the ballroom felt sunny and alive from the brilliant light of the sparkling chandeliers and the upbeat melody of a four-piece band. The tables were covered in beautiful cream-colored linens and large ornamental baskets of jeweled fruits. An aroma of cinnamon, apples and something sweet floated through the ballroom, making me want to open my mouth to taste the air. Glasses clinked, trays passed and laughter ensued. It was exactly as I had envisioned and more.

But my heart skipped a beat when I finally focused on the people —*hundreds* of wealthy Mondarian residents—foreigners and visiting dignitaries covering nearly every square inch of available floor. Women wore long gowns with plunging necklines and dripping jewels. Men wore tuxedos in every shade and style. Every guest donned either their own mask to match their outfits or took a generic silver mask from baskets placed around the room.

My fingertips touched my own mask, suddenly grateful for the additional coverage of my real identity.

"Time to mingle." Reese dropped my hand from his arm and disappeared into the sea of people.

I froze, unsure of which direction to take. Darden dazzled a couple with a card trick in front of me and Genevieve bobbed her head with a concerned look as she listened to an old woman speak about some spot on her hand.

"Let's find a court member to talk to, dear!" shouted a woman to a man beside her. They were both dressed in brown and had grey feathers affixed to their masks, reminding me of some sort of fowl.

"Can you believe we were finally invited here to see the King's 100?" she asked the man I assumed to be her husband. "I can't wait to tell the ladies at the club about this. Oh, there's a court member there doing a magic trick right now! Hurry!"

To avoid the threat of conversation, I made my way to the perimeter of the ballroom, avoiding eye contact with every guest I passed. Finding an open spot next to an empty food-tray on a stand, I bounced to the swing of the band's music and hoped I could avoid conversation until our call to dinner.

But then I felt a tap on my shoulder.

"Excuse me, miss. Can you break a bet for us?"

I turned to see two tall men with hefty mustaches. "My pleasure," I said with my practiced voice and smile.

"The trim in this ballroom—it's imported Hulgredeon limestone, is it not? Colonel Wexley here seems to think it's Mondarian quartzite."

We weren't required to know the material for the trim of the ballroom, but I'd studied enough geology to answer such a simple query.

I raised my eyebrows and pulled my shoulders back. "Well, then I'd say you owe the Colonel a drink." I smiled as the men continued their ridiculous banter about the territories of The Lands. I acted like I deserved a place in their conversation, when I was as visible to them as the oxygen molecules that filled the room—a feeling that was all too familiar being the invisible sister to the queen of Capalon.

Needing something to do with my hands, I shoved them in my dress pockets and felt the corner of something sharp. I pulled the object out of my pocket to find a small, sealed envelope with the name PARIS in capital letters.

Unable to read the letter in front of my mustached guests, I dismissed myself from their conversation and snuck out a side door to the hallway. I leaned my back against the wall as I tore open the envelope and read the note.

PARIS,

YOU NEED TO LEAVE MONDARIA BEFORE THE KING FINDS OUT WHO YOU ARE.

FROM, A COURT MEMBER WHO KNOWS YOUR SECRET

My knees buckled and all the hairs raised on the back of my neck. Somebody else other than Darden knew my true identity, but who?

It could have been any of the girls in the dressing room. It could have been Reese. In reality, it could have been any singer, drummer or magician passing me during the Social Hour to speak with guests. And unlike Darden, the court member who wrote the note wanted me to leave—either as a helpful warning or as a threat.

Dizziness and heat took over my body. I removed my mask and slid down to the cold floor, waving air into my face with the envelope and mask. Two people knew who I was, and I had to hope that they both had no intentions of telling the king.

Breathe. Focus. Breathe.

But my breathing only intensified. I was about to order Chip to help talk me down when I heard approaching footsteps beside me. I crumpled the note in my fist and shoved it inside the pocket of my dress.

"Paris?"

My brain took a second to register that the tuxedo and mask-clad boy was Ari Novak. His stance, his face, his very energy was taller in his black tuxedo. He looked around, then took a few steps toward me and bent down, removing his mask. "Are you okay?"

"Yeah, I was just...taking a break. I was getting dizzy from standing in one spot for too long."

He nodded but his face stayed serious. "You're probably dehydrated. Here." He handed me a water bottle—*his* blue aluminum water bottle.

Capalons never shared utensils or food to prevent the passing of germs. But I had noticed in Mondaria, sharing things like a water bottle wasn't out of the ordinary. So, to look Mondarian, I accepted Ari's offer and placed his water bottle to my lips. "Why are you out here?" I asked as I capped his water bottle and handed it back to him.

"Drummers' line up for the king's entrance."

I nodded, feeling like a fool for thinking that maybe there was a chance he was in the hall waiting just for me.

"Everything will be okay, Paris. Your table guests will love you. Just don't call any of them an ignoramus," he said with a wide smile that folded curved lines of skin at the corners of his eyes.

Ari thought I was nervous about talking with my table guests, which I guess was a partial truth—I had no idea who I would dine with and I could be seated with the one person in all The Lands who recognized me.

He wished me luck, then turned to head back toward his line-up.

"Ari?"

He turned his head, and I felt my throat tighten. I didn't know why I stopped him. But there was something inside me that wasn't ready to let him go. "Are you nervous?"

He shoved his hands in his pockets and took a few steps back to me. "Kind of. But think about the guy who *should* be nervous—the king." He freed one hand from his pockets and leaned his weight on one leg. The pose made him look like a debonair royal guest, rather than a young teenage drummer. He rubbed his jaw, which was freshly free of stubble. "We're just the ones to help him look good while he has to do the dirty work. Say I mess up tonight and make a fool out of myself, but the king messes up too. Maybe he does his whole speech with spinach stuck to his teeth or something. What are people going to talk about when they go home?" Ari folded his arms across his chest and shrugged. "The one drummer kid who missed a beat or the king who looked like he had grass stains on his teeth?"

I nodded and took a deep breath, feeling my heart settle back into its normal rhythm. "That makes sense." My final words to him from the night before pinched me with guilt. "Ari, I'm sorry I was short with you last night. I just wasn't feeling well after the dinner. Layla probably told everyone that I vomited out in the courtyard."

Ari's face twisted. "If she did, I didn't hear it. Wow, I'm sorry, Paris. That had to suck."

"Yeah. It sucked," I said, enjoying the sound of the last word. It wasn't used in Capalon, but it summed up the feelings of a less than desirable situation.

"Probably time for you to head back." Ari extended his hand to help me up, and I accepted, fully aware of the tingling jolt through my body from his touch. After checking my dress to make sure it was free of dust, I caught Ari's eyes lingering on me. "What is it? Do I already have grass stains on my teeth?" I showed him an exaggerated smile.

Ari laughed. "No, I just think you look," he cleared his throat, "um, you look...put together."

"Oh," I said, feeling my throat go dry. "You look...put together too."

Ari fidgeted with his gold tie. "Have a good show, Paris."

"Yeah, you too."

I reentered the ballroom and took a sip out of the nearest water goblet, breaking a major rule out of the court handbook. I set it back down on the table and lifted my head. My eyes scanned the room and they should have been searching for a suspicious court member or a blonde-haired woman who resembled my mother, but they refused to focus on anything other than a thought that tugged at the back of my mind.

The way Ari looked at me...

It wasn't aggressive like the way Felix looked at me during the welcome party. And it wasn't disconnected, like Darden's or Reese's faces, seeing me out of necessity for a friendship based on a mutual partnership around magic or music.

Ari looked at me and I felt...*beautiful.*

Agnes passed, reminding me and the other lingering court members that it was time to take our seats. I put my mask back on and headed to my assigned table near the back of the ballroom and greeted my guests. I stood behind my chair until all guests were present and took a seat. We had just completed our circle of introductions when three loud knocks on the closed main doors to the ballroom drew everyone's attention.

The doors opened and drumsticks tapped three times before the whole drumline fell into a loud cadence, sending an exciting energy throughout the ballroom and under my skin. The beats pinged off the arched ceiling and deep into my chest as they marched down an open aisle between the rows of tables. They separated into two even lines on either side of the aisle and one drummer played a steady roll.

"Ladies and gentlemen," boomed the Chancellor's voice through the ballroom's speakers, "please stand for King Orson Anders of Mondaria."

I stood with the rest of the ballroom and watched as the leader of my enemies walked the drummer-lined aisle to the head table at the front of the ballroom. I took a deep breath, knowing that my life hung on the hope that the stout man with a full head of golden hair and a trimmed beard would never know the enemy princess of Capalon was a member of his court. For some reason, I expected more from his ensemble but he only wore a black tuxedo with a silver tie. At the table, he lifted a chalice to his lips and took a sip. "For Mondaria."

He sat and the rest of the room followed suit except for the singers of the King's 100. Maestro stood at the edge of the head table to direct us in the Blessing Song and although I had been nervous at the thought of singing in front of my table guests, the thoughts in my head overtook my nerves as I watched Maestro.

What if the note came from Ari? What if he secretly knew who I was and he was trying to be helpful? In a way, I hoped it was him— that he was seeing me for *me* and not as Paris Marigold, the Mondarian. But I wasn't about to ask him if he knew I was a Capalon, just to have him run away and tell the king to execute me.

And what if Darden had been deceiving me? Or my own roommate? Reese? Genevieve?

The possibilities followed me throughout dinner and to the dance floor, where we were required to find a guest to dance with once the king and queen completed their solo dance as a couple. They bowed, signaling for everyone else to join them on the dance floor.

I had been so focused on the anonymous note, that when we started to dance, it took me a minute to recognize the familiarity of a nearby aroma. Then the connection hit me like a Capalon speedcraft —peppermint, lemon and lavender oil—a smell I had known since birth, belonging to my mother.

My dance partner winced. "Miss, yeh done stepped on mah foot."

I opened my mouth to apologize, but I was too shocked to respond. My mother was alive, and she was somewhere with me on King Orson's dance floor. My head swiveled, desperate to find her but it was too hard among the sea of masked faces and elegant gowns.

"Wouldn'ah be the firs' time I've been stomped on durin' a dance," he chuckled. Mr. Haggis continued to tell the story of some other lady he danced with back in his kingdom of Hulgrede but my attention could only focus on finding my mother.

As we traveled around the dance floor, I caught brief moments of her scent. I searched for a blonde head of hair but there were so many with all their faces covered in masks. My pattern turned to dance, look, smell, dance, look, smell.

Where was she? If I could smell her, why couldn't I see her? And why hadn't she noticed me yet?

But I was masked and with a different hair color. For all I knew, she had a new hair color too to avoid being recognized as the dead queen of Capalon.

Another partner. More spinning. More looking.

Eventually the maestro took the stage to cue the singers in our goodbye song. At the conclusion of the song, the king and queen made their formal exit, and as a court lady, I was expected to follow suit. But I didn't want to leave when I knew my mother was within feet of me.

"Honey, aren't you supposed to follow your comrades out the door?" asked my last partner, a rail-thin elderly man.

I nodded and stepped forward to catch up to my cohorts, looking behind me one final time, but no one broke free of the crowd to chase me. I could have allowed myself to feel miserable that my mother didn't recognize me, but the only emotion I could feel was pure elation.

My mother was alive, and I was right. I took the risk to enter Mondaria for a reason, and I wouldn't leave until my mother was safely with me.

CHAPTER 13

I bounded forward to catch up to Darden before we approached the stairwell to the dressing rooms. "Rehearsal studio. Now," I whispered in his ear, hiding my smile.

"But Miss Marigold, we're not supposed to go anywhere else in our court uniforms, other than—"

"This is an emergency, Darden." I wiggled my wrist just enough for him to get the message.

He followed me to the magician's rehearsal studio and shut the door.

"What's the emergency?" he asked.

"She's here," I said, letting my smile show itself without restraint.

"The Capalon you were looking for? She was at the ball?"

I nodded. "She didn't recognize me, but who would with my new hair and mask?"

"Wow, Mondaria now has *two* Capalons within its borders." Darden took a deep breath. "I'm happy that you're happy, Miss Marigold, but is this information so important it requires breaking a rule out of the court handbook?"

"Oh...no, I guess not. But there is something else." I handed him the note I found inside my pocket. "Any idea why somebody would write this?"

He read it and shook his head. "I know what you're thinking but I swear to you, I haven't told anyone." He handed the note back and looked in my eyes. "You don't believe me."

I chewed my bottom lip. "I do. I mean, I *want* to believe you, but how else would somebody know?"

Darden shrugged. "Maybe it's from your roommate. Do you talk in your sleep?"

"No. And knowing her, she would have preferred to accuse me herself in person. She's not one to avoid confrontation."

"I've noticed." Darden lifted his hands to crack his knuckles. "I promise I'll do what it takes to keep your secret safe, Miss Marigold."

"Thank you, Darden."

"Because I really need your brain for my illusion," he said with a smile, dropping his hands behind his back.

I sighed. "Of course, for your mystery girl."

"I told you—she's the queen of hearts. You just haven't found her yet."

A grin stretched across my face. "And here I thought we were the first to form a peaceful bond between two enemies."

Darden tilted his head to the door. "Enemies or not, we really need to change out of these clothes before we get in trouble."

❦

LATER THAT NIGHT in my room, I still couldn't get the note out of my head. I stared at Layla's vacant desk from my bed, littered with Mondarian coins, jewelry and a notebook with an artistic depiction of a rainbow. If one of the court members knew my secret, were they sharing the information with their friends?

The door opened and Layla put her toiletry tote away in her closet before taking a seat at her desk.

I leaned forward, eager to interrogate my roommate. "Layla, have you heard any rumors about me from other court members?"

She swiveled in her chair to face me. "Like what, princess?"

"I don't know exactly. I just...have this feeling that maybe I'm not fitting in here."

Her brows knitted together. "Yeah, because you don't."

My heart skipped a beat. "What do you mean?" I swallowed, fearing an accusation of my real identity.

She shrugged. "None of us fit in here. We weren't raised to be royalty, so we're all just putting on a facade when we're out there in our gowns and tuxedos."

I nodded as my heart rate settled. "But there's nothing strange you've heard about me specifically?"

Layla shook her head. "No. Just that you hang around Darden McCray a lot."

"Oh. Well, he asked me to be his date to Grape Stomp."

Layla lifted her brows. "Mr. Manners? Have a great time with that one."

"Who are you going with?"

"Simon Zacher."

"Is he that boy you played cards with at the welcome party?"

"Yes, ma'am. He's a Fourth Season drummer, and I *almost* beat him at the push-up contest."

Simon's age sparked a theory. "Layla, when you said you were interested in older men, *how* much older did you mean?"

Layla opened a small porcelain blue box and placed a pair of earrings and necklace inside it. "I didn't necessarily mean older. I just meant somebody who wasn't a scared, hormonal boy who doesn't know how to stand up with his own backbone."

I nodded and chewed on my thumbnail. "So...you're not interested in somebody like...Maestro?"

"EW! Who do you think I am, Paris?"

"I know, I'm sorry...it's just...I think I saw Maestro with a woman. Or possibly a girl our age. I can't be sure."

Layla's face twisted. "Maestro actually convinced somebody to be attracted to him? That's the sickest thing I've ever heard."

It *was* a disturbing thought to think there was somebody out there who wanted to kiss the maestro. And I was happy to finally rule out Layla as his potential lover. "Have you dated a lot of boys to give you the impression that they're all...what was it, spineless and testosterone-driven?"

"Close enough, and I've only really dated one. He broke my heart. And now I hate him. End of story."

Layla's broken heart reminded me about Darden's mystery girl. "Layla, what card did you get from Darden's trick?"

"A heart."

"I know, but which one? I got the two of hearts."

Layla reached for the baggy original jacket in her closet. "Seven. Is there more to the trick? Oh, did one of us win the unfortunate prize of attending Grape Stomp with him?" she asked with a wink.

She stepped out of her slippers, climbed into her bed and turned off her lamp, allowing the light of the moon to dance across our faces. I shut my eyes but my head was filled with too many questions to drift off to sleep:

Which court member wrote me the note?

Who was Maestro's mystery woman?

Who was Darden's queen of hearts?

And most importantly, how was I going to get my mother to notice me?

My thoughts then drifted to Ari standing above me in his tuxedo —his tall stance, the way the black of his attire matched his hair and brows, the way he looked at me—making me feel as if I had been truly seen for the first time in my life.

I took a deep breath, fighting the urge to allow the strange thoughts and emotions to fill my head. Maybe my match in Capalon would be handsome. Attraction was acceptable once a match was made for the sake of reproduction, but nothing more. Perhaps my match would feel the same desire for me and we could hide our attraction behind closed doors, like Xavier. Or maybe I was getting weak and allowing the Mondarians to brainwash me with their unnecessary attention to physical appearance and romantic feelings.

That had to be it.

Romantic feelings weren't real or necessary for the sake of humanity. I was being brainwashed. I took another deep breath and shut out the image of Ari but his words from our conversation lingered, the sound of his voice ingrained in my ears like the embedded speakers I had implanted since childhood.

And then something he had said forced my eyes open—if I wanted my mother to notice me, I had to be the offbeat drummer. I needed to stand out from the other members of the King's 100 so she would know who I was and take me back to Capalon where we could be a family again with my sister.

I just needed a plan.

CHAPTER
14

The next morning at breakfast, Layla left me again after the food line to go to the rehearsal studios so I took a seat next to Heather and Genevieve. I turned my head to catch a black head of hair sitting among some other First Season drummers. Feeling relieved that Ari chose to sit with them instead of me, I ate my breakfast. I didn't need to be tricked by emotional illusions into thinking that I had developed an attraction to him.

There was only one person I needed to be thinking about at all times, and that person was my mother. Genevieve and Heather bantered back and forth about their experience at the Harvest Ball, and I served as a spectator of their conversation.

Deciding I needed one more donut, I headed back up to the food line but on my way, Ari leaned back from his seat at the table to block my path. "So, you wanna go on that moose statue hunt with me after breakfast?"

"Yeah."

"Okay, meet you in the Lounge," he said with his smiling brown eyes.

No. I meant no. Why did I say yes? "Actually...I just remembered I have something to do after breakfast."

His shoulders slumped. "Oh. That's too bad."

What was that look behind his eyes? Hurt? "But I can talk for a few minutes now. Want another donut?"

He swiveled his legs around his seat and stood. "Definitely."

And that was the kick-off for my new routine in the Mansion for the following weeks—I would go through the food line with Layla, sit with Genevieve and Heather, then if time allowed talk to Ari for a few minutes over my second donut before wandering off to do some investigative work around the mansion or brainstorming in my room. Combined rehearsals followed, along with lunch and sectionals. Dinner was with Layla and *only* Layla—that was her strict policy for me which I didn't mind. Then depending on the night, magic planning with Darden or singing with Reese.

I must have walked the Mansion close to one hundred times, unable to spot a single clue about my mother. I even made a few more visits to the Records Room, but came up short for information leading me in the right direction. My time alone in my room involved conversations with Chip and recording my ideas for how to get my mother to notice me. They ranged from re-dying my hair back to blonde, leaving secret messages for her around the Mansion and traveling to surrounding towns on my off-days.

Chip had access to the chemical compound of hair dye but obtaining the ingredients was easier said than done. Darden said the keys to the Mansion's salon were kept by the salon's manager who kept them on her at all times. I asked Genevieve if she would go with me to the salon in the Village but she refused and pleaded with me not to do it for fear that Maestro would kick me out. And with guard patrols in the Mansion, I didn't know what kind of message to leave that wouldn't get traced back to me. So instead, anytime Layla wanted to go to the Village, I would join her, hoping that I would run into my mother.

One day, after sectionals, I was planning to head to the Village with Darden since Layla signed up for solo auditions. We passed a trembling Heather in the hallway behind the ballroom. Genevieve stroked her hair and spoke calming words.

"Heather, are you okay?" I asked, placing a hand on her shaking shoulder.

"She's nervous about the singers' solo auditions," Genevieve said.

"What do you have to be nervous about?" I asked Heather. "You sound great! I listen to you sing all the time and you help me so much with the notes."

Heather lifted her head. "Thanks, Paris. But I have a tendency to screw up when I'm nervous. I'm surprised I'm even here for how much I sucked at my court audition."

I shook my head. "I don't believe it. You just have to tell yourself you can do it. And Heather, I *know* you can."

"But I'm the only New Lady soprano auditioning for solos. It just feels like a lot of pressure. I'm just going to make a fool out of myself in front of everyone else auditioning."

I smiled. "I'll audition too."

"Really? Weren't you two headed somewhere?" Heather asked, looking at Darden.

We all waited for Darden to respond, but he suddenly lost the ability to communicate.

"It can wait." My words stabbed a pang of guilt in my gut because what I was really saying was 'my mother can wait.'

But Heather looked at me with hopeful eyes.

I reached for Heather's hand. "You'll sound amazing compared to me and the maestro will be sure to pick you. I'll just be there for moral support." I turned to Darden. "You can go on to the Village without me."

He hugged his chest. "I...um, I'm just going to head back to my room. Good luck with the audition, ladies."

I blinked and Darden was gone.

Heather flung her arms around me and pulled me into a hug, then led me to the rehearsal room where the maestro conducted the auditions. She waved goodbye to Genevieve before we entered and sat on the risers.

Reese and Layla were by far the best new singers but there was still a spot open for a soprano solo in the auditorium show. It was open for any season but Heather heard a rumor that the maestro wanted a New Lady to showcase for the king.

I auditioned with no fear of the maestro, knowing that my presence was solely for someone else's benefit.

Heather was the last to go. I wished her luck as she stepped up to the piano. Maestro signaled Francis to play, and Heather missed her intro.

"I'm sorry, can I start again?" she asked as she nervously wrung her hands.

Maestro nodded and Francis played her intro.

My heart fluttered with excitement when she made her entrance on time and gave a powerful performance up until the end when she took a breath in the middle of a sustained note.

Maestro nodded at the conclusion of her audition.

"You were great," I whispered, as she sat down next to me.

She rubbed her temples. "I screwed up twice. Maestro hates that."

I shook my head. "Not anything you can't fix. And it's such a tiny thing, nobody other than Maestro would notice it."

She smiled and leaned into my shoulder.

We sat in silence with the other singers as we waited for Maestro to make his decision. After a few minutes, he posted the list to a board, then walked out of the room. I stood but didn't approach the board with the rest of the group.

"Hey Layla, we're scheduled to sing a duet at the New Year's Eve Ball," Reese said.

Layla scoffed and left the room.

"It's a pleasure to sing with you, too!" he shouted at her. He slung his bag over his shoulder with a grunt and headed out.

Heather turned and picked up her bag with a sour expression. "I didn't get it."

I offered her a sympathetic look. "I'm so sorry, Heather. You sounded great. He's probably just more familiar with the returning members' voices."

She shook her head as I followed her to the door. "He didn't pick a returning member," she said. "He picked you."

CHAPTER
15

I followed at Heather's heels. "It had to be a mistake. Or one of his mind-games. We all know you're a better singer, Heather. I don't—"

"You don't need to make me feel better, Paris. I'm okay."

"Let me talk to him."

"No. Please don't. Thanks for auditioning with me, but I'm kind of tired now. I'll see you later." She headed into the Lounge and I considered following her, but comforting Heather wouldn't change the fact that I was given the solo. Only one person could make the change, so I headed to his office.

When I arrived in the Administrative Wing of the Mansion, I followed the sound of piano chords punching out a repetitive rhythm. I peered into Maestro's office and where a desk should have been, a baby grand piano sat in its place, taking up nearly the entire room. One of his hands sat on the keys while the other scribbled notes with a pen. The faint smell of something sweet and woody tickled my nose. The maestro didn't flinch when I knocked on the door but moved his eyeballs in my direction.

"Why are *you* here?" he asked as he poured some brown liquid into an empty glass on the ledge of the piano.

"I wanted to—"

"I know why you're here." He spoke to his full glass.

My heart increased its tempo against my chest.

"You want something." Maestro tilted his head back and the brown liquid disappeared from the glass. "I have one hundred miserable, empty kids who will perform to their highest caliber because they *all* want something—money, adoration, fame, fancy dresses, an education...what do *you* want?"

"Maestro, sir, I came here to talk to you about—"

"You said you were 'attracted to joy' at your audition and you feel most like yourself when you sing." He nodded as he poured himself a second glass. "It was a good answer. You want to be happy, and singing does that for you. I get it. But what I can't figure out is why living in this dump of a house would *make* you happy?" He clutched the glass and slammed his free hand on the surface of the piano. "WHAT DO YOU WANT?" The piano strings vibrated under the power of his hand and the roar of his voice.

Breathe. Focus. Breathe.

"Sir, I want to talk to you about the solo auditions."

He shook his head. "That's not what you really want, but...okay." He crossed his legs and leaned forward. "Let's talk."

I sucked in a breath. "Why didn't you pick Heather? She's a better singer than me. She deserved it."

His eyebrows formed two uneven mountain peaks at the base of his forehead. "First of all, nobody deserves *anything*. And this court isn't always about who's the most talented. I need people on that stage I can rely on and at this moment in time, I can't rely on Miss Romaine."

"But she has so much more experience and—"

"LA LA LA LA LA!" The maestro shoved two fingers in his ears. "STOP! PLEASE! My ears can't handle the sound of whining! This is *my* court, not yours. End of story. Now go." He turned and swallowed the last of his drink, slamming down the empty glass.

I clenched my trembling hands and tried to steady my breathing but anger took over. "And I was under the impression this was the *King's* 100."

The maestro's hands hovered above the piano keys. "Miss Marigold, as far as I'm concerned, I *am* your king. And if you say one more word to me, I swear on the entire Royal Family that I will dismiss you and you'll be in the first auto-taxi back to Green Heights. So, any final words? I'd love to hear them." His menacing eyes held me like a snake hypnotizing its prey.

My jaw twitched, but I kept my mouth shut, knowing better than to poke the monster.

"That's a good court lady. Now get out. Get out!" Maestro's hands pounded all the piano keys under repetitive shout-singing of "GEEEEEEEEEEET OUT! Get oooout! GET OOOOOOOOOOUT! GET OUT! GET! OUT!"

I hurried out of his office without a destination in mind—I just needed to get away from the crazed man. I desired a way to stand out from the other court members of the King's 100 but I never wanted a solo. I was still getting used to the idea of singing, let alone singing by myself in front of an audience of thousands. My feet carried me back to the Lounge where Genevieve pounced on me.

"Paris! Come on, you'll miss it!" She tugged my arm forward.

"Miss what?"

"You'll see. I've been looking for Heather, but can't find her anywhere."

I didn't have the heart to tell Genevieve that I caused her best friend's disappearance.

Genevieve pulled me outside the back door of the Lounge, where a gaggle of girls and a couple boys sat on the grass. A few yards away, the drummers rehearsed their marches under the direction of their Fourth Season drum captain, Sanjay Dane. Only the boys were shirtless and the girls wore athletic undergarments beneath their snare harnesses.

"It's the last outdoor rehearsal day of the season," Genevieve said. "I wouldn't have wanted you to miss it, especially on your *birthday*," she said with a playful smile.

"It's not my birthday."

"You can't fool me, Paris! All our birthdays are listed on the court roster, remember?"

Of course. Paris Marigold's birthday was listed on the roster, not Piper Parish's real birthday. "Oh...you're right. But, isn't this kind of...weird?"

"No! Look around you! The returning members were the ones who told me about it. It must be a tradition—one that Robert doesn't have to know about," she said in a whisper.

Of the few drummers I had come to know, Staci Ringer glimmered under the hot sun, the normally pallid skin of Simon Zacher radiated a deep shade of red and then...I saw Ari. "Genevieve, I should go. I...need to rehearse."

"No, stay with me! They're almost done, anyway." She looped her arm through mine, forcing me to watch the hypnotizing way Ari's arm muscles tensed with each hit of his snare drum.

"Robert has nice arms but they're not *drummer's* arms," Genevieve said softly in my ear.

When the drummers finished their rehearsal, the other kids in our group let out loud calls and whistles. Genevieve stuck two fingers in her mouth and blew a whistle so loud it could have turned the heads of every citizen in Mondaria. And to my horror, it garnered the attention of one of Mondaria's black-haired citizens, who turned and waved at me.

"Bye, Genevieve," I said, peeling myself away from her.

"Where are you going?" she asked.

And then there were heavier, quicker footsteps behind me. "Paris, hold up!"

I paused and closed my eyes, refusing to turn around.

"How did it go?" asked Ari.

I felt him brush past me and I forced my eyes to open. I focused on the sweat above his brows, but against my will, my eyes traveled down to his steadily rising chest and glistening toned abdomen. "It was great!" I said with too much enthusiasm, unable to control the volume of my voice. "Wait, how did what go exactly?"

"Solo auditions. Darden said you were going to audition."

"Right, the solo auditions," I said with a nod. "Maestro gave me the open soprano solo for the auditorium show."

"Wow, that's great! Congrats, Paris." Ari held up a wide palm. "Hey, don't leave me hanging." He grabbed my wrist and hit my palm against his—a 'high-five.'

I felt like an idiot, having seen the action done multiple times in the Lounge, only to forget what to do in front of a half-naked Ari.

He dropped my hand and wiped his brow. "So, I'll see you tonight at Grape Stomp?"

"Yes, sir! I mean, yeah." I felt uncomfortably twitchy. "And I look forward to meeting your girlfriend." I said the word 'girlfriend' as if I was verbally reminding myself of the important fact.

Ari put his hands on his hips. "She's actually not coming."

His new hand placement drew my eyes to the visible iliac crests of his hip bone. "That's too bad," I said, surprised by the upbeat tone to my voice.

"But Heather said she'd go with me in her place. Maybe we can all sit together—you, Darden, me and Heather?"

I had the sudden urge to know if he asked Heather to Grape Stomp or if Heather offered to go with him. And if he had known Tasha wasn't able to make it, why hadn't he mentioned it to me before? "Yeah, I think that's a great idea," I said, deciding the best thing for me was to exit the conversation. And before Ari could respond, follow me with his scent or naked torso, I darted away with a short "Bye!"

Genevieve caught up beside me and looped her arm through mine. She talked about how excited she was to see Robert when my mind ran away with the thought of Ari and Heather together at Grape Stomp.

Why had the thought of them together bothered me when I already knew Ari had a girlfriend? Ari and Heather were friends, just how Darden and I were friends. Well, friends based on an agreement to impress his queen of hearts.

I stopped in my tracks.

If Heather was Darden's queen of hearts, then I could tell Ari. I promised Darden I wouldn't tell anyone, but I trusted Ari to not say anything. We could make something up. Say that Maestro told us to change up our dates for whatever reason. And then Darden could enjoy his evening with Heather, tell her he had feelings for her, and I wouldn't have to help him finish his complicated illusion.

Genevieve tapped the side of my head. "Paris, hello? What's going on in there?"

"What card did Heather get from Darden's hearts trick?"

"I don't remember."

I pulled Genevieve forward as I picked up our pace to the dormitories. Heather *had* to be the queen of hearts.

Genevieve giggled as she quickened her steps to keep up with me. "I still maintain that you were in on his numbers trick."

I huffed and reached for the Lounge door, but Genevieve's following words froze my muscles.

"And if it matters to you," she said, "*I* got the queen of hearts."

CHAPTER
16

Genevieve appeared at our door as Layla and I were on our way out to meet the rest of the King's 100 for the Grape Stomp call-time. "Happy Birthday, Paris!" she shouted, as she extended a paper-wrapped item.

"Today's your birthday?" asked Layla.

I shrugged, taking the gift from Genevieve.

"Damn, I suck."

I shook my head. "Really, Layla, it's okay. I don't—"

"Yes, you *do* suck," Genevieve said.

Layla stuck her tongue out and left me alone with Genevieve, who clapped her hands. "Go ahead and open it!"

I unwrapped the pink paper to find a pair of brand-new blue jeans. "Oh, you didn't have to do that, Genevieve."

"You're the only person I know who doesn't own a pair of jeans. And...they're actually from me and Heather, but Heather's...she's just not feeling well right now."

Guilt coursed through me at the reminder of Maestro's flawed decision. I set the blue jeans on my bed, then gave Genevieve a hug—the appropriate gesture when receiving a gift from a Mondarian. "That was nice of you two. Thank you."

She bounced on the soles of her feet. "Let's go! I can't wait for you to meet Robert!"

I followed Genevieve through the back door of the Lounge and over to the Mansion Lawn. Our attire for the evening included knee-length black knit skirts with purple collared shirts and the men wore black shorts with purple shirts. Guests were invited to wear casual attire but to keep their bottoms above the knee for the grape stomping.

Genevieve leapt into the arms of a husky boy with brown curly hair. After receiving a slew of Genevieve's kisses, Robert scanned the event as if he had stepped into a dream—a feeling the two of us shared. Rows of white draped tables covered the typically empty green lawn under a huge canopy of twinkling string lights. A black and white dance floor sat at the entrance of the event with a band playing lively, upbeat music. Large wooden barrels filled with grapes framed the tables, mixing the tart scent of berries with pine needles. The sun cast a deep orange hue against the backdrop of the mountains and a breeze caressed my arms with its final breaths of autumn air.

I spotted Darden and headed his way, exhaling a sigh of relief that I wasn't required to play the role of table host for the evening. Grape Stomp was once a day of labor for everyone at the Mansion, including the King's 100. Court members were instructed to bring friends for more manpower to assist with the stomping, but over time, it became a traditional day of celebration rather than work.

But my relief was short-lived when I remembered I would sit at the same table with a girl who managed to go from loving to hating me over the span of a day.

Darden waved his hands in the air and presented a small bouquet of yellow flowers. "Marigolds for Miss Marigold. Happy birthday."

"Today's your birthday?" asked Ari.

Heather turned her head as if the sight of me made her feel ill.

I nodded. "Yeah."

Ari smiled. "Happy birthday. Sorry I didn't know."

"It's okay. I—"

"Paris, today is your birthday?" asked Raya, a Second Season singer.

I nodded as Reese took a seat beside her as her date.

"I'll make sure to do an extra special challenge for you," Raya said.

Darden pulled out my chair.

"Challenge?" I asked as I sat down.

But Raya struck up a conversation with the girl on the other side of her—a Second Season magician named Jasmine. Jasmine's date, Eli was the only outsider date at our table. His expression was like Robert's—as if he had just discovered a hidden treasure. He complimented Jasmine at every opportunity and couldn't stop looking around, as if the king's Mansion would disappear if he didn't monitor every detail.

Jasmine left the table to speak with Agnes, leaving Eli alone for a minute. "So, Jasmine says you guys practice every day?"

"We don't practice, we *rehearse*," Darden said. "Our maestro likes to remind us that 'practice is for drooling toddlers and—'"

"Rehearsing is for professionals!" Ari and I both jumped in at the same time to finish Darden's sentence.

"Which one is your maestro?" he asked.

"You'll find out soon enough," Jasmine said as she slid back into her seat.

Raya tapped her glass and cleared her throat. "To make tonight more interesting, we'll play a little game of Truth or Dare." Raya flashed a wicked smirk. "And you must follow through. If you don't, you'll have to face your punishment."

"What's the punishment?" I asked.

"You have to take a drink from our Witch's Brew! It's a concoction of mystery liquids." She pulled a glass bottle with a stopper from under the table, filled to the top with a liquid the color of mud. Raya revealed a wine glass with her other hand. "I'll fill up the wine glass to the top and you have to chug the whole thing."

"What's in Witch's Brew?" asked Eli.

"Don't worry, you don't have to play," she said. "Just our newest court members."

Eli made a dramatic sweep across his forehead, which elicited a giggle from Jasmine.

"And I can't reveal the mystery ingredients—that would ruin the intrigue. But this game is a tradition among the Second Seasons. Rumor has it one year somebody added urine. It could have been made up or...it could have been Witch's Brew!" Raya leaned her head back and cackled.

"That's repugnant," muttered Darden.

"Is there alcohol in there?" asked Heather. "It's against my religion to drink."

I nodded because in a way, it was against my religion too as a health-obsessed Capalon.

"Then to be safe, you'll just have to follow through with your truth or dare, *Miss Romaine.*"

Ari raised a finger. "What if we don't want to play?"

"You have to play. It's tradition. In fact, let's make *you* our first victim." Raya set the bottle and wine glass on the table, then rubbed her hands together. "So, Ari. Truth or dare?"

"Um, truth?"

Jasmine whispered something to Raya, who nodded. "Ari, how far have you gone with your girlfriend?"

Ari's face paled, and I suddenly wanted to hide at the bottom of a grape barrel.

"Can I have another question?" he asked.

Raya shook her head. "Nope, this is the game, *New Man.*"

Ari's mouth fell open.

Raya tapped the tabled. "Oh, come on, how long have you been dating?"

Ari ran a hand through his hair. "On and off for two years."

Raya's eyes widened. "Two years! Well I'm sure you've at least gone past Stage One."

"I don't know what that is."

"You know, up here." Raya made a circular motion with her palm over her chest.

Ari didn't respond.

"So that's a 'yes'? You have to answer or you chug the Brew!"

I found the grape stompers to be quite entertaining in that moment. I even spotted the maestro taking a turn, willing him with my eyes to fall and chip a tooth on the edge of the barrel.

Raya and Jasmine let out 'ow-ows' in response to whatever response Ari gave, causing my stomach to churn.

Raya cleared her throat. "Okay, who's next? Heather—truth or dare?"

"Dare."

Raya convened with her cohort and had to calm her giggling before she gave her instructions. "Heather, Ambassador Lane over there just recently returned from a climb up to the top of Mt. Forrestin. He was boring me with the details earlier. We dare you to ask him about his climb up *Mt. Foreskin* tonight!"

"Ew, no. I'm not saying that to a guest. Maestro will kill me."

"You chose a dare, Heather. So, you must follow through or—" Raya flashed the bottle of brown-orange liquid.

Heather winced.

"What's your decision?" asked Raya.

Heather groaned. "I'll do the dare."

"I'll be watching you to make sure you do it, *New Lady*."

"Yes, ma'am."

I rolled my eyes at Heather's unnecessary politeness.

Maestro called the court to attention, instructing us to line up for the presentation of the Mondarian Anthem.

"Paris," whispered Raya. "You're safe now. But be ready."

After our performance, I watched with Raya and Jasmine as Heather approached Ambassador Lane during a casual Social Hour.

"Good evening, Ambassador. I heard you enjoyed a recent climb of Mt. Foreskin?"

Jasmine and Raya's faces lit up, and I had to bite my own lip to keep from laughing. The Ambassador answered the question as if he didn't hear the intentional slip.

As I listened to a guest talk about his sea-faring kingdom's recent acquisition of an antique collection of ferry boats, I pondered which option I would select for Raya's game.

What if I revealed myself on accident by requesting truth?

What if I revealed myself on accident through a dare I had to perform on a guest?

I had rehearsed lying about my identity enough to make up artificial facts on the spot. Holding my composure with a stranger was a risk I wasn't willing to take.

Truth. I had to pick truth.

When the maestro instructed to take our seats, Raya congratulated Heather on her follow-through, then turned to me. "I haven't forgotten who's next! Paris, truth or dare?"

"Truth."

Raya whispered to Jasmine while I held my breath.

"Describe your first kiss in detail."

My whole body relaxed. "I've never been kissed. So, who's your next victim? Reese?"

Raya lifted her hand. "Wait, you're sixteen and have never been kissed?"

"She's seventeen today," Darden said. "Remember, it's her birthday?"

"Seventeen!" she laughed so hard, she had to hold on to Jasmine to keep from falling off her chair.

Had I revealed too much with my honest answer?

"Okay, okay," Raya waved her palms to calm herself and Jasmine from their laughter. "Your answer doesn't count, so...I dare you to get your first kiss tonight!"

I shook my head. "That's not fair. I answered the question."

Raya's eyes hardened. "No, you nullified the question so as the game leader, I'm initiating a dare."

I clenched my fists under the table. "But in mathematics a null is a value of zero, which is still—"

Darden thought it was a great time to clear his throat and shoot me a warning glare, throwing me off my explanation.

Raya sat tall in her seat and crossed her arms. "Paris, you'll kiss a court man at the after-party in the Lounge tonight for all of us to see, or you chug the Brew."

I slouched low in my chair, hiding my face behind a balled fist.

"Don't look so mortified, Paris. It's a fun dare!" Jasmine said.

"It's an unfair game of manipulation," I murmured.

Raya moved on to her next victim, Darden, who chose dare.

"I dare you to let us read a page out of that notebook you're always scribbling in."

Darden tightened his grip on the notebook full of secret magic tricks. "Hand me the Brew, please," he answered, without skipping a beat. Darden chugged the wine glass full of the mystery liquid. When he finished, Raya instructed him to tip it over his head to prove every drop was gone. The table applauded his effort and I swear Darden's dark skin turned a shade of green.

Agnes approached our table. "Your table's turn to stomp,"

"Yes, ma'am," we responded as a group.

My heart pounded with fury as we headed to the grape barrels.

Who does Raya think she is?

I've never kissed a boy and I definitely can't kiss a Mondarian boy.

Urine is sterile, right?

Darden and I removed our shoes and climbed into a large wooden barrel, full of red and purple grapes. After forty-five minutes of stomping with guests, I took a water break at our table, where Reese sat by himself.

I smiled between sips of water as I watched Layla prance around in circles, arm in arm with a guest in a nearby barrel.

"Somebody's enjoying this party," Reese said, watching Layla with me. "Too bad she'll find a way to insult that poor guest and crush his soul by the end of the night."

I set down my glass. "She's not that bad."

"Not that bad? She insults me every chance she gets. Just this morning in the Lounge, she asked if I could stop practicing my songs because they were 'melting her brain.'"

"Consider it flattery. She only insults the people she likes."

"So, you're telling me she likes Genevieve?"

"Well...not exactly..."

"By the way, if you need to complete your dare, I'm more than willing to help." Reese flashed a smile. "You know, in the sense of strictly helping you to avoid drinking a liquid that might be part piss." He shuddered.

I scratched my face to hide my flushing cheeks. "That wouldn't upset Raya?"

He shook his head. "Nah. She's got a thing for some Third Season. She was telling me all about it in our barrel, which was why I felt the need to excuse myself."

"Oh. Well, thanks for your offer."

"Time for us to return to the barrel," Darden said over my shoulder.

"Yes, sir," I said with a sigh.

Guests trickled in and out of our barrel, some full of laughter, others disgusted with the feeling of the grapes between their toes. I found the wet, squishy bottom therapeutic against my sore feet. I nearly slipped and Darden caught me just in time before I landed on my rear end, when I heard booming laughter.

I knew that laugh.

I turned to see the Duke of Pallerdon heading straight for our barrel. I was practically invisible to anyone who visited Capalon, but one time at a product-trade dinner, the Duke of Pallerdon insisted that I sit with him. He proceeded to tell me the details of his divorce from the Duchess of Pallerdon and how he had moved on to a younger, healthier version of his former wife. "Darden, give me your glasses."

"What? Why?"

"Because that man knows me," I said, tilting my head toward the salt and pepper-haired man and his young wife. "Not me, Paris, but the *real* me."

"This one, Lilac! Come on dear, the help will assist us," boomed the Duke's voice.

"Darden, now," I said in a sharp whisper.

Darden reached for his glasses, but then his hands changed direction, pressing hard on my back, knocking me to the floor of the barrel. Holding me down with one hand, he used the other to smear grapes across my face.

I shrieked, sending the Duke into a roaring laughter.

"Oh, that's going to take a while to clean off, missy! Ha! Come, Lilac, we'll give this barrel some space. Let's try the next one."

I wiped juice off my eyelids and spat out sour bits of grape skin. "What in the name of the Ancient Data was that for?"

Darden spoke in my ear. "Hey, you wanna keep your Capalon swearing down? You really thought putting on my glasses would hide your face?"

My chest swelled with anger. "It was all I could think of!"

Darden's attempt to stifle his laughter failed. "Come on, I'll help you up."

"No, I got it," I said, reaching for the edge of the barrel, only to slip and fall again, on all fours.

The tables closest to our barrel took notice of my messy mishap and responded to their entertainment with a mix of laughter and applause.

Heat scorched my skin. "I'm going to clean myself off and don't even think about following me."

"But we have to be two to a barrel."

"I don't care!"

I finally made it out of the barrel and marched to a white tent set up with hoses and towels. When I entered, I was greeted by a giggling Heather, who wiped grape juice splatter off Ari's forehead. When they saw me, Heather burst into laughter and Ari's jaw dropped.

I turned my back and buried my face in a towel.

"Wow, Paris, you really took a tumble in there," Heather said behind my back.

I ignored her and pulled grape bits off my face and out of my hair.

"I'm going to grab some more food," she said to Ari. "Wanna come?"

Ari said something I couldn't hear and Heather exited the tent— her perfectly clean, blonde hair bouncing behind her.

"Are you okay, Paris?" Ari asked, his voice close to the back of my neck.

"Yeah, I'm great," I said in a deadpan response.

He rounded the front of the bench and extended another towel to me.

I reluctantly accepted, using it to wipe my arms.

He shoved his hands into his pockets and leaned against the post of the tent. "You know you don't have to do Raya's dare."

"I know. I'm just...thinking about it."

"What's there to think about? Raya's just being manipulative."

I untucked my shirt from my skirt to watch grapes spill onto the grass around my feet. "I get it, Ari. What's your problem?"

"I don't have a problem, I'm just trying to help."

"I don't need your help." I twisted the knob of the hose, but my hand kept slipping over the brass.

Ari reached over and twisted on. "But it's your first kiss. Don't you want it to be on your terms and not Raya's?"

"It's just a kiss," I said, splashing the cold water over my legs. "It doesn't mean anything."

"I just don't think you should be afraid of the consequences. Darden pretty much chugged that drink, so it can't be that terrible."

I expelled a sharp laugh. "*I* shouldn't be afraid of the

consequences?" I shook my head. "Aren't you contradicting yourself?"

"Why, because I didn't take the drink?"

"Not only that, but...never mind." I dried my hands and shut off the water.

"No, I want to know. Please, enlighten me," Ari said with a less than pleasing sarcastic tone as he crossed his arms.

"Okay. The drum solo auditions—Staci said you have the best roll out of anybody but you didn't audition because you didn't want to take the opportunity away from a returning court member. And your stipend money—you feel like you're responsible for your dad, when you should be taking care of your own future. Your dad is an adult and he can pull himself out of his own mess if he wants to, which clearly he doesn't." I couldn't stop as I gesticulated with a hand-towel. "And on top of it, you're with a girl who cheated on you and you took her back because you blame yourself for some reason." I opened my arms and looked around. "Where is she, Ari? Is she really at a family reunion or is she sneaking around behind your back again? Look at the outsider dates—they're having a fantastic time! Why? Because it's the *king's* Mansion! VIP's from other kingdoms *beg* to have an invitation to come here and your girlfriend chooses a family reunion?"

Ari's jaw tensed. "Maybe I don't enjoy hurting people, okay? I've seen my dad do it too many times to count and I refuse to be like him."

"But when are you going to take control of your own life? Start doing things for you and not what's going to make other people happy?"

He shook his head and forced a curt laugh. "This is coming from the girl who refuses to think about anything other than what her family wants her to do."

"Unlike you, I don't have a choice."

"Yes, you do. Everyone has a choice, Paris. And I choose to not hurt people to benefit myself, but apparently you have no problem with it."

"What's that supposed to mean?"

"Heather. She told me all about how you talked your way into getting her solo."

My hands strangled my towel. "That's not at all close to the truth and if you believe that, then you really are a dumb drummer."

We stared at each other until Ari turned and marched out of the tent.

I hurled the dirty towels into a basket.

"Paris?" Darden emerged from the shadows, making my heart jump.

"My *helpful* date, there you are. Thanks so much for dunking me in the grapes. That was just so...so smart. And now I'm a purple court member. What's Maestro going to say when he sees me?"

"The event's almost over, so hopefully nothing. But we should get back to the table for our official dismissal."

"Yes, sir, Mr. McCray. Hey, wait up."

Darden didn't slow his pace, causing me to have to hop over the tent's staked ropes to catch up to him. "So, let's do it at the beginning of the after-party. That way we can get it over with and I can shower."

"Do what?"

"Kiss! You're obviously my pick since we're supposed to be 'spending more time together.'"

Darden shook his head. "I'm not kissing you."

"Why? It's just a kiss. Then I can get Raya off my back."

"No."

I stopped Darden. "Why?" I lowered my voice. "Are you still mad about the whole pepper spray thing?"

"I *do* still have pain around my eyes from that stuff, but no."

"Then what's your issue?"

Darden looked up at the twinkling lights. "It's not *my* issue."

"Okay, you'll have to be more clear because I don't speak magician."

Darden's mouth opened and closed a couple times until he finally spoke. "I'm required to be perceptive to be a superb magician."

"Yeah, so what?" I said with crossed arms.

"Ari's my best friend."

"What's Ari got to do with this?"

Darden sighed. "I'm not kissing you, Miss Marigold."

"Yeah, well, then I'm not helping you with...*you know*...secret magic that requires my help. And I found out who she is, by the way. For how perceptive you are, you missed a huge detail by picking a girl who already has a boyfriend."

Darden's jaw tensed. "Fine."

"*Fine?* So just like that, our little deal is off?"

"Yes, ma'am."

"You're a true weirdo, Darden McCray."

"No, I'm a true genius. Hey look, the Queen of Capalon." Darden looked past my shoulder and I turned to see a sea of empty tables. When I turned back around, Darden had disappeared. "Damn magician."

I plopped on the chair back at our table and avoided eye contact with anyone else.

Raya approached me and I cut her off before she could give me another warning about her ridiculous dare. "I'm taking the punishment."

"Really? With all your *attractive* options on your birthday of all days? Bad decision, New Lady." She scanned my face. "And what happened to you? Did you go for a swim in the grapes?"

"Just give me the stupid drink, Raya."

Raya pressed her palms against the table and leaned over me as if I was a misbehaving child. "We might be playing a game, but I still have seniority over you. Do you understand?"

I wanted to shout back that I was actually the Princess of Capalon and if anyone held the most authority, it was me. But instead, I sucked in a breath and narrowed my eyes. "Yes, ma'am."

Raya grinned and retrieved the bottle of brown liquid from under the table, then filled the wine glass to the top.

Blocking any attempts of further logic or reasoning from my mind, I lifted the glass to my lips and forced myself to chug the drink until it was gone. A variety of identifiable tastes washed over my tongue like orange, toothpaste, hot sauce, coffee, curry and chocolate. There were others that weren't as recognizable—something berry-flavored, something that burned at the back of my throat and something that reminded me of the smell of the Mansion's freshly cut grass. The liquid had a grainy texture and a few gooey lumps that were the hardest to swallow. I held the empty glass upside down over my head, sending a ripple of applause around the table, including Ari.

"Tastes like garbage, right?" Darden reappeared and handed me a glass of water.

"This is your fault," I said, wiping droplets of water from my mouth. He shrugged and took a seat beside me.

Raya dealt out her final dare to Reese. "I dare you to give me three compliments."

"That's so unfair!" Heather said. "I had to say the word 'foreskin' in front of a guest!"

"This is my game, so we'll play by my rules," snapped Raya.

As our table listened to Reese rattle off three quick compliments about Raya, I stared at Ari, who rested his cheek on his palm as he tapped a spoon against the edge of the table. Even though half of his mouth was covered by his hand, I could tell he was smiling.

His joy irritated me. Of course, he was smiling—he wasn't the one who had to drink a glass of vomit-flavored juice.

Raya told a story about a drunk guest who followed her around like a lost puppy until Agnes gave us the official dismissal. Court members said goodbye to their dates and then we all headed across the lawn back to the Lounge. Within minutes, music boomed to the top of the wooden rafters and bodies crowded a makeshift dance floor.

I said goodnight to Darden, then pushed through a group of people standing in front of the door to the Ladies' Dorms when I stepped face-to-face with Ari.

"Good job standing up to Raya," he said before taking a drink from his familiar blue water bottle.

I tilted my head and plastered a sarcastic grin. "Yeah, my ingestion of a foul liquid proved that I have the upper hand to an arrogant court member."

"Ari! Come dance with me!" shouted Heather from the dance floor.

Ari raised a dismissive palm to Heather, but she grabbed his arm and pulled him away from me.

I squeezed the bridge of my nose. A headache threatened to take over and I couldn't place if its cause was due to the long day or the mystery contents of the Brew. In need of water, I took a swig out of Ari's abandoned water bottle just as Reese jumped out from behind me, shaking his hips. "You can't *not* dance to this song, Paris!"

I laughed and let him lead me on to the dance floor. The beat of the music pulsed in my bones as I danced to the rhythm and threw my arms above my head, mimicking the other bodies around me. Reese took my hand and spun me around, causing giggles to bubble out of my chest.

I caught Ari's eyes watching me dance with Reese and another giggle escaped, even louder. Reese's hands knew when to find mine and where to lead me in a set of fluid dance moves. Our movements to the music sparked something inside me that urged me to pull him closer.

Reese *was* handsome by definition. If I was playing the role of a real Mondarian teenager, then it *was* about time I had my first kiss.

And it was my birthday.

He shouted something in my ear.

I laughed too loud, wrapping my hands around his neck.

Ari's eyes found mine.

I pulled Reese's head down and pressed my lips against his.

It was hard. Our teeth clinked. His tongue poked into my mouth, which I didn't expect, so I pulled back. The surrounding court members around us let out whoops and howls. I smiled and let Reese spin me into a dramatic dip. I glanced over at Heather's dance group to see that a black-haired drummer had taken notes from his magician-roommate and mastered his very own disappearing act.

CHAPTER
17

E ven though I slept in until just before the afternoon call-time for soloist rehearsals in the auditorium, my body dragged the day after Grape Stomp. Maestro only threw one dagger at me, telling me to look less constipated and more regular.

During hair and make-up in the dressing room, I was happy to listen to Layla describe the guests she met at Grape Stomp to avoid thinking about my oral impulsivity on the dance floor the night before or my impending first solo in front of thousands of people.

"How was *your* night?" asked Layla with a hairpin clenched between her teeth.

I twisted my hair back for a third time, finally settling on the look by shoving in a hairpin. "It was okay. Tell me more about that guest with the goatee. Did anyone ever tell him he had a shrimp tail stuck in it?"

Genevieve popped her head up on my other side. "Just okay? I saw you make-out with Reese in front of everybody on the dance floor!"

Layla's arched brows shot me a glance through the dressing-table mirror.

I sucked in my bottom lip. "Oh...yeah."

Genevieve leaned her elbows on my dedicated portion of the table. "Is he a good kisser? Are you guys a couple now?"

I inserted another hairpin. "I wouldn't know if he was a good kisser because it was my first kiss. And no, we're definitely not a couple."

Layla huffed. "You would know if he was good. Doesn't surprise me he's a lousy kisser."

"Okay, I'm confused," Genevieve said. "You kiss the *hottest* New Man and shut down any chance of being a couple?"

I checked the seat on the other side of Genevieve to make sure Heather wasn't around, then explained the whole Truth or Dare game to both Layla and Genevieve.

"So, you *do* have a thing for Reese. Otherwise you wouldn't have kissed him after drinking that gross stuff." Genevieve returned her focus to own mirror and finished applying her lipstick.

I shrugged. I didn't have a solid reason for why I did it.

"Oh, Paris." Genevieve capped her lipstick.

"What?" I looked at her reflection in her mirror.

She turned, meeting my eyes face-to-face. "You did it to make another boy jealous, didn't you?"

Remembering that I still needed eyeliner, I turned around and searched through my emptied makeup bag contents splayed across my portion of the table. "No, why would I do that? In front of all those people, that's crazy."

"Hey Genevieve, instead of creating idiotic drama for you and your herd of sheep to giggle over, how about you take care of that lipstick on your teeth?"

"Yeah right, I don't have," she looked in the mirror, "Oh no." Genevieve sprang from her chair and headed to the bathroom.

Layla sighed. "Man, I can't stand that girl. She *is* right, though. You're not into Reese, otherwise you would be bouncing off the walls all twinkle-eyed like these other weirdos."

I nodded. "Exactly."

"You've got a thing for Ari."

My mouth opened, unable to produce sound for a beat. "No, that's—"

"And you're in a tizzy because making Ari jealous doesn't feel as good as you hoped it would."

"No, there was something in the Brew that toyed with my judgment and I'm just upset because I embarrassed myself in front of half the court." I slammed down my compact. "Where is my damn eyeliner?"

"Fine, you don't like Ari." Layla held up my missing eyeliner. "He has a girlfriend, anyway."

I grabbed the black stick out of her hand. "I know. We're just friends."

"And Maestro is an angel."

I stepped into my auditorium performance dress—a long, form-fitted black dress covered in sequins and capped sleeves. According to Maestro, the aesthetic for auditorium shows represented the kingdom's bird with court members serving as its black beating wings and Maestro as its red body. According to Raya, Maestro wanted every eye in the auditorium on him so he wore a bright red tuxedo jacket for every show.

My heart pounded from Layla's stubbornness, causing my fingers to slip on the dress's zipper. Ari was my friend and nothing more. Why did everything with Mondarian girls have to center on their romantic interests? Why did they have to assume that every relationship was built on attraction?

Backstage of the auditorium, I had a whisper-conversation with Reese before the singers took the stage for our set. "Hey Reese, I'm sorry I kind of attacked you last night."

"I didn't completely mind it," he said with a smile. "I *was* surprised since you already drank the Brew."

"I know. There was something in that drink, and I just got carried away with the music. I don't feel any sort of...I mean, you're my friend, so—"

"It's okay, you don't have to explain," Reese said. "And if I remember correctly, I might have attacked you back. Raya slipped me some drinks throughout Grape Stomp, so at the end of the night, I was a little buzzed. But if you really want to make it up to me..." Reese lifted his brows with a suggestive smirk.

I punched him in the arm.

"Ow! I was going to say 'sing with me.'"

The music and lighting changed—our cue to take our positions. Even though I sang to an auditorium full of two thousand people, I worried about the one girl who stood beside me on the risers. I hated that I was the one to step up to the mic to sing a solo and receive a verbal "good job" from the man in the pit donning a bright red jacket.

It should have been Heather.

But Heather lied to Ari.

I allowed myself to enjoy the applause and the way the light danced across the sequins on my dress, making me feel like a glittering star. The show concluded with the entire court of the King's 100 filling the auditorium with our powerful finale. The audience stood with a cheering ovation and I found myself intoxicated with the thrill of such exuberant adulation.

When we returned to the dressing room, I pulled out my chair to find a lavender rose with a note tied to it.

Your solo was beautiful, just like the woman you are...

I tucked the rose under the table and into my new court-issued bag, so nobody would see it. I struggled to breathe.

Layla touched my arm. "Paris, are you okay?"

"Yeah," I said. "I mean...no. I'm not feeling well. I'm going back to the room."

"Okay, well Staci and I were going to the Village, so I'll be back late."

I felt Layla's eyes upon me as I changed out of my performance dress.

"Are you sure you're okay?" she asked. "Do you need me to hold your hair back or something?"

I pulled the bag strap over my shoulder. "No, I just need to rest."

When I entered my room, I did nothing but stare at the card for the hours that Layla was gone. I traced the handwriting, smelled the paper and read the message hundreds of times. "Chip, do you have any copies of my mother's handwriting?"

"No, Princess. I only have archived audio files. Would you like to hear them?"

"No." I didn't want to hear my mother's voice until I saw her for myself. I smelled her at the Harvest Ball and she sent me a note for my first auditorium show. She was in Mondaria.

But even better, she knew *I* was in Mondaria. And aside from the excitement of another sign that my mother was alive, I felt relief in knowing my mother would be the one to take over the planning for our reunion. I no longer had to focus on plotting to find her.

She was alive.

The Queen of Capalon would take back her title.

She had a plan.

I just had to wait.

CHAPTER 18

At breakfast the following morning, I unrolled my silverware from its napkin to find yet another handwritten note:

MEET ME IN THE MAGICIAN'S REHEARSAL STUDIO
AFTER BREAKFAST

Rather than eat anything at all, I left Genevieve and Heather as soon as I finished reading my message. I passed Ari at his table of drummers on the way out. He turned his head as soon as I passed, like he hadn't noticed me.

I held my breath as I opened the door to the rehearsal studio, only to find Darden tossing a coin in the air. I groaned. "Did you really need to surprise me with a note in my silverware? I thought our deal was off."

"It is. I just need intel." The coin disappeared from one hand, then reappeared in the other.

"What kind of intel?"

"Tell me what she likes. Does she have an affinity for a certain flower? Dessert? Bird?"

I leaned against a bookcase. "I'm really not in the mood for this right now."

The coin reappeared across Darden's knuckles. "I just don't think a three-dimensional video of me doing magic will be tailored enough to *her*. I want her to be swept away to a place in her heart that is truly magical."

I let out a groan. "Fine. Paris."

Darden squinted through his frames. "Is...your name?"

"She has this obsession with the ancient city of Paris. Goes along with the whole culinary interest I guess."

Darden nodded and reached for his notebook. "Paris...city of love."

"City that no longer exists."

"Doesn't matter." Darden closed his notebook. "So why are you still here?"

"We're done? Okay, good, I can go eat my breakfast."

"No, I mean why are you still in Mondaria? I thought you said you located your target."

I fidgeted with a box with several latching sides. "Well...it's more complicated than that. I think I've done what I need to do on my end. I'm just waiting for that person to make their next move."

Darden nodded. "Well, I hope you're here long enough for me to complete the trick. If it works, you'll get some satisfaction from her reaction, too, since you were involved."

I nodded, but I suddenly felt a strange mix of emotions. I should have secretly disagreed with Darden's comment. I should have thought that I didn't want to stay long enough to see his trick because I wanted my mother to take us back to Capalon as soon as possible.

But aside from my mother, there was something else I didn't feel ready to leave—something that felt too...*unresolved.*

✎

I SPENT the following weeks prowling the Mansion halls at late hours and revisiting the Records Room, only to come up short with information and signs of my mother. I convinced myself I would receive another message from her, but it never came. The pain of waiting for another note was matched with the pain of not having spoken to Ari since Grape Stomp.

We had been purposefully avoiding each other at breakfast and our busy schedule of rehearsals and shows didn't exactly encourage time to talk. And even if I mustered the courage to speak with him, I didn't feel well-versed enough in the realm of friendships and resolving conflicts to initiate a conversation.

It helped that Layla forced me to take trips with her to the Village on our down time, so I wouldn't be tempted to linger in the Lounge and stare at the back of Ari's head, wishing I knew the Mondarian way to fix what I'd damaged. And even though my deal was off with Darden, I continued to see Reese for our singing sessions and the occasional late-night solo work with Maestro. I kept busy interacting with people—just not the people who were on my mind the most.

I suggested a trip to the Village with Layla one day after Sanjay announced to the dining hall that it was Ari's birthday. He forced Ari to stand on a chair while the whole room sang 'happy birthday.' Heather mentioned that the drummers planned to throw a birthday party for him in the Lounge that afternoon but I assumed Ari preferred I didn't attend.

Layla loved going in and out of every shop in the Village, forcing me to smell scented candles that stung my nostrils or watch her try on articles of clothing she couldn't afford. After eating hot ham and cheese sandwiches at a cafe called *Melty Mountain*, we passed a woman on the street standing as still as a statue next to a mailbox. She wore a casual brown jacket with sunglasses, blending in with the fall attire of the other shoppers, but there was something about her that felt familiar.

Layla watched me pause and look over my shoulder.

"What is it?" she asked.

"Nothing." And then it hit me—the woman was one of our Compound's patrol officers back in Capalon. I hurried forward toward the auto-taxi stop.

"Slow down, Paris. Did you see like an old ex or something?"

"Something like that. Just...don't turn around, okay?" I didn't slow my pace till we reached an available auto-taxi.

Layla leaned her head back as she caught her breath in the auto-taxi. "You know...some people—like you—try to avoid their exes. I get it. But...my strategy is to be right up in their faces so they can see the huge mistake they've made."

I declined any further invitations to go to the Village after that incident. If my sister had Capalon Patrol officers in the Village, it would only take one look at my face for them to sweep me away back to Capalon. And I wouldn't be able to cause a scene for risk of exposing myself, the Patrol officer and the whole reason why I was there in the first place. I would disappear from the court and leave my mother without being able to say hello or goodbye.

One day after another rose-less auditorium show, Layla begged me to go to the Village with her to start some early Christmas shopping. I stepped into the blue jeans from Genevieve and Heather after getting out of my performance dress. "I'm just going to stay at the Mansion today. I need some down time."

"Suit yourself," Layla said as she wiped her lipstick off with a solution-soaked cotton ball. "I heard Heather say she and Ari are going."

I looked at her through the dressing-table mirror.

She smirked. "You sure do perk up when you hear your *friend* is hanging around another girl."

Rather than spending time alone in my room, I felt the need to do something with my hands, so I headed to an open rehearsal studio with a piano. Between Chip and a few music books I took from the Lounge, I learned all the notes in C and D Major. I even managed to play a few basic tunes by reading notes in both the treble and bass clef.

After returning to my room, Little Bernie the cat paid me a visit, and I calmed as he purred in my lap. He only stayed a few minutes until he heard Agnes call him. I headed to the bathroom to wash my hands when the girls from the Village trip entered the hallway. "Have a good time?" I asked as they were about to pass by.

Layla led the pack with an arm full of shopping bags. "Yeah, it was great," she said with a smile. "Especially the part when Ari punched Felix Adaire in the face and broke up with his girlfriend."

CHAPTER 19

My limbs went rigid, and I considered the chance that Layla was lying until Heather bounded forward and followed us into our room. "You should have seen it, Paris! We were all coming out of this coffee shop when Ari passed his girlfriend, who was hand in hand with Felix Adaire—remember him from like our first day here?"

I nodded and sat on my bed as I anxiously awaited more details from the girl who had been avoiding me since the solo auditions.

Heather spoke with an animated face. "So, it turns out Tasha didn't go to Grape Stomp with Ari because she spent that whole weekend with Felix! Ari said they were officially done, and we started to walk away when Felix said something insulting to Ari and the next thing you know, Ari punches Felix in the face! Felix was about to hit him back when a wall of smoke forms and Ari disappears!"

Knowing Ari's best friend and his affinity for smoke bombs in emergency situations, I assumed Darden whisked him away into an auto-taxi back to the Mansion.

"Have you seen him since the fight? Is he okay?" I asked.

She shook her head. "No, but now Ari is officially single. And since you guys are friends, I was wondering if you could tell me what he might like for Christmas? I was thinking about buying him some new shirts since all he wears is flannel."

I stood up. "You know what Heather, I have a headache, so maybe we can just talk about it later."

"Oh, okay. Night!" she bounced out of the room and I felt Layla's eyes upon me.

"What?"

"Better call dibs."

"Call what?"

"Dibs. It's what you gotta do in situations like this. Remember what I said about girl code? That way you and Heather don't become enemies."

"I'm not doing that," I said as I plopped onto my bed and pulled out a book I borrowed from Layla—*The Passion of Drake and Daniella*—the first book in the series. Whatever word the book shop owner in Badger River had used to describe it was accurate. It was eye opening, with adjectives I had never imagined being matched with body parts and human intimacy. And yet, I couldn't bring myself to stop reading it.

"Suit yourself. I'm heading to the rehearsal studios to work with Reese on our duet for the New Year's Eve Ball. Hopefully he'll make it back to his dorm at the end of the night with all his boy-parts intact," she said with a devilish grin.

I nodded and waved goodbye. I tried to read my book, but no matter how hard I tried to concentrate on Drake's exquisite palms against Daniella's porcelain skin, I couldn't keep my mind off Ari.

Was he okay?

What did Felix say to him?

And why did I have to be right?

I normally felt triumphant whenever I bested my sister, which was rare. But with Ari, I just felt sick—like I had manifested the fight for him.

I eventually put my book down and closed my eyes, listening to the sound of soft rain against my window. It was open just enough for a gentle stream of cool air to blow in the smell of the cold mountain air. I felt myself dozing off into a light sleep when knocking at the door disturbed my relaxed state. "Come in!"

But the handle didn't move. Three more even taps sounded against the door.

I got off the bed, ready to scold Layla for forgetting her key when I opened the door to see a shirtless Ari, wearing only red flannel pajama pants and a lazy smile.

"Miss Paris Marigold!" he said, holding out the last syllable of my name a little too long.

"Ari, what are you doing here? Are you crazy?" I asked in a frenzy of motions—checking behind him to make sure nobody had seen him in the hallway, to pulling him inside and locking the door.

"Yes, I'm probably crazy. But aren't we all? I mean, we take direction from a man who very closely resembles Satan. Haven't you seen his horns?" Ari placed his index fingers next to his temples, displaying a bandaged hand as he laughed hysterically. His body swayed toward me and the scent of alcohol filled my tiny room.

I instinctively held my palm out to prevent his body from falling onto me, causing my fingertips to touch his firm abdomen. I pulled my hand back and shoved it in my jeans pocket. I blushed when Ari caught me looking at his rows of muscles. Again. "Where's your shirt?"

Ari looked down at his bare chest. "Oh yeah. I couldn't figure out how to get my shirt on with one hand. The clinic didn't give me anything for the pain so Sanjay told me to take a shot with him. Or was it two? I can't remember. But the good thing is I don't feel pain anymore. See?" Ari lightly punched me in the shoulder with his damaged hand. The act resulted in him cursing and doubling over.

I directed him to sit on my bed and helped prop him up against my pillows. I then moved to the foot of my bed. "Ari, why are you here?"

He smiled and spoke with a booming voice. "To serve His Majesty, King Orson—"

"Shh!"

"Sorry. Shh..." Ari attempted to put his index finger to his lips but only touched the corner of his mouth.

I stifled a laugh. "Why are you in my room, Ari?"

He looked at me through lowered eyelids. "Paris Marigold, I am here because I needed to tell you that you were right. I should have ended it with Tasha a long time ago. And now look." Ari held up his hand, as if showing me the bandage for the first time. "She's been with that jerk Felix since pretty much the day Maestro kicked him out." He shrugged. "You were right. The beautiful Paris Marigold was right."

Heat rushed to my cheeks. I opened my mouth to speak, but Ari cut me off and continued his slurred speech. "And I asked Layla about your solo. She told me the truth. It's pretty obvious that Heather...well, she's a nice girl, but...anyway, Paris Marigold of Green Heights, I'm sorry. I'm in your room because I wanted to say sorry and tell you that you're right. You're beautiful and you're right."

"Ari, you're intoxicated," I said, trying to ignore my fiery cheeks.

"How do you know I'm drunk?" he asked with a playful smile.

"Well for one thing, you're slurring your words and you also reek of alcohol." I failed to mention that he called me beautiful—*twice*. "You have to leave before anyone sees you here and you get us both kicked out."

"But I want to talk to you. I miss talking to you," he said with round, pleading eyes.

I felt myself getting lost in swirls of chocolate and gold for a moment until a loud belch from his mouth brought me back to reality. "We can talk later, when you're sober. You need to leave!"

But Ari only yawned and didn't move an inch. "You didn't come to my birthday party. I was hoping you would, but you didn't."

"Oh yeah...I'm sorry about that." I chewed on my thumbnail and stared at my feet. "I guess I didn't think—Ari, don't you dare fall asleep!" Ari's eyes closed, so I stood to tug on his uninjured arm.

"Would sleep be such a bad thing? Your bed feels nice. And I would keep you warm." He pulled me onto the bed with the arm I had been tugging. My skin tingled under his tense muscles and I felt intimidated by his strength—*drummer's arms.*

His fingertips lightly touched my hip bone under my shirt, making the hairs on my back slowly prickle up to my neck. The dim lighting, the smell of the mountain air pushing through under my window and Ari's warm touch made me want to melt into him. To tell him that yes, I would be fine if he slept in my bed and kept me warm. His breathing slowed and his hand slid lower down my thigh. His other arm raised above his head, showing off every row of muscle under his firm chest.

I turned my body to get a better hold on his shoulders and prop him up, but my eyes fell to his lips. My awkward kiss with Reese didn't sell me on the hype of kissing that the Mondarian girls couldn't stop talking about. But like the Mondarian snowflakes I longed to see, maybe every kiss was different in its own intricate design with each couple. Maybe with Ari...

I shook the thought out of my head. Ari needed to return to his room, so neither of us would be dismissed from the court. I tightened my grip on his shoulders to pull him forward when the door swung open.

"Paris, what the hell?" Layla asked, shutting the door behind her.

I pushed Ari's torso off me and struggled to stand on my own two feet when I hadn't ingested an ounce of alcohol. "It's Ari." I felt absurd stating the obvious. "He's intoxicated, and he's fallen asleep on my bed."

Layla smiled. "That's one way to get him to date you."

I lifted a finger to my lips. "Shh!"

Ari softly snored, but I didn't want the risk of having him overhear something that wasn't true.

Layla stared at Ari for a moment as she chewed on the tip of her straw from the cup in her hand. "I didn't see anybody's door open on the way in. Just wake him up and take him out."

Waking Ari up was no easy task. I tried shouting his name and shaking him. Layla opened her cup and dumped ice over his chest.

"Darden, what the—" he sat straight up. "Wait, where am I?" Then he met my eyes, followed by Layla's. "Oh, crap on the king." His forehead fell into his palms.

"Time to leave, drummer-boy," Layla said. She threw her empty cup away and turned her back to us.

"Are you okay to head back on your own?" I asked Ari, my heart racing from almost following through with my kiss research.

Ari slowly moved himself to the edge of my bed and examined his bandaged hand. "Yeah, I'm good. I can get myself back to my room."

I picked the ice cubes off my bed, then offered my hand. "I should make sure you don't pass out in the Lounge on your way there."

He took my outstretched palm to help himself up and let me loop my arm through his as I escorted him down the hallway and into the stairwell.

"These stairwells have great acoustics. Echo, echo," Ari said, tilting his head back.

I covered his mouth with my hand, feeling the roughness of light stubble on top of his lip and chin, then opened the door to an empty Lounge. "Okay, hopefully you can get yourself upstairs to your room. Goodnight, Ari."

I turned to head back upstairs but his strong hand gripped mine.

A mix of grey-blue moonlight and dark shadows danced across Ari's face. "I know who you really are, Paris Marigold. You were right about me and I think I might be right about you."

I blinked in disbelief, entranced by the illuminated specs of gold in Ari's eyes and the feel of his hand enveloped around mine. Was he the one who slipped me the note at the Harvest Ball like I had hoped?

He licked his lips. "You've been homeschooled your whole life and now you're on your own but you're afraid to let go. What's holding you back, Paris? Just let go..." His eyes bounced from my eyes to my lips, sending my heart into a fierce cadence against my chest.

"I...I have to go to bed," I said, breaking his hold on me. "And you do too."

He smiled and performed a sloppy court bow. "Good night, Miss Marigold." He turned, and I waited until the door to the Men's Dorms closed behind him. Still under Ari's trance, I slowly made my way up the stairs. When I opened the door to our room, Heather sat on my bed and leapt up when she saw me.

"Paris! I had another idea for Ari—"

Without thinking, I let Layla's suggested words fall out of my mouth. "Heather, I have dibs on Ari."

"Oh," she said, rapidly blinking her eyes. "I thought you liked Reese?"

"You heard the court lady, Heather. She's got dibs." Layla ushered her out the door, then turned and crossed her arms. "So, you're admitting it then?"

"Admitting what?"

"That you have a thing for Ari."

"No, I just know that Ari isn't interested in Heather, so...I'm protecting her from getting her feelings hurt."

"And his abs have nothing to do with it?"

I tossed a pillow at Layla and after laughing together, settled into my bed and fell asleep with the comfort of Ari's scent surrounding me.

CHAPTER 20

I woke gasping for breath.

During my phase of rapid eye movement sleep, my brain thought it was vital for me to experience a nightmare of my mother calling to me from the Polaris Auditorium stage. When I ran down the length of the aisle to meet her, she transformed into Ari who proceeded to strangle the life out of me.

I looked over to the other side of the room to see no Layla, and glowing clock digits indicating that I had slept into the late morning. I pressed my palms to my head as imagery from the night before replayed behind my eyelids—playing the piano, being surprised by a half-naked Ari and telling Heather I had 'dibs.'

What was I thinking?

I had no right to claim Ari for myself. I allowed myself to get lost in his eyes and be mesmerized by his lips—things that had no purpose in a productive Capalon way of life.

Whoever gave me the note at the Harvest Ball wanted me to leave before the king discovered me, but the truth was, I needed to leave before something far more dangerous happened—like developing romantic feelings for a Mondarian drummer.

After I dressed, Heather happened to open her door at the same time. She fidgeted with something on her sweater in an attempt to avoid eye contact but I caught up to her and tapped her arm. "Hey, Heather. I just wanted to say sorry about the whole 'dibs' thing. Layla told me to say that to you and I didn't know what it meant."

She opened the door to the stairwell. "So, you *don't* like Ari?"

I shook my head. "We're just friends."

She perked up with a smile, then her face twisted. "Why do you hang out with Layla so much? You should hang out with me and Gen more." Then she looked at my messy hair and pajama pants. "You know we have sectionals today, right?"

"Yeah, I'm going to eat and run. See you in sectionals."

I left Heather in the Lounge and headed to the dining hall. When I approached the food line, I saw that I wasn't the only one who slept in.

Ari signaled for me to sit by him after I filled my plate with the leftover bits of food from the pans on the buffet line. His hair stuck straight up on the crown of his head and dark circles framed his eyes.

But he managed to get a shirt on.

He leaned forward and whispered. "Did I really go to your room last night?"

I nodded and touched my neck at the reminder of his fake grip on me from my nightmare.

"I'm so sorry," he said, massaging his temples. "I shouldn't have let Sanjay convince me to take those shots with him."

"I'm just glad neither of us got caught."

He took a sip of his hot chocolate. "Did I say...or do anything I shouldn't have?"

You called me beautiful. Twice.

"No."

He looked as though he didn't believe me and then Sanjay came up behind him. "Hey Novak, still on for your solo tonight or do you need a sub?"

He nodded. "I'll be fine. Play through the pain, right?"

Sanjay slapped him on the shoulder, then exited the dining hall.

"Solo?" I asked Ari.

"Yeah, Maestro wasn't happy with Simon Zacher on the solo, so he opened auditions again and...I got it."

I smiled. "That's great, Ari. But can you play with your injured hand?"

"Yeah, I'll be fine." His eyes lingered on his bandaged hand, so I bent my head down to eat my cold eggs. "Hey, I'm sorry that I've been kind of distant the past few weeks."

A fluttery feeling tickled my insides. I continued to stare at my eggs and poke them with my fork.

Ari's fingers tapped the side of his cup. "Tasha and I were fighting after Grape Stomp. I tried to work things out, but we weren't getting anywhere. I was dumb to think it didn't have anything to do with Felix."

I lifted my head to meet his eyes. "Were you in love?"

Ari's eyes widened slightly as if my question may have been inappropriate. But his answer remained calm. "I don't know, honestly. I know that's a weird answer but we've known each other for so long, I'm not sure if it was love or just...*knowing* each other." Ari shook his head. "But it doesn't matter what it was because it's over."

Agnes walked up to our table. "Paris, you know we have sectionals today, right?"

"Yes, ma'am." I waited till Agnes walked away to let out a groan. "Sorry Ari, I've gotta go get ready for..." I put my fingers to my temples, mimicking Ari from the night before.

He smiled. "Right. Talk to you later."

I said goodbye and lifted my tray from the table.

"Wait, Paris? I know people say they'll 'talk later' all the time but things have a tendency to get in the way around here, so...what if we made a pact to see each other at least once a day to catch up?"

The fluttery feeling in my stomach intensified. "Okay. When?"

"Well, I can barely keep my eyes open at the end of the day so how about in the morning—before everyone else wakes up. I'll set a fire in the Lounge and we'll just catch up before the day takes over."

I nodded. "Yeah, I'd like that."

"Okay, it's a deal."

I walked my tray to the conveyor belt with a smile on my face. I would start everyday talking with Ari—my *friend*. There was no harm in friends talking. Sure, he had called me beautiful, but he was also intoxicated. He probably would have acted the same way around Heather if he had chosen her door to knock on instead of mine. And whatever effect his eyes and smile had on me, it was just something I had to learn to suppress.

Ari was just a nice boy who wanted to talk to a friend.

And I happened to be the one he picked to fill the position.

THE MAESTRO WAS on good behavior for our sectionals that day, having only hurled one pen into the risers when the basses missed their entrance.

Layla walked out of the rehearsal room with me when we finished. "Reese is driving me crazy, working on this duet together."

"Still can't talk without fighting?"

"Even worse. Now he's saying things like 'I love our blend' and 'thanks for pointing out that fermata.' He even stayed to watch me play piano after our allotted rehearsal time together."

"And this is bad because?"

"Because he's treating me like I'm one of the girls who swoon over him. It's like he thinks his long arms and eyes draw these girls in and he's so proud to have everyone under his spell."

I tapped my chin. "Oh yeah, what color are his eyes again? Brown?"

"No, they're like a grey-blue, with a hint of green."

I turned to look at Layla with raised brows and a playful smile.

"What's that look for?"

"Nothing. Just that you had to be looking at him pretty well to know the exact pigmentation of his iris."

"That's not...I wasn't looking like that. We just look at each other a lot while we sing."

"Funny, I thought Maestro specifically told you two to *not* look at each other in sectionals today?"

She let out a groan. "You know what I mean." We took a few steps together in silence. "Did you know that his dad is a ski coach? If he didn't get into the King's 100, he was going to try to be a competitive skier."

I shook my head and watched the floor below us change from smooth stone to glassy marble. "We don't talk to each other when we sing other than about the music. We just sing."

"He's probably just making up lies to pose as a normal human. It's easier to seduce a girl when you come off as normal."

I laughed. "Layla, Reese is being nice to you because he's a genuinely nice guy. He's not trying to seduce you. Unless...you *want* to be seduced?"

"No! And by him of all people? He's so egotistical and maybe he's a good singer, but he's a lousy songwriter, just like he's a lousy kisser."

"I never said he was a lousy kisser—you did. But I'm sure there's a way you could find out for sure."

Layla pushed against me with her shoulder. "What about you and Heather? You looked all chummy in rehearsal today for putting dibs on her crush last night."

I scratched behind my ear. "Yeah...that's because I told her I didn't mean it this morning."

Layla's brows creased.

"Layla, Ari and I are *just* friends. You have to believe me."

She nodded. "You're right. Maybe giving him a rebound is a good thing."

"A what?"

"A rebound—the first person you date after a breakup. Normally it's fleeting and means nothing. But it's a way to heal before moving on to your next relationship."

I sighed. "So many things I learn from you, Layla Tanvi."

Layla wrapped her arms around me as we continued to walk the hall. "You know you love me, princess."

I giggled and hugged her back.

Maybe I was forgetting that I was a Capalon and she was Mondarian. Or maybe I was just playing a role. Whatever I was doing, it didn't feel forbidden or wrong. I just felt like a teenage girl.

CHAPTER
21

The next morning when my alarm went off at too early of an hour, I was somehow full of energy. I kept on my pajama pants and put on a sweatshirt on over my t-shirt. I bounded down the stairs to see Ari blowing air into a small flame in one of the fireplaces. The sun hadn't bothered waking up with us, keeping the Lounge in a few more minutes of darkness. "You were serious when you said you would start a fire," I said, impressed with Ari's willingness to do physical labor at such an early hour.

"Only for you, Paris," he said with a polite smile.

When the sound of popping and hissing reached my plush chair at the hearth, Ari took his own seat opposite from me. He tapped his armrests, then leaned back. "So, where should we start?"

FOR THE NEXT COUPLE WEEKS, we answered each other's questions ranging from 'how many donuts do you think you could eat before puking' to 'how many children do you want to have someday?' He would tell me about his family back in Badger River. I would tell him about my mother or funny things my sister and I used to do. And anytime a conversation turned too specific about Green Heights, I would remind him I didn't get out much being homeschooled or switch the conversation back to him. And no matter how hard of a day we had the night before, we kept our promise and met at the same time every morning with Ari starting the fire. I didn't mention my morning chats with Ari to anyone, not even Layla. I would open the door to our room, just as she was waking up, so it looked like I was returning from the bathroom.

One night while Layla was in the rehearsal studio, I asked Chip to walk me through the process of starting a fire. The following morning, I had a flame that insisted on going out every time I got the log to light.

"What can I say? I'm impressed," Ari said as he knelt down beside me to see the flame of my efforts. "You just need to blow some air on it to really get it going." He signaled for me to bend down with him and we both blew air onto the flame. Our mouths were so close together, I could have turned my head and our lips would have touched.

He was the first to sit back on his heels. "Hey, what do you think about a campfire party outside tonight? I've been wanting to have one before it gets too cold."

"Yeah, I think that would be fun. Oh wait, I told Reese I would sing with him after the ballroom show tonight."

"Why don't you guys just sing for us at the campfire? I'm sure Reese wouldn't mind an audience."

"I'm sure he wouldn't. Okay. I'll let him know."

The conversation that followed included listing our top five favorite desserts, other instruments we wished we knew how to play and Ari's description of horseback riding.

Later that day before singers' sectionals, I was thinking about what questions I wanted to bring to our chat the next morning when Heather tapped me on the shoulder.

"Have you seen Ari lately?" she asked. "I can't seem to track him down."

I had been seeing so much of Ari, I forgot I had given up my 'dibs' on him to Heather. "No," I said with a high pitch to my voice. "But I heard he's having a campfire party tonight. You should come."

Heather agreed to attend the party and planned to bring Genevieve with her. After sectionals, I walked up to Reese and Layla who were arguing in the hallway.

"Hillary March won the moguls championship last winter, not Eloise Howell," Layla said.

Reese spoke with open palms. "No, I'm telling you, I was there, and it was Eloise."

"Maybe you were there, but Hillary spoke at my ski team's end-of-year banquet and I specifically remember her saying that she won the moguls."

"*Two* winters ago."

"*Last* winter!"

"You were on a ski team?" I asked Layla.

Layla tore her eyes off Reese to recognize my presence. "Yeah, I'm a record holder for my school. And I'm positive I would kick Reese's butt on a moguls hill."

Reese smiled. "Like I said, I'm willing to put it to the test, if you are. But if you're too chicken, we can just admit that I would have won and call it a day."

"Oh, it's on, Olsen."

Layla and Reese shared competitive glares with a reverent undertone. I cleared my throat to break their silent connection and tell them about Ari's campfire party.

As predicted, Reese was thrilled for the opportunity to have an audience for his new songs. "It'll be something fun after tonight's boring State of the Kingdom Dinner," Reese said. "But Prince Corbin will be in attendance tonight, so you girls better perform your best if you want to win your way to the throne."

Poor Reese, if you only knew my secret.

Layla's smile faded and her face paled. "I have to go."

"Wait, are you coming or not?" I shouted.

Layla shouted back a series of responses as she hurried away. "No! I mean, yes. Maybe. I don't know! No."

"I think you need to mark Layla as 'tentative,'" Reese said.

The two of us watched her disappear around the corner.

"I've never seen her that flustered," I said.

Reese smirked. "I have that effect on women."

"Then I bet you could give Prince Corbin a run for his money."

Reese shook his head. "No, you know me, Paris. I'm all talk. And the prince...he's a true man-whore."

I told Reese I would see him at the campfire party and said goodbye when he stopped me.

"Paris?"

"Yeah?"

"Layla is a cool girl."

And that's when I saw it—the smile that Genevieve used when she talked about Robert—the same smile Darden used when he plotted his magic for Genevieve. And the same smile that I tried to suppress every time I was around Ari.

Reese wore *his* smile for Layla.

CHAPTER
22

The State of the Kingdom Dinner lacked the dancing of the themed balls—something every court member was thrilled to do without. Our dresses were navy blue satin with a crisscross neckline. It was simple but sophisticated and reminded me of something my sister would love to wear—if Capalons wore dresses.

Most of the girls in the dressing room buzzed about the princes being in attendance for dinner that night, but the two girls closest to me never mentioned the word 'prince' once.

Genevieve bragged about some plumbing problem Robert helped her father solve for a big client of his. I expected Layla to jump in and make a smart comment multiple times during Genevieve's story but she stayed silent. Layla finished her hair and make-up early, then disappeared, only to return for our line-up in the hallway.

"Layla's acting weird," I said to Reese. "What did you do to her?"

"Nothing! Last time I saw her I was with you."

"You better be telling the truth," I whispered as we entered the ballroom. Agnes handed out our assigned table numbers on small square cards and after the Social Hour, I made my way to the front of the ballroom to a table that sat directly in front of the stage below the head table.

A jolt of nerves coursed through my body.

What if somebody in the Royal Family recognized me?

"Paris, I need you to switch seats with me." I turned to see Layla staring at me with red-rimmed eyes.

"I thought we weren't allowed to switch seats."

"I know, I know, but I just...well, the Mansion event planner told me to switch with you."

"Really?"

"Yeah, she didn't tell me why but here's my table number, now give me yours."

I hesitated but the urgency behind Layla's eyes moved my hand. She took the card out of my fingers, then slipped past the people in front of me.

I felt relieved as I neared the back of the ballroom to Layla's table, but what was the Event Planner's purpose for switching our seats? And who was the Mansion event planner, anyway? She wasn't anyone we met on our tour and anytime she was mentioned, she was only referred to as 'the Mansion event planner.'

The Chancellor's voice boomed through a microphone. "Please rise for the Royal Family."

Already standing, I turned to face the stage. The Royal Family took their positions behind their chairs—Queen Marisol, Prince Corbin and Prince Taran. The queen wore a navy gown, covered in glittering crystals and a sparkling tiara sat atop her dark head of hair. Both princes wore the same navy tuxedos with silver ties and shared the same golden hair as their father but that's where their similarities ended. Prince Corbin held a smirk as if he found the event to be comical and stood with a lazy stance and untamed hair. Taran was about a head shorter than his older brother and tilted his chin up, mimicking his mother's stern features.

Three knocks pounded against the ballroom doors to begin the drummers' cadence. The drummers separated into their two even lines, then one drummer dropped into a roll as the king entered the ballroom. My eyes should have been focused on the king but they drifted to the soloist. I had been listening to Ari play his solo for the past couple of weeks but my heart fluttered as if each performance was his debut.

The remainder of the evening was boring, to say the least. Not one, but two guests dozed off at my table and the only thing keeping me awake was that Ari sat within my line of sight. A couple times, he'd turn his head, meet my eyes, smile, then return his focus back to the king. It was quick, but it was enough to send enough electricity to my brain to stay alert.

When the show was over, I planned to talk to Layla about the elusive event planner, but when I returned to my chair in the dressing room, I found another lavender rose. Not taking the time to read the message, I stuffed the rose in my bag and changed out of my dress. Unable to wait till I got to my room, I pulled the rose out of my bag and read it in the Administrative Wing.

You'll soon see how big my love for you truly is.

"What are you doing with the Queen of Capalon?"
Unable to breathe or speak, I turned my head.

A young woman with frizzy hair stared up at me as she fumbled with a key ring in one hand and clutched a clipboard in another. She tilted her head to my flower. "The lavender rose. One of the first queens—I can't remember who—hated lavender roses and nicknamed them the Queen of Capalon. Sometimes we still get a few that pop up in our greenhouse."

"Queen of Capalon," I said through a raspy whisper. I gathered my composure and cleared my throat. "Are you the Mansion Event Planner?"

She nodded and tucked the clipboard under her armpit so we could shake hands. "Scarlet Koon. I've been asking Bernie for years to be added to your training day tour, but he sees no value in it."

Instead of introducing myself back, I asked a question. "Why did you make Layla Tanvi switch seats with me at dinner tonight?"

She crinkled her brows. "I didn't switch any seats at this dinner."

"Oh."

She clicked a pen and pulled up her clipboard. "What was the girl's name? Court members aren't allowed to make seat changes on their own. Everything has to go through me."

"Never mind. Nice to meet you."

I left with gratitude for having learned two things—that Layla lied to me about switching seats and my mother signed her name with a rose.

CHAPTER 23

I was right again—my mother had a plan.

But her message delivered uneasiness as opposed to relief—that 'soon I would see how big her love for me truly was.' How big was the thing she was planning? Was she going to overthrow Mondaria? Did she intend to hurt people in the process with a rebel uprising or would she carry out her plan peacefully? And why couldn't she just talk to me about it? Why all the notes? Was she being held against her will? My head spun with all the unanswered questions, but my mind eased when I remembered Ari's campfire party.

I saw Darden on the way through the Lounge. "Hey, are you coming out to Ari's party?"

"No, ma'am. I have work to do." He held up his notebook and exited the Lounge.

I headed to a large orange flame burning in the center of the dormitory lawn. Without the heat from the bonfire, there was no way I would have agreed to stay outside. Heather, Genevieve, Reese and Staci sat on logs around the fire while Ari stood.

"You made it," he said with a smile. "Just in time for me to give you the official food of a Badger River campfire party—a marshmallow."

He handed me a stick with something white and round at the end of it. Ari placed his hand on top of mine, directing my stick away from the flame itself and closer to the glowing embers where it browned from the heat.

I didn't want to leave his touch, but I felt Heather's eyes upon us. "Heather, have you had a marshmallow yet? Ari can show you how it's done."

I retrieved the gooey ball of fluff and stuffed it into my mouth, savoring the melting sugar over my tongue. Ari helped Heather with her marshmallow and I waited to see his hand guide hers as he did with mine, but he kept a distance between them.

Reese called me over to sing with him and our audience applauded after each one. At the end of a song about being lazy on a rainy day, I followed Reese's eyes to see Layla.

A sweatshirt covered the top of her dress from the dinner and she clenched her fists. "Oh, I made it just in time for your crappy music," she said, staring at Reese.

"Don't listen to her, Reese," Genevieve said. "Your music is great."

Layla's lips tightened into a thin line. "You're right. That's a *wonderful* song. Should get you at least ten pairs of panties."

Layla's sarcasm wasn't lost on any of us.

"Cut the crap," snapped Genevieve. "Reese is a talented songwriter."

"No, he's a *lazy* songwriter." She focused on Reese. "Want to know why your music sucks? Beautiful music or *real art* is created from emotion—raw pain, intense desire, devastating loss...you sing and it's like wrapping a wet blanket around our ears."

"Layla, stop," I said, sending her a warning glare.

"No, she's right," Reese said. "Here's a song filled with *lots* of emotion..." Reese strummed some violent chords and sang choice words directed at Layla.

She straightened her neck, but I noticed a twitch in her bottom lip. She turned and left the campfire. The others laughed at Reese's song but I shot him a disappointed look before chasing down Layla. I followed her to the rehearsal studios, where she picked an available piano.

Her small body moved up and down the keyboard as she played a dark and rapid melody. "He's a jerk!" she shouted over the piano. "He wouldn't know good music if it hit him in the face!"

"Layla, please stop so we can talk."

But Layla continued to play. "See, it was all an act—him being nice to me."

"You're the one who insulted him!"

"He's just so...so—"

Our heads turned to see Reese's body in the doorway, with his guitar slung over his back. "Talented? Handsome?"

Layla slammed the lid of the piano down over the keys. "What are you doing here?"

Reese lifted his chin. "Thought I'd do some songwriting. I'm feeling pretty fired up, thanks to you."

"Well, you have to go to another studio because this one's taken."

"Fine, I will."

"Fine, thanks for gracing us with your presence."

I waited for Reese to leave the studio but he and Layla stood their ground, not taking their eyes off of each other. It was a confusing scene for me to dissect—I would have imagined their expressions to be angry and threatening, but instead, they looked ravenous. Reese finally left, shutting the door behind him.

As soon as he was out of sight, Layla slumped over the lid of the piano and cried. I sat next to her on the piano bench and touched her back. "Layla, what's going on?"

After a few minutes, she sat up and wiped her cheeks with the sleeve of her sweatshirt. She opened the lid of the piano and stared blankly at the keys. "If you love somebody, you go back to them. You *always* find a way to go back to them."

"Who are you talking about? Reese?"

She looked at me with two black rivers under her eyes. "You were right to pass Ari off to Heather. Love isn't worth the pain."

She opened the piano lid and her right hand played a slow rhythm of sad notes.

I spoke softly. "Layla, I know you lied about the event planner switching our seats. I talked to her. If there's something going on, I want to help."

She sniffed. "Just leave me alone, Paris."

"But I'm just trying to—"

Her notes stopped, and she shut her eyes. "If you're really my friend, you'll go away right now and leave me alone."

I stared at the piano keys for a beat. "Okay," I said. "I'll go."

She turned her hand back to the keys, adding her left hand to the melody.

I headed back down to the campfire and plopped down on a log as Staci finished a story about an embarrassing incident with losing both her sticks at a recent show. The remaining people at the campfire laughed at the conclusion of her story, then we sat in silence, listening to the popping of the fire.

I was lost in thought about my roommate and my mother when Staci cleared her throat. "So, Paris...there have been some rumors about you and a couple court boys," she said.

I whipped up, not expecting to be the next form of entertainment at the party. "What?"

She nodded. "Yeah, Reese and Darden." Staci leaned her elbows on her knees. "So, what's going on? Are you dating one of them?"

My eyes darted across the flames to see Ari poking at the fire with a long stick. "For the record, Reese and Darden are just friends."

"But you kissed Reese at Grape Stomp," Heather said, interjecting herself into the unnecessary conversation. "We all saw it."

"Ladies, Paris doesn't have to talk about who she likes if she doesn't want to," Genevieve said.

I looked at Genevieve. "Thank you, Gen. But I don't—"

"I know who it is, but I won't say anything." Genevieve brushed her red hair behind her shoulder.

My mouth hung open for a beat. "Genevieve, I don't—"

"Miss Marigold, would you please join me for a stroll?" I turned around to see Darden staring down at me with his hands in his pockets.

I groaned at his horrible timing.

"Oh, a *stroll*," Genevieve said with a wink, sending the other girls into laughter.

"Darden, tell them we're not dating," I said with pleading eyes.

Darden chewed on his bottom lip. "I...don't talk about relationships, whether they're my own or others'."

His comment sent my audience into a roar of accusations, except for one.

Ari broke a few sticks in half and added them to the fire.

I rolled my eyes as I stood up from my log. "Let's go, Mr. McCray."

When we were inside, I punched Darden in the shoulder. "What kind of response was that?"

He winced. "The kind that wouldn't cause any trouble for either of us. Once this trick is done, I'll swear up and down that I find you incredibly repulsive."

"Trick? I thought our deal was off."

He smiled. "I finished the calculations on my own. I just need you as look out."

I followed his steps down the hallway and into the rehearsal studio suite. I looked in the clear windows expecting to see Reese and Layla, but they were both gone. He stopped in the small kitchen inside the suite and tossed a bag of popcorn inside the microwave, setting it for eight minutes longer than it needed.

"Right now? You're doing it NOW?" I asked, shocked at my delayed realization.

He held his finger to his lips and continued forward.

When I caught up to him, he handed me a pitch pipe. "G for Genevieve," he whispered.

Darden took a deep breath as we neared the magician's rehearsal studio.

I turned my head to ask him a question.

"I'm not nervous, Miss Marigold, so don't ask me. You just need to do your job and I'll do mine."

I rolled my eyes. "Yes, sir, Magician McCray. I'll be the perfect assistant."

I took a deep breath and paced in front of the door when I heard footsteps behind me.

"Paris?"

Before I acknowledged Genevieve, I blew the G loud enough for Darden to hear.

"What are you doing back here?" she asked.

I tapped my nails on the pitch pipe. "Um...rehearsing. This hallway has good acoustics and after Darden showed me a new card trick, I thought I'd do some rehearsing."

Her brows furrowed. "Well, that's what I'm here to do. I've had my name on the magicians' studio waitlist for a long time."

The door behind her opened a bit more, and she was about to turn her head.

"You're right," I said, grabbing her arm. "I *do* have a crush on a court man. I just don't want you to talk to the other girls about it."

Her face lit up. "Of course! So, who is it? I want to know if I'm right."

I watched as Darden silently moved out of the magician's studio into an empty drummer's studio across the hall.

"Actually, I think I have a stomachache from all those marshmallows. See you later, Genevieve."

"But wait...oh, never mind," Genevieve said as she stepped into the studio and closed the door behind her.

I whispered "good luck" to Darden and left before burning popcorn triggered the fire alarm.

CHAPTER
24

A ri was late to our chat the next morning, so I started the fire on my own. I wasn't around for the end of the campfire party, so my mind wandered.

Did Ari stay up late talking to Heather?

Had he made a visit to her room?

Was he *still* in Heather's room?

But then the sound of footsteps calmed my nerves.

"I'm so sorry, Paris. I blame being late on the marshmallows. Darden and I talked for like two hours after I got back to our room. He was in this super-chatty mood and I was hyped up on sugar."

I smiled and blew air on the low flame. "It's okay. I didn't even need your help."

Ari flopped his legs over the arm of the plush chair. "Nicely done. So, is chopping wood next on the list?"

"I'll stick to the fires. But you owe me the next one."

"You got it, Paris."

I turned my head to see Ari smiling at me and there was something that felt so comfortable between the two of us. Like we weren't inside the king's Mansion, but at his house in Badger River, waking up for a day of hot chocolates at Dan's and hiking in the woods. I was tempted to crawl into his armchair with him and let him wrap his arms around me as we watched the fire together.

Is that what Tasha felt when she was with Ari? Or how Genevieve felt with Robert? Was having romantic feelings for someone as simple as being comfortable with another person? Or was there more to it?

I felt comfortable with Darden and Reese, but not the same way I felt with Ari. It was a different kind of comfort. I just couldn't match a word to it.

I headed to my designated chair on the opposite side of the fire and asked Ari why Darden was in such a chatty mood, even though I knew the real reason why. Then the conversation took off to card games, Ari's grandmother who got drunk playing a card game once, and my ability to multiply large numbers in my head.

Layla skipped her normal breakfast in the rehearsal studio and sat with me, Genevieve, and Heather for breakfast. Genevieve called over Staci Ringer from the drummers' table, as well as Jasmine. She described Darden's trick for everyone in detail.

I couldn't help but smile, knowing that Darden pulled off an amazing illusion using a projector, a tilted pane of glass, and speakers. Darden had wanted me to stay at the Mansion long enough to for him to do the trick, and I knew why—because seeing Genevieve's expression was *real* magic.

Genevieve's eyes twinkled as she spoke. "I stepped inside the rehearsal studio and I saw a huge vase of red roses with a message that said 'for my love, Genevieve.' And then hovering above me was the Eiffel Tower from the lost city of Paris."

"I've never heard of it," Jasmine said.

"It was a real thing a long time ago. And it was sparkling. And it was so real, it was as if I could reach out and touch it. Beautiful music played from an instrument I had never heard before and fog danced across my feet. It truly felt like I was standing in the city of love." Genevieve paused to suck the last of her milk up with a straw. "And I would have stayed to see who did it, but the fire alarm went off because somebody burnt a bag of popcorn. I even went back after the guards cleared the studios and there wasn't a shred of evidence left. It *had* to be a Fourth Season Magician."

Jasmine shook her head. "I've never heard of an illusion like that. It's almost like your magician is using illegal technology or something."

Genevieve's face soured. "My secret admirer is *not* using anything illegal. He's just brilliant." Then her eyes shifted back to that glazed-twinkle look. "I just feel like I'm floating in a dream. I live in the king's Mansion, I wear gorgeous gowns on a regular basis, and I have an amazingly talented secret admirer."

"And a boyfriend," said Staci.

"Yes, and a boyfriend. Of course, I can't tell Robert, but it's fun knowing that I have two boys interested in me. I just love being loved."

"Well, there goes my appetite." Layla stood and lifted her tray.

Genevieve ignored Layla's exit. "It's perfect timing too. I think Christmas is one of the most romantic times of the year. In Paris, they would say, 'Joyeux Noel!'"

I gave Genevieve a hug to share in her excitement, then followed Layla out of the dining hall. "Hey, are we going to talk about last night?"

"No. Never."

"Layla, I'm trying to be serious here."

"And I *seriously* need you to never *ever* bring up last night again, okay? There are some things that friends keep secret, and this is something that's my secret."

I could reason with secrets. "Okay. But what about Reese? You were pretty mean to him, Layla."

"Fine, I'll give him a basket full of rainbows next time I see him."

I raised my brows.

"Paris, we're just going to have to agree to disagree on this one. I think his music sucks. Your voice is pretty on the harmonies, but it's not enough for what he needs if he's serious about a career as a songwriter."

I sighed. "Just...go easy on him."

"Why?"

"I just...well, I can't be sure, but I think he likes you, Layla."

Her cheeks reddened, but she kept a straight face. "Well...he can't. I won't let him." Layla hurried forward. "Whatever you do, Paris, don't let me stand under any mistletoe with Olsen."

I took a few quick steps to keep up with her fast, short legs. "Why would standing under a poisonous plant be harmful to you and Reese?"

She smiled and slowed her pace. "Nothing good ever comes from standing under mistletoe, princess."

Genevieve and Heather passed us in the hall.

"Don't listen to her, Paris," Genevieve said over her shoulder. "Mistletoe is one of the things that makes Christmas such a romantic time of the year. It's the kissing plant! You've never heard about mistletoe in Green Heights?" she asked.

Layla and I said a unison, "Homeschooled."

Heather's blonde head poked around Genevieve. "But everybody knows what mistletoe is. My cousins are homeschooled and they all know. How do you not know, Paris?"

I wanted to say, "Because I'm the Princess of Capalon, *Heather*," but Layla ended the conversation for me by telling Genevieve and Heather to duck-off. Or was it something else? Buck? Whatever it was, it was a conversation ender that I wanted to remember for the future.

Backstage during an auditorium show that night, I congratulated Darden in a whispered conversation. "Genevieve was *mystified*, just as you wanted. So, when are you going to reveal yourself to her?"

"Never."

"What? After all that work?"

Darden adjusted his black tie. "In my opinion, love's better left as an illusion. Once you know the secret to the trick, the magic loses its luster."

"You don't give yourself enough credit, Darden."

"I don't mean it as *me* specifically. I could be the most attractive guy in all of Mondaria and the same rule would apply. You imagine love to be greater than it is in reality, so when you finally get it, you end up disappointed in one way or another. And I happen to be most comfortable under illusion."

"Says the magician," I said with a smile.

He shrugged. "Hey, don't mess up tonight. The king and queen are in their box."

I gave him a thumbs up, then took the stage with the other singers for our set.

As I sang, I pondered Darden's explanation. Was I happier with Ari hidden under the illusion of my fake Mondarian identity? If he knew who I really was, would he still make campfires for me or would he hand me over to the guards?

But then the faint smell of something familiar tickled my nose after I finished my solo. My mother was nearby but to my disappointment, she continued to stay hidden, failing to reveal herself backstage or after the show. I had to be ready at a moment's notice for her to appear and dissolve the illusion of Paris Marigold.

WE DIDN'T CELEBRATE Christmas in Capalon, so the Mansion's transformation into an indoor forest of pine trees was fascinating. I also noticed how the decor and the holiday seemed to make everyone a bit more cheery. Ari especially couldn't contain his joy for the atmosphere.

The next morning, he stood in front of an empty hearth with a huge smile plastered on his face.

"Where's my fire, Mr. Novak? And why do you have a coat on?"

"It's a surprise. Go get yours and meet me outside."

I bounded back up to my room and ran into Agnes and Little Bernie in the hall on the way back out.

"Why are you so happy to be going outside this early?" she asked through lowered eyelids.

I bent down to give Little Bernie a pat on the head. "Um...just excited to start the day."

"Uh-huh. Just remember he's not allowed in your room." Agnes ducked into the bathroom before I had to construct a lie that didn't involve seeing a boy.

The cold air bit at my face when I stepped outside but Ari grabbed my hand, melting away any ill thoughts of winter.

"So where are we going?" I asked. "Oh, did you finally find the moose?"

"Nope. Something even cooler."

We walked across the Mansion lawn hand-in-hand, only for Ari to gently drop our connection when we approached a circular barrier surrounding a frozen pad of white ice.

"They've set up a temporary ice rink for the Christmas guests. And we'll be the first ones to test it out," Ari said, slapping a hand on the barrier as if he was showing off a prized discovery.

I recalled Layla talking about ice rinks and ice skating, but the activity required some sort of special shoe. "Don't we need equipment?"

He shook his head. "Just our shoes. You don't need ice skates to have fun on the ice." He helped me over the barrier and held my hands as we stepped onto the ice. I slipped, but he caught me, preventing me from falling on my butt.

Ari performed a series of spins and slides and I followed suit, laughing and forgetting all the obligations, risks and threats that waited for me outside the ice rink. When Ari performed the Mondarian waltz on his own and fell on his rear end, I reached down to help him up but I shook with laughter and fell down next to him. When our laughter subsided, we stayed seated on the ice to watch the sun peek over the mountain tops, sending a coral haze across the lawn.

I turned to Ari, expecting him to say something about the rising sun but he was looking at me.

"Your ears are bright red," he said. He huffed hot air into his hands and placed them over my ears. We looked into each other's eyes and I wanted to tell him that his mouth looked cold and that maybe covering it with mine would—

"Hey, get out of there! This is for Mansion guests only!" shouted a Mansion employee.

Ari helped me up without any slipping and boosted me over the barrier, cursing under his breath. He pulled me by the hand as we sprinted and laughed all the way back to the Lounge.

When we stepped inside, court members were emerging from the dorms.

Heather was the first one to see us. "Where have you guys been?"

"Just out for a walk," Ari said. "I'm gonna hit the shower. See you ladies later." Then he pointed at me and raised one black brow. "Stay out of trouble, Paris."

Heather eyed something on the chair behind me. "Isn't that Ari's water bottle?"

She reached for it and read his initials out loud. "Yep, A.P.N. I wonder what his middle name is?"

"Phillip," I said without hesitation.

One morning, Ari and I talked about middle names and how he tried to go by Phil for a while when he was little because he didn't like the name Ari. I slipped and told him my real middle name, hoping he didn't think to check Paris Marigold's ID.

Heather gave me a sideways glance.

"At least, that's my guess. You should ask him when you give it back to him."

She smiled and headed to the dining hall with the water bottle in her hands.

But as I watched her walk away, I couldn't help but feel that she was taking something that belonged to me.

CHAPTER
25

That night before dinner, I decided it was time to return the Records Room key to the guards. I planned to tell them I found it on the floor of the hallway but when I approached the guard's station, the words "Capalon in custody" hit me in the chest like a bullet.

The guard who offered me a 'special arrangement' from our Mansion tour spoke to a heavy-set female guard. "Yeah, they got this guy locked up for questioning. He's not talking. News will spread like wildfire soon enough though."

"How'd they catch him?" asked the woman.

"Suspicious innkeeper called the cops, and they got him with a tech-scanner."

"Do we have any of those?"

"We did. I can't find it so don't tell the captain." The guard leaned back in his chair. "Can't imagine the look on that slimy glow worm's face when they caught him."

I didn't stay to listen to the guards' conversation and headed toward the Records Room. There would have to be a new file in the DETAINED filing cabinet that would tell me who they caught. If it was another patrol officer, then my sister had multiple people looking for me.

When I turned down the hall, I heard approaching footsteps from the opposite end. I ducked behind a fake Christmas tree to see Maestro approach the Records Room door. He knocked softly twice, and the door opened. He looked both ways before stepping inside and closing the door.

Who was he meeting?

I considered opening the door to see if my mother was in there with him, but if I was wrong, I'd reveal my stolen access to the Records Room. And that revelation would bring about a full interrogation by Maestro and the sweaty captain, and potentially spur a war between two enemy kingdoms.

I walked to the dining hall for dinner in a cloud of thought which followed me through the food line and to the table with Layla. Since Layla's fight with Reese at the campfire, I had been the one to steer our dinner conversation, talking about things like how pretty the Mansion looked, the design of our dresses for the Christmas Ball, and Maestro's latest outbursts. But sitting with the knowledge that one of my own citizens could be executed because of me placed us both in silence.

We kept our heads focused on our food until guitar chords echoed through the dining hall. Layla looked past my shoulder and I turned to see Reese standing on a chair with his guitar. Normally when Reese sang one of his songs, he smiled and nodded his head along with the audience. His lyrics were light and simple and easy to memorize after hearing a couple choruses.

But on the chair, he kept his eyes shut and sang quick lyrics above powerful guitar chords. As the song climaxed, Reese belted the final notes, raising the hairs on my arms and the back of my neck. As he sustained his last chord, Layla ran out of the dining hall. Reese followed, and I fell into step just a few feet behind.

I found Layla at one of the six hearths with her palms against the mantle, staring into the fire. Reese stood behind her.

I leaned against a bookshelf so it didn't feel like I was intruding on their conversation. A few other court members in the Lounge turned their heads but Reese and Layla were never ones to shy away from an audience.

"Why did you do that?" Layla asked, keeping her back turned to Reese.

"What, sing?"

"No. Why did you listen to me? That song...the words...and your voice...I've never heard you go into that register before. It was strained, but *beautiful*."

"Because you were right. I finally had something to be angry about and I put it into a song. You challenge me to be better and...I like you, Layla."

Layla hit the mantle with her palm. "Dammit, I swore I would never let this happen again."

Reese pulled the guitar around to rest on his back. "What, listen to my singing?"

She finally turned to face Reese. "No. You...you like me. And I... don't entirely despise you, which means...which means we could fall in love."

Reese let out a short laugh. "What's wrong with that?"

"Everything! Something terrible will happen and we'll end up miserable and broken."

"You don't know that for sure, Layla."

"Yes, I do. I've been through it before and I'm not going to let it happen again. Trust me Reese, I'm doing us both a favor. You should just date Heather. Or Raya. Or any of those girls who—"

Reese wrapped an arm around Layla's waist and pulled her into a kiss, bending his tall body down to meet her lips. Layla held his face in her hands and kissed him back before taking a step back. "I can't give you what you want, Reese. I'm sorry." She stepped between pieces of Lounge furniture, leaving Reese alone at the hearth.

I followed Layla up to our room as my mind connected the dots to the source of Layla's broken heart. I sat next to Layla on her bed and handed her a box of tissues. "That day in the auto-taxi, you said you would make yourself visible to your ex so he could see what he was missing. You switched seats with me at the State of the Kingdom Dinner so Prince Corbin could see you."

She blew her nose. "Close. Try the other brother."

"Prince Taran? But I thought you said you liked older boys?"

"That's something I *would* say after getting my heart crushed by a boy our age."

Layla told me the story of how she and Prince Taran met over the summer when she was working as a server at a restaurant in Wisteria —her hometown and location of Mondaria's military school. Prince Taran would visit her at the restaurant in his downtime and they fell in love in a matter of weeks. Word got back to the king about their relationship and he forced Taran to put an end to it.

"I was at Taran's apartment when he got the call and I heard the whole thing. The king said I was a poor mountain girl who wasn't politically right for him. He said that Prince Corbin at least had the dignity to follow his manhood to the girls who weren't trash. And that's all it took. Taran asked me to leave, and it was over."

I chose my words carefully. "Maybe he broke up with you out of love. He knew that taking it any further would just hurt you more."

She shook her head. "Next time I saw him in the restaurant, he ignored me. And it was like I could *feel* the love erased from his soul. I was furious with Taran but I wanted revenge on the king too. And the best revenge I could think of on both of them was getting into the King's 100. The king has to keep me inside his Mansion and watch me perform almost every night without knowing I'm the trashy girl who took his precious son's virginity. And Taran..." She forced a laugh. "The look on his face when he saw me at the State of the Kingdom Dinner..." Layla smiled and shook her head.

"What did Taran say to you after the dinner?"

She scoffed. "You think he *actually* tried to speak to me? Paris, if somebody loves you, *truly* loves you, they come back for you. Taran had two chances—after he broke up with me and after that dinner."

"And Reese?"

She shook her head. "What about Reese? I can't give him my heart when it's been ripped out."

I sighed and wrapped my arms around her. "How can I help, Layla?"

She rested her head against mine. "Be Reese's kiss partner for the New Year's Eve Ball."

After Reese's and Layla's duet for New Year's Eve, the other singers join them for the countdown and traditional kiss, followed by the final song of the night. I was relieved that it was a tradition only for the singers because I overheard Heather ask Agnes if she could kiss a drummer.

I shook my head. "No, you have a duet with Reese. It would make more sense for—"

"It doesn't have to be us. Maestro already said that." She leaned back to look at me. "I can't kiss Reese again. I don't trust myself. Bad things will happen if I kiss Reese again. I'll tell him that you're his new kiss partner and I'll ask Bradley Wafer—that's who asked you, right?"

Bradley had continued to be the most uncoordinated New Man since dancing with him during our Mondarian Waltz instruction. When I told Ari I would be kissing him on New Year's Eve, Ari joked that he might miss my mouth and go straight for my nose.

I looked into Layla's red-rimmed, hazel eyes. "I'll do it, but just because you asked me to. If at some point you change your mind, you *have* to tell me, okay?"

Layla smiled. "Yes, ma'am."

I offered to give Layla some space and headed back down to the Lounge, where Genevieve called me over to a group of new members playing cards.

"Paris, want to play Sink the Stiff with us?" she asked. "I made brownies..." she said with a song in her voice as she lifted a plate of chocolate squares.

In need of a distraction from Layla's sadness and from my own nerves about the recent Capalon in custody, I took a seat next to her on the couch. "Sure. Gotta find who has the king of spades, right?"

Heather explained the other steps of the card game and then we started—me, Heather, Ari, Genevieve, Darden, and Staci. Ari was the last to take his turn. He caught my smile but didn't say anything. I collected all of Ari's cards, including the king of spades, winning the round.

"You knew from the very beginning. How did you know?" asked Ari as he stuffed a piece of brownie in his mouth.

I shrugged and bit my lip to prevent my smile from stretching too wide.

The next few rounds came down to the last hand. If I successfully went out without losing all my cards, I would beat Staci and win the game. I thought I had it in the bag when Ari sunk me with his last card.

"What did you do?" I shouted at him. "You didn't bother coming after me till the last card, that doesn't make any sense!"

"I wanted you to think you were going to get away with it," he said with a cocky grin.

Out of retaliation, I snagged the last of his brownie and stuffed it in my mouth.

"Oh, you'll pay for that."

And before I could swallow, Ari stood up from the couch and lifted me over his shoulder, carrying me out the door and into the cold. He set me down, then slipped inside the door, using his strength to keep it closed.

I was trembling so hard I couldn't tell if it was from my laughter or the cold. "Ari Novak, you open this door right now!"

Ari gestured as if he couldn't hear me through the transparent window.

"It's freezing out here!"

"Say Ari is the best at Sink the Stiff."

"Ari is the best at Sink the Stiff! Now open this door!"

He cracked the door, just enough for his head to poke through. "Now say I'm the best drummer in all The Lands."

I hugged myself and jumped on the balls of my feet. "You're the best drummer in all The Lands and...all the galaxies! Now let me in!"

He opened the door, but instead of allowing me entry, he made his way outside, leaning his body against the door. "I like this game. One more compliment on your own and you can come in."

I should have taken a step back, but I stood my ground. We were close enough that I felt the heat of his body. "You're nice."

He rolled his eyes. "Boring."

"Ugh! Fine, you're...fun to talk to." I made the mistake of allowing my eyes to lock on his. "You always put me in a good mood even if I've had a terrible day."

Ari's playful grin softened into something more serious and genuine. I spotted a tick in his jaw muscle.

"And..." My brain and inhibitions were numbing from the cold. I leaned forward, so my crossed arms rested against his warm chest. For some reason I thought back to what I said to Maestro the day of my audition. It didn't seem completely true anymore. Singing was no longer the one thing that made me feel like *me*. "...I've never felt more myself than when I'm with you."

Ari's eyes sank into mine until I heard the door click and he stepped aside. "You cheated. I said one compliment, and you gave me three."

I took a sharp breath, returning me to reality. I ducked my head under his arm as I stepped back inside the Lounge. "I guess I can't be trusted," I said with a mocking grin when he stepped in behind me.

"If you can't be trusted, Paris, then no one can."

His smile grew and mine faded.

Heather tugged on Ari's arm. "Ari, let's be partners for the next game!"

Ari's eyes broke from mine. "Um, ok...we can take down Paris together."

I rubbed the back of my neck. "Actually, I'm going to turn in."

Heather's face couldn't have glittered more with the news of my intention to leave.

I waved goodnight and watched Heather tug Ari back to the game table before I retreated to my room. I repeated a reminder to myself as I climbed the stairs back to my room.

He doesn't belong to you and he never will.

CHAPTER 26

I woke up before my alarm went off. I had a repeated nightmare about my mother on the stage, only to be killed by the strength of Ari's two hands. I shivered as I headed downstairs to wait for Ari but a fire roared in our regular hearth. Ari stared blankly at the flames from his armchair.

"How long have you been down here?" I asked.

"Not too long." He rubbed his eyes. "Didn't sleep too well last night."

I took my seat across from him, folding my legs under my bottom. "Something on your mind, Mr. Novak?" I asked with a smile.

Ari nodded but didn't smile back. "That day in the Village when I ran into Felix, he said I was destined to be a failure just like my dad." He ran a hand over his stubble. "After what you said to me at Grape Stomp and rolling Felix's words around in my head for the longest time, I finally wrote my dad a letter. I told him I could no longer be the one person in the family he could lean on because I had my own future to take care of. And...he didn't take it well."

I hugged my waist tighter, wishing my arms wrapped around Ari instead. "I'm so sorry, Ari."

Ari rubbed his palms on the armrests. "He wrote back this long letter, saying all these terrible things and I know they're all lies, but there's always some truth in a lie, right?"

Paris Marigold was a lie but there was definitely truth behind my fake identity. I might not have really been Paris Marigold from Green Heights, but I definitely loved to sing. I liked my new friends. And I was absolutely fighting the most *real* feelings for the boy sitting in front of me.

I agreed with what Ari said but I refused to nod my head, not knowing what terrible things Ari's dad had said to him. "I think you just have to choose for yourself what you want to believe. And if what your dad said is all bear crap, then it's all bear crap. And if you think it's bear crap, then I think it's bear crap."

The corner of Ari's mouth by his scar turned up. "That's a lot of bear crap."

"Yeah, but it's true. Screw what your dad says. What do *you* believe about yourself?"

He lifted his eyes from the fire to meet mine. "I believe...that a girl from Green Heights has helped me more than she probably knows. And I have no way to return the favor. Other than help you build a fire which you've proved you can handle just fine on your own."

Ari's sad smile melted me from my head to my toes. A slew of responses sat idly on my tongue:

You've helped me by just knowing me.

The first time I saw you, I remembered what it was like to feel joy.

And I don't ever want to leave when I'm with you because just being around you feels so good.

I hated the safe response I chose. "You introduced me to Dan's hot chocolate. And now all other hot chocolates pale in comparison."

He nodded. "I did do that. But what else? What does Paris Marigold want?" Ari leaned forward, resting his elbows on his knees.

I swallowed and stared into his eyes. I knew what I wanted when I first came to the Mansion, but I felt like something was taking the place of that goal. Why should I be a part of whatever grandiose plan my mother had up her sleeve? I just wanted to sing on the King's 100 and talk to Ari every morning. My lips moved, threatening to form forbidden words that didn't involve finding my mother or returning with her to Capalon. "I...I want..."

Our heads turned to the sound of the door opening from the Ladies' Dorms. Eric emerged and walked past us. "Uh, you two didn't see me."

We said a unison "yes, sir" and then burst into laughter when the Men's Door closed behind him. Our conversation moved away from what I wanted to guesses of whose room Eric visited. But at the end of the conversation when we stood up, Ari stretched his arms out for a hug.

"You didn't tell me what you wanted, but everyone wants a hug."

I stepped into his embrace, enveloped by the warmth of his flannel-covered arms and the scent of campfire. I wished he could read minds and feel the satisfaction emanating from my chest.

Right now, this is what I want. Please don't let go.

And he didn't. Not until another door opened.

✎

JUST BEFORE OUR combined rehearsal in the auditorium that day, Heather stopped me in the hallway.

"Paris! I want to talk to you about Ari. When do you think I should give him his Christmas present? Tonight, or tomorrow?"

My stomach flipped. "You got him a Christmas present?"

"Yeah, I found a couple of non-flannel shirts I think he'll like from the Village. I was thinking about giving them to him tonight after rehearsal. Or maybe I would ask him to meet me early tomorrow morning, so—"

"No." I didn't mean for my response to come out as forceful as it did, but it was strong enough that Heather's head jerked back. "Sorry,

I just mean that Ari's not really a morning person. You should give it to him tonight. Or tomorrow night."

Heather thanked me, then caught up with Ari, tickling him at the sides. Ari didn't tickle her back, but smiled.

I swallowed down my jealousy when an arm looped through mine.

Genevieve whispered in my ear. "There's a culinary phrase called '*mise en place.*' It's French for 'set in place.' It's when chefs chop all their vegetables or meats and set them aside for the recipe that's to come. It's a productive way of preparing for something that could otherwise be messy and without order."

I gave her a sideways glance, but kept walking.

"Paris, I'm talking about your boy situation. It's about time you try some *mise en place.*"

I opened the door to the Green Room. "I told you, Gen; Darden and Reese are just friends."

"I'm not talking about them," she whispered. Her eyes traveled to Heather and Ari. "I don't think you want a mess on your hands." She kissed me on the cheek, then bounded off to the other side of the stage for the magicians' positions.

I waited in the dark wing of backstage, feeling guilty for not having thought of getting Ari a Christmas present and also turning Genevieve's words over in my head. Did I have a mess on my hands? It wasn't like Ari had any romantic feelings for me; I was just his friend. Maybe I had developed some feelings of attraction for him, but I could hide those feelings without letting them get in the way of our friendship. Heather could give Ari a present—there was no harm in a present. As far as I knew, there was no romantic attachment to gift giving...or was there?

The drummers started the rehearsal from their entrance at the back of the auditorium when a voice spooked me.

"Hey, Paris."

I reached for my heart. "I know you're a magician, Darden, but do you always have to be so sneaky?"

"Sorry."

"And now that you've gotten what you need from me, I'm Paris and no longer *Miss Marigold*?" I smiled and waited for a smart response from Darden, but he sucked in his lips and fidgeted with the strap of his watch. "What's wrong, Darden?"

"Um..." He rubbed an eyebrow. "I don't...I'm so sorry...I don't know how to say this."

My heart drummed against my chest. "What did you do?" I stepped closer, hoping my deepest fear wasn't hidden behind Darden's eyes. "Did you tell somebody about me? Did you...tell Ari?"

"Um..."

"Darden!"

"I lost my notebook. Or someone stole it. And aside from recording all my magic secrets, I also recorded all of my...personal secrets."

I touched my temples. "Are you saying you wrote about me in your notebook and you don't know who has it?"

He winced. "Yes?"

Images of Mansion staff and court members reading Darden's detailed interactions with the undercover Capalon princess raced through my mind. "Darden, I've never wanted to kill a Mondarian more than I do now!"

"I know. But I'll find it."

My jaw clenched with tension. Finding the notebook was imperative for both of us since Darden would be found guilty of harboring my secret. "Where was the last place you had it?"

"Sectionals. Or the dining hall."

I crossed my arms. "Well, which one was it?"

"I don't know! It'll turn up. It has to."

The music cued the singers' entrance. "Meet me after rehearsal. You're going to walk me through every one of your last steps, and we'll find that thing."

"Yes, ma'am."

As I took my position on stage, my head flooded with worry.

What if Ari was the one who had Darden's notebook? Would he turn me into the guards? Or would he continue chatting with me every morning, not caring that I was from Capalon? If he was the one who slipped me the note from the Harvest Ball, maybe he was keeping Darden's notebook so nobody else would find it. Maybe he was protecting me. Or maybe he had already turned me in and it was just a matter of time until Captain Murphy fired a bullet into my head.

The maestro's voice boomed through the auditorium speakers in the middle of our number. "No, no, no. Shut up! Shut up! My ears! I can't take it! Francis, stop playing!"

The piano music ended, and we froze in our positions to take whatever insulting corrections Maestro planned to fire at us.

"The sopranos are going flat on the first five notes in measure twelve. Actually, it's not all of you, it's one of you, and I'm going to find out who." He called all the sopranos to the foot of the stage and directed us from his stand below us in the orchestra pit. One by one, he instructed us to sing our five notes individually.

After my turn, the maestro smiled. "And I've found our culprit. Again, Miss Marigold."

I took a deep breath. *"Sing for the kingdom..."*

"Wrong. Again."

I shifted my stance. *"Sing for the kingdom..."*

The maestro cut me off with a dramatic wave of his arms, then he spoke into his mic, filling the auditorium with his voice. "Everyone! Come out on stage!"

A few people trickled out from backstage

He lifted the mic to his mouth again. "'Everyone' means that all drummers, singers and magicians of the King's 100 need to be on my stage NOW!"

Within seconds, the stage filled with the entire court and dread weighed down my shoulders.

"Ladies and gentlemen."

"Yes, sir."

"Miss Marigold insists on singing flat on a few simple notes so we're all going to wait till she gets it right." He let the mic fall onto his music stand, sending a boom through the speakers. "Measure twelve." He leaned forward and narrowed his sharp eyes on mine. "Do you really think you belong here?"

"Yes, sir."

"Then sing like your *life* depends on it." The maestro cued Francis to play my starting pitch, then directed my line as the King's 100 watched behind me.

"No, no, no!" Maestro hopped off his podium in the orchestra pit and darted over to Francis's piano. He leaned across Francis's frail body and pounded the notes into the piano. "Sing for the kingdom," he sang as he lifted his eyebrows and pointed to invisible notes in the air.

He had me sing the five-note sequence so many times, I lost count. Maestro moved around the orchestra pit as he continued to direct me. At one point he sat in his conductor's chair and laid his head down on the music stand, pretending to direct me in his sleep. Another time, he stood on a chair and hit a tambourine on each of the five notes.

When he finally cut me off, he hopped up onto the low wall of the orchestra pit. His legs dangled behind Francis's head. "Francis, go home. This is going to take more time. Everyone, say goodnight to Francis!"

"Goodnight, Francis."

I felt the jealous energy of the court as we watched Francis exit the auditorium. During a normal rehearsal, we would have all been done for the night and heading to dinner. But what the maestro was doing was anything but normal.

"I bet you're all hungry. Well, you can thank Miss Marigold for that." The maestro smiled, and I wanted to disappear.

My heart pounded, terrified at what words would come out of his mouth next.

"Crunches until Paris can get this right. Now!"

Court members behind me and on the wings of the stage dropped to their backs.

"You're included in 'everyone,' Miss Marigold."

"Yes, sir." I dropped to my back and kept an eye on the maestro. He directed me through my line as I lifted my body through rhythmic crunches. I had no idea how many crunches I had done when the maestro dismissed the court for a water break. My abdomen ached and my mouth was parched, desperate for water.

"Where do you think you're going?" he barked at me. "You don't deserve a water break. You're still doing crunches and singing!"

I swallowed and pressed my back to the floor, continuing to crunch and sing through the pain and thirst. Footsteps fell around my head as the court slowly returned to the stage.

"Hey gang, Miss Marigold still isn't getting this. I'm so sorry for her inability to follow direction. Paris, apologize to your court."

"I'm sorry," I said between crunches from the floor.

"What was that?"

"I'm sorry!" I shouted.

"We'll forgive you when you can sing ON PITCH. Jumping jacks! Everyone!"

I scrambled to my feet and sang my line through the bounce of my body. My stomach growled so loud that I swore Maestro heard it.

Minutes passed and the maestro finally sent everyone to dinner. "But sopranos need to come back to the stage in an hour. Hopefully Marigold will have it right by then and can sing it once all the way through with her section." He bit into a granola bar.

An hour.

I wanted to sob. I wasn't sure if I could even sustain five more minutes of the maestro's torture, let alone an entire hour.

Feet shuffled behind me as the court cleared the stage.

I spotted Darden in my periphery. "Excuse me, Maestro, I believe Miss Marigold deserves a—"

"She deserves nothing, Mr. McCray. Now get off my stage."

"Yes, sir." Darden disappeared from the stage in the matter of time it took me to blink.

Layla stepped forward and her mouth opened, ready to aim some of her own fire at the maestro, but Reese bent down to whisper something in her ear. Whatever he said convinced her to stay silent. But before she left the stage, she turned to me to mouth "sorry."

"Paris, this is just one of Maestro's games." Ari's whispered voice caressed the back of my sweaty neck. "Don't let him get to you. And—"

"Get a move on, Mr. Novak."

I heard Ari walk away, leaving the scent of a campfire to linger in his wake. The auditorium emptied, leaving the maestro and myself as its only occupants. Maestro exited the orchestra pit and climbed the steps to the stage. He stood in front of me as I continued to bounce and flail my arms, singing the same five notes over and over again.

He put his hands on his hips. "You're still not getting this. Follow me." He jogged back down the steps and continued up the side aisle of the auditorium. "What's taking you so long, let's go!"

I forced my feet to jog down the steps and catch up.

"This isn't hard, Miss Marigold! Jog and sing till you get it!"

I jogged the auditorium through the route the maestro created for me, singing my same five notes the whole way. The maestro sat on the edge of the stage and scribbled in a notebook between shouting insults at me.

My shins throbbed and a pinch in my side pierced me like a knife. I was so hungry. And so tired. Whatever the maestro was trying to prove, I wasn't getting it. Maybe I wasn't cut out for the court after all. Maybe I didn't deserve my spot on stage with the other singers. I let out a cry as my hip slammed into the back of one of the auditorium seats.

"Why are you slowing down? Pick up the pace and keep singing!"

I moved my legs forward, but I wanted to quit. I didn't belong in

Mondaria. I didn't belong in the king's Mansion. And I definitely didn't belong inside an auditorium with a crazed maestro.

"If you quit now, Paris, you're quitting the court. Are you ready to quit?"

I moved forward at a walking pace and stopped singing.

Maestro stood and manufactured a concerned look on his face. "Please tell me if you're quitting because I'll need to phone the guards."

The sopranos returned to the stage and Maestro invited them to take a seat. "Miss Marigold is thinking about quitting, ladies. Heather, would you be able to take her solo for tomorrow's auditorium show?"

"Yes, sir." I glanced up at Heather who smiled, not at the maestro, but at me.

The maestro had said that everyone could be replaced. Heather would replace me as a soloist if I quit. And perhaps she would also replace me as Ari's friend for his fireside chats. Ari would build fires for her, take her ice skating and hold her close in warm embraces.

I was replaceable.

But on the reciprocal, the court was replaceable. I would go back home to Capalon and I could find friends to replace Layla, Darden, Reese and Genevieve. And my match would replace Ari.

Ari could be replaced.

My head shook, disagreeing with my thoughts as I picked up my pace and ignored the insults from the stage.

I knew deep in my heart no one in Capalon could take the places of my Mondarian friends. What would a Capalon know about the joy of harmonizing, the thrill of staying up late just to talk about frivolous topics or the simple pleasure gained from the sound of a crackling fire with a marshmallow-coated tongue? And aside from my new Mondarian friendships, I still hadn't reunited with my mother and *she* certainly wasn't replaceable.

Ari was right.

Maestro was playing a game I refused to lose. I still needed to help Darden find his notebook, be a shoulder for Layla to lean on, and watch the snowfall on Christmas morning with Ari. And above all, I needed to find my mother, regardless of whether I agreed with her plans. Something or *someone* had to be holding her back from connecting with me and it was my job to help her.

Maestro Leto was just a bitter Mondarian. And I was a Capalon. I was the princess of the greatest kingdom in The Lands. I had to beat the maestro at his own game for Capalon. For my sister, the queen. For my mother, the former queen who was hiding in the shadows. And for my new friends.

I wasn't ready to give up. I wasn't ready to quit. I had to keep going and keep fighting the maestro at his ridiculous game. Because if I quit, I was telling all the people who were important to me that not only I was replaceable, but that *they* were replaceable too.

Breathe. Focus. Breathe.

I'm a Capalon and I control my emotions.

I smiled.

"Yes! Sing it out, Paris!" shouted the maestro.

I ran, I sang, I smiled.

Maestro clapped his hands. "Sopranos, from the top!"

I bounced up onto the stage. The other girls had full stomachs and looked tired.

But I was awake. Alive. Full of energy.

We sang the whole song a cappella.

Mine was the loudest voice.

Then the song ended.

"Good. See you tomorrow!" Maestro left the pit, and we were done. It was late at night. I had missed dinner, but we were *finally* done.

And then I was dizzy. And so tired.

A few of the older sopranos congratulated me as they left the stage. My feet were heavy and refused to move as a blossoming question anchored me to the stage floor.

Why *me*? Why had the maestro selected me for his game? It was almost as if he was punishing me. Almost as if....

Black spots filled my eyes. I spoke the words out loud to myself. "He knows..."

Somebody shouted. I felt the ground crash against me. I smelled a campfire.

My sight faded to black.

CHAPTER
27

My sheets felt starchy and thin. The smell of sanitizing solution pricked at my nose. I opened my eyes to see Layla's posters and colorful knickknacks replaced with stark white walls, and railings appeared on my bed overnight.

"Good, you're awake." A woman wearing a white coat spoke to me from beside a sink and a set of cabinets. "You fainted. You need to do a better job of eating and staying hydrated. What did you have to eat today?"

I rubbed my head and spoke to the doctor from my borrowed clinic bed. "Um...a couple donuts for breakfast and a salad for lunch." Then the maestro starved me during the rehearsal from hell.

"You know now that you're away from home, you have to take care of yourself, right? You're lucky you don't have a concussion. Just a bump on your head. Drink this before you go see Bernie." she handed me a white bottle with some sort of pink milk. "He told me you needed to go to his office as soon as I discharged you."

"Why?"

She shrugged. "I don't know. I'm just the lady who tells him that his performers are too ill or injured to perform and he doesn't listen. Oh, and will you take your friend with you? I have to lock up."

"My friend?"

She nodded. "The boy who carried you here."

What boy? There were no boys left with us on stage at the end of the rehearsal. But after forcing down some strawberry flavored milk, I walked into the waiting room to see a black-haired drummer slumped in a chair.

"Ari," I whispered. "Ari, wake up. The doctor has to lock up."

"Hm?" His eyes opened and blinked a few times. "Paris, hey, how are you?"

"I'm okay. I guess I was just dehydrated and hungry."

"And run down by an evil maestro." He lifted a flat square box off his lap. "I saved you some pizza."

We moved into the hall and I ate a piece of pizza, washing it down with the remaining milk. "This is so good, Ari. Thank you."

"Want to head to Lounge?" he asked.

I shook my head. "I've been instructed to go see Maestro."

"I'll go with you."

"Don't."

Ari's black brows furrowed.

"I mean, I don't want you to get pulled into any of my trouble. In case he kicks me out."

"He won't kick you out. I won't let him. After what he did to you—"

"It'll be fine," I said, touching his arm. "And if he *does* kick me out, I'll visit you all on your down time in the Village."

Ari and I looked at each other, both knowing that I was lying. Meeting court members on their down time was next to impossible. And if I was back in Capalon, any visitation would *absolutely* be impossible.

I sighed. "But if he doesn't kick me out, I'll see you tomorrow morning. Normal time, normal place. You should get some sleep before your favorite day of the year tomorrow." I smiled, but the gesture was not reciprocated.

Ari reached for my hand. "So, if I don't see you in the morning, this is it?"

I nodded and tried to memorize the feel of his fingers against my skin—rough in some spots, but soft everywhere else.

"Paris, I—"

"I'll see you tomorrow, Ari." I squeezed his hand and took off for Maestro's office.

CHAPTER
28

I knocked on the maestro's door.

He invited me to sit, then turned around and locked the door.

"What are you doing?" I asked, wishing I hadn't wasted my vial of pepper spray on Darden.

"Just want to have a private conversation without interruption." He sat down at the piano and poured his alcohol into a glass. "You're stronger than I thought you were, Miss Marigold. That rehearsal would have sent any of those other girls home in tears. But not you. You're *special*."

My skin crawled at the sound of the word 'special' from his mouth.

"Would you like a glass?" he asked, showing off the bottle of alcohol.

I shook my head.

He lifted the glass to his lips and smiled as he sat it down. "That's right," he said with a nod. "Capalons don't drink. Wouldn't want to damage your precious minds."

Blood drained from my head. "I don't know what you're talking about," I choked out. But my worst fear had been confirmed—the maestro knew my secret.

"Don't lie to me now." Maestro slid a framed photograph across the table—a photograph from the walls of the Records Room.

I looked down, expecting to see only my father's face among the group of rulers and their spouses but I was shocked to see both my parents. They were so young, the picture was faded and of all the faces, only my mother's mouth was turned up into an almost-smile as her hand rested on her pregnant belly. I never thought my mother and I resembled each other, but in the photo at her young age, we would be indistinguishable if my hair hadn't been dyed brown. I assumed my father kept her away from the Assembly Meetings the entirety of their marriage, but he must have put an end to her attendance once my sister was born.

I shook my head in disbelief. Her face was so small among the rest of the group in the photo, there was no way Maestro would have been able to pick out our resemblance so easily.

"As I hear, Capalon is still being actively ruled by Queen Evelyn, so that makes you Princess Piper."

I reached for Layla's conversation-ending words. "Duck-off."

But the maestro only roared with laughter. "You can't even use our curse words properly! Oh, this is too much," he said, wiping his eyes.

Breathe. Focus. Breathe.

Observe the facts.

"Your accusation is based on some facial resemblance. It hardly bears weight." I kept my voice steady and refused to let my eyes linger on my mother's face. "And how do you know so much about the enemy family? Perhaps you—"

But before I could react, Maestro clutched my wrist in his cold fingers and held a device above it. A small screen displayed a vivid-green outline of my veins and the square piece of tech that sat comfortably between them. "Shall I escort you out of the Mansion myself, *Princess?*"

I pulled my hand away as he chuckled. "I'd love to call the guards on you, I really would, but I'm in no mood to start a war or let

Captain Murphy have his glory." He sipped the last of his drink and leaned back in his chair. "Well, go," he motioned with the back of his hand. "What are you waiting for?"

"No," I said, wrapping my fingers around the seat of the chair. "I'm not leaving until you hand over my mother. I know she's here."

"Oh, Princess. Is *that* why you're here?" He leaned his back against the wall and stretched his legs out on the piano bench. "So now I know what you want—you want your mother back." He shook his head. "So tragic—you actually believe that we have your mother. I can assure you she's dead. Mondarians are terrible at keeping secrets and if there was even a sliver of possibility that she was alive, I would have heard about it."

"I don't believe you. I have evidence to believe that—"

Maestro interrupted me with a long whistle. "I knew Capalons were wacky in the head but you're screwier than I could have ever imagined. And you view *us* as the stupid ones?" He smiled, then poured himself another drink. "Princess, you know we've captured one of your citizens, right? You're willing to let one of your own people be executed because of *your* delusion? I think that places *you* as the evil one."

I thought of commands for Chip, but what good could he do? If anything, using Chip would make matters worse. My mother's eyes looked up at me from the faded picture as if she was trying to offer her help.

Think, Piper, think.

"You're not moving." He reached for the phone and sighed. "I guess the captain will finally have his day."

If only I knew the identity of his secret lady. I looked at the maestro and at the picture from the Records Room.... The Records Room. The only people who had access were guards and Royalty. It was only a hypothesis without any concrete evidence but I had no other options to support my case. "You and the queen," I spat out. "I know about your secret affair. I even have audio evidence." I lied with conviction and raised my wrist with a balled fist. "I could start my own war between you and the king. Everyone can be replaced—even maestros."

He smiled and placed the phone back on its dock.

Adrenaline coursed through my veins at the shock of my confirmed accusation.

"So, we have damning secrets on each other? What an interesting turn of events." Maestro sat up and leaned an elbow on the ledge of the piano. "At least in my situation, the other party knows who I am. In your case, you've brought other people onto the game board with you. And one day when you get caught by Captain Murphy, you won't be the only one to lose." He slid me the framed photo. "Do what you wish with it. I just wouldn't recommend hanging it up in the Hall of Memories."

I grabbed the photo and headed to the door, then stopped. "I want Darden's notebook back too."

The maestro pretended to choke on his alcohol. "Whozit's whatsitz? I don't give a damn about Mr. McCray's personal diary. Oh, unless he has a magic trick that makes Capalons disappear."

If the maestro didn't have Darden's notebook, then who did? I opened the door.

"Oh, and Miss Marigold?"

I paused, not giving him the courtesy of eye contact.

"Don't even think about mentioning my situation to anyone else."

I squeezed the door handle. "Or what? You'll kill me, Maestro?"

He chuckled. "Like I said, I'm in no mood to start a war." I heard him take a sip and slam his glass on top of his piano. "But I *will* kill Ari Novak."

My head snapped to see his face curl up into a wicked grin. "Merry Christmas, Miss Marigold!"

CHAPTER 29

My head ached, but I pulled myself out of bed to meet Ari. I found him standing in front of a roaring fire, wearing a red and green flannel shirt and a red hat with a white ball on its tail. "Merry Christmas, Paris." He handed me a gold and green paper box.

I opened it to see a small moose carved out of wood.

"Since we could never find the mystery moose on the lawn, I thought I'd make you one."

I ran my thumb over the smooth antlers of the moose and inhaled the scent of the soft pine. "Ari, I love it. I'm so sorry, I didn't get you anything."

"That's okay, Maestro gave me the best gift by not kicking you out."

My cheeks flushed, but I didn't jerk my head to hide them. Instead, I looked up into Ari's eyes, wishing he could feel the gratitude pouring from my heart.

"And I have one more gift for you but you have to follow me." Ari bent his arm like a proper court man and after tucking the moose safely inside my pajama pants pocket, I accepted his escort like a proper court lady. We left the Lounge and walked down the hallway toward the Stardust Ballroom.

Ari held his hands over my eyes before we stepped through the doorway. When he removed his hands, I opened my eyes to see the ballroom had been transformed into what I would call the very essence of Christmas—large garlands strung across the tall arched ceilings, ornamental evergreens lined the walls and the most striking sight were the lights—thousands of small lights gave the ballroom a soft glow in the absence of the powerful luminescence of the chandeliers. "It's beautiful," I managed to say in a whisper.

"The staff finished setting it up last night, and I wanted you to see it before it was full of people. Come on." He held my hand and walked me through the ballroom until we were in the center of the dance floor where all the garlands met under a centerpiece of pearl berries and flat green leaves.

Mistletoe. The kissing plant.

My heart leapt into my throat. "This is all so amazing, but don't you think we should leave? We'll probably get in trouble again."

"Nah, we've got to take advantage of this empty ballroom for just a minute longer." Then he cleared his throat, straightened his back and bowed. "Hello miss, my name is Ari Novak."

I curtsied, playing into our standard dance routine. "It's a pleasure to meet you, Mr. Novak. My name is Paris Marigold."

"Miss Marigold, may I have this dance?" Ari held out his hand and after a beat, I accepted.

He led us in the Mondarian Waltz. "Pretend that instead of court members, we're guests of the king. You're wearing a multicolored ball gown and I'm wearing...a red and black flannel tuxedo."

I wrinkled my nose.

"Awesome, right? We're enjoying the king's free food and drinking his wine but not *too* much wine, of course. I'd like to remember this dance."

Our quick waltz eventually slowed to a gentle sway, bringing our bodies closer together. The warmth of his hand in mine, his scent lingering in front of me and the softness of his flannel shirt under my fingers sent me to a place between a dream and a deep sleep. I rested my head on his shoulder and closed my eyes as I wrapped both hands behind his neck. He mirrored his other hand on my waist so we held each other in a moving embrace.

I felt a thick rope tug a curtain open inside me, just enough to let flecks of gold light peek through the small space between the heavy fabric. The light was safe and warm, pulling me closer into Ari's chest, his breathing matching mine. I didn't want to be anywhere else or with anyone else—only in my friend's arms, holding on to him like he was the most real, alive thing I had ever touched.

My friend.

My friend with soft black hair and brown eyes the color of truffles and butterscotch. I felt the curtain pull back just an inch more and suddenly the word 'friend' didn't feel right—that there might be another word I wanted more intensely. That there just might be...*more*.

More than friends.

My eyes flashed open, catching a glimpse of one of the chandeliers, dull and massive, hiding behind a thick strand of twinkling garland. The other chandeliers hid in other dark spots of the ceiling. My eyes jumped from one to the other as my mind jumped from thought to thought.

What if we weren't *just* dancing? What if all the nice gestures Ari had been doing for me—the ice-skating rink, waiting for me at the clinic, the moose, the ballroom—hadn't just been nice things he would do for any friend? What if...Ari had opened a curtain on his side of the stage as well?

"Ari?"

"Mmhm." He moved his mouth closer to my neck, the heat of his breath warming my body in unreachable places.

I fought the urge to turn my head and position my mouth next to his and focused on a grey chandelier. "Why do you go out of your way to do nice things for me?"

Ari pulled me in closer, his lips brushing my ear. "I think you know why," he whispered.

I tilted my head back just enough to look into his eyes. Beneath the swirls of brown and gold, I saw someone who saw something more in me than just a court lady or princess, only, he didn't really know *me*. He only knew Paris Marigold.

I felt jealous of the fake girl Layla created on an application—the girl who glittered with the flip of a switch, but in the dark, her truth was as tangible as cold crystal.

Ari's fingers brushed a strand of hair behind my ear, the sensation of his touch sending a tingle across my skin. I focused on his soft lips but the maestro's words drove a knife through my heart—I had Ari on the game board with me.

I was Piper Parish, Princess of Capalon.

And Ari would always be a Mondarian.

Paris Marigold was the girl who had convinced a drummer she was worth caring for, *not* Piper Parish. Every ounce of my body wanted to taste Ari's lips, but as much as I hated the maestro, his words rang true in my ears. As soon as Ari found out who I was, he would lose Paris Marigold and I would lose Ari.

Unless...

I licked my lips. "Ari, were you the one who gave me the note at the Harvest Ball?"

Ari's eyes focused on mine as my fingers curled against the soft hairs on the back of his neck. I wanted him so badly to say 'yes,' that he had known all along and he didn't care I was Capalon.

But his brows furrowed. "What note?"

Air caught in my throat as I reached for my last hope that Ari knew the truth. "And Darden's notebook? Are you the one who has it?"

His eyes answered before he formed the words. "No, I didn't even know he lost it."

Splinters pierced my palms as I pulled the rope, closing the curtain and dampening the glow of the gold light. I stepped out of Ari's embrace, the cold hitting me instantly and dissolving the warmth from his body. "I can't...I can't do this," I forced out in a raspy whisper.

"I'm sorry, is there something I did to—"

"I like Reese." My false words hung in the stale air of the massive ballroom, the sad chandeliers looking down on me in disappointment.

Shadows danced across Ari's face as butter-yellow sun slowly poured in through the ballroom windows.

Before the tears fell and before I changed my mind, I spoke the most untrue sentence since stepping foot in Mondaria. "I'm sorry, Ari. I don't have feelings for you...we're just friends. Nothing more."

I sprinted out of the ballroom, through the Lounge and up to my room, slamming the door shut behind me. I fell to the floor and sobbed into my hands.

Layla sat up from her bed. "Who was it? Maestro? Genevieve? I'll kick her a—"

"No," I said through a cry, "It was me. I did this to myself. Ari likes me. And I told him I like Reese."

Layla jumped out of her bed and her arm wrapped around my shoulders.

"I can't like Ari and he can't like me because...because..."

"Because you're Capalon?"

I stared into her hazel eyes. "You know?"

She shrugged. "Yeah, I searched through your stuff and found the Capalon currency like the first week we were here. Nobody in Mondaria has that. Paris, I tried to warn you to leave, but you stayed."

"Wait, so you were the one you gave me the note at the Harvest Ball?"

She nodded.

"Why didn't you just tell me to my face?"

She smiled. "We're enemies, remember? I didn't want you to know it was me in case you decided to slit my throat in the middle of the night."

I sniffed. "What about the other notes—the ones with the roses?"

"I don't know about those—I just did the one."

"Do you have Darden's notebook too?"

"No...why would I have that thing?"

I rubbed my temples. "Have you told anyone?"

She shook her head. "At the beginning, I left you lots of opportunities to steal from me or turn me in for dumb stuff and you never jumped on it. So as long as you weren't trying to do anything horrible to me personally, I was okay with it." She sighed. "Honestly, I was kind of hoping you were here to do something to the king."

"Why? He's your king."

Layla clenched her jaw. "He also doesn't think I'm good enough for his son."

"But—"

"Paris, I know where you're from you haven't seen all the things that love can do to a person. And maybe it's better that way. But when you fall in love with someone and you're rejected, it can nearly kill you." She sighed. "I know your situation with Ari sucks, but I promise you, it could be a million times worse. I think you're doing the right thing. It's best for both of you that you just stay friends." She raised her eyebrows. "And using Reese as your fake interest helps my case too. Who knows, maybe Reese will start liking you, so he can get over me." Then she perked up. "And you already agreed to be his kissing partner for the New Year's Eve Ball. From my experience, he's definitely not a lousy kisser, so you might enjoy it. It's like you're solving all our problems with a kiss," she said with a smile.

I shook my head. "I told you I don't want to do it."

"But you will. Because you love me. And...because you love Ari." Layla rubbed my back as more forbidden tears fell. "You know you're the coolest Capalon I've ever known?"

I laughed and wiped my eyes. "I'm the only Capalon you've ever known."

"Oh, I forgot to tell you! I think your conspiracy theory about the maestro having a secret lover is true! The other day when he was working with me and Reese, I swear I saw lipstick on his collar. Who do you think it is?"

The maestro's threat to kill Ari sent a wave of panic through me.

"It's no one. I was wrong. It was...one of the guards with an older court member, not the maestro."

"But you said—"

"It was early in the season when I didn't know him that well. So, let's just drop it, okay?"

"Okay, fine—Maestro doesn't have a secret lover." Layla handed me a box of tissues.

I blew my nose into a tissue. "Can we just not talk about anything that has to do with lovers or kissing please?"

"Yes, I thought you'd never ask." Layla hugged me, then headed to the dining hall to bring back breakfast to have together in our room before the auditorium show that afternoon.

When we finished our meal together, I threw my body across my bed. Layla wrote the note from the Harvest Ball. I exhaled, relieved it hadn't been anyone else. But it still didn't solve anything about my mother, and my birthday was quickly approaching. I told my sister I would be back in time for my match ceremony, but my mother still hadn't arranged to meet me.

Was Maestro right? Was my mother truly dead? Had I followed a trail of false hope? I clenched my fists and blinked away a few more tears.

She *had* to be alive. If she wasn't alive, I would have broken Ari's heart for nothing. I took a deep breath and asked Chip to play my recorded evidence to settle my aching heart.

❧

THAT AFTERNOON, we performed our auditorium show and Maestro acted pleased with both my solo and the soprano section despite having nearly killed me over it the night before. After the close of the curtain, we changed for the Christmas Ball later that evening. I had been anxiously waiting to wear the bright red Christmas Ball gown for weeks. The strapless bodice sparkled with a starburst of crystals, and the flowing chiffon skirt danced with each movement. I couldn't wait to see Ari's reaction when he saw me wearing a gown in his favorite color, but after Layla zipped me up, I refused to look at myself in the mirror. The Christmas Ball was supposed to be one of the happiest occasions of the year but I felt like a stone throughout the whole event.

Having been swept away by the ballroom's elegant decor just that morning, now I hated it—every light, strand of garland and Christmas tree, wishing it would all just disappear. Even worse, I had to put on a happy face with the guests and say things like "You'll have to come back for a Mondarian snowfall, there's nothing like it," even though I had yet to see a single snowflake. And I danced with men under the same mistletoe where Ari and I had held each other in a tight, swaying embrace only hours prior.

I tried to stay focused on other things—like the fact the queen was absent due to a sudden illness, causing the king to leave the event before the dancing began. Or that Layla laughed with every dance partner and I assumed her joy revolved around the princes not returning to the Mansion until after the New Year. I made the mistake of staring at the back of a woman with blonde hair, only to see her spin around, dancing with the one boy I was trying not to look at the whole night.

Ari saw me and smiled with closed lips.

I wished he had looked at me like he hated me and wanted me to leave the Mansion. But his smile was kind, which was Ari to the core. Even after a girl rejected him, he was kind enough to offer her a smile and break her heart into a hundred more pieces, multiplying the already broken pieces by—

"May I have this dance?" Darden tapped my shoulder after I said goodbye to a guest.

"We're not allowed to dance with each other, Darden."

"But I have updates on a certain lost notebook. We'll stay in the middle of the floor where we'll be hidden."

I stared at his red tie, hating the color staring back at me. "Make it quick."

Darden pulled me to the center of the dance floor and led me in the Christmas Waltz. "After retracing my steps, I know for sure I had it in the dining hall *before* sectionals, so it had to go missing *during* sectionals."

"You think another magician has your notebook?" I asked as Darden lifted his arm to twirl me.

"It's possible. But I think it's been lodged between something backstage or dropped under a seat and nobody has taken it."

"Why's that?"

"Because of the content, Miss Marigold. If a magician read the notebook and knew about a certain *person* on the court, they would have notified the guards immediately."

"*You* didn't notify the guard."

"But I had an ulterior motive. And my ulterior motive led to an unexpected friendship," he said with a smile.

But I only squinted. "So, nobody has the notebook because I would have been arrested or killed by now?"

"Yes! This is something to be happy about, Miss Marigold. Where's your Christmas spirit?"

I sucked in a breath to keep the tears at bay. "It died this morning."

"You need to find other dance partners. Now." Agnes glared at us before switching her face back to jovial court lady.

Eventually the torturous evening ended. As I closed my eyes for the night, I was thankful for only one thing that had nothing to do with Darden's notebook—that Christmas was over.

❧

MY DREAMS over the next few days were all the same—a performance of myself sitting in the middle of the auditorium stage, crying. My brain forced me to live in my own sadness, even while I slept.

"You don't look good." Layla packed a small bag on her bed.

I was supposed to be packing too, but the only thing I thought to take was a book.

"You're like a sad, pale flower. I just want to set you out in the sun and tell you jokes till you perk up. You need some cheering up."

I plopped my butt on her bed. "I have plenty of cheer. I'm a court lady. I'm full of cheer."

She looked at me through her eyelashes. "Clearly."

Somebody knocked three quick taps on our door. Layla opened it and I heard Agnes's voice. "Have you guys seen Little Bernie?"

Layla looked at me and I shook my head.

"Nope, no cat sightings here," Layla said.

Agnes sighed. "Okay, well let me know if you see him. And call-time is in the Lounge in two minutes."

"Yes, ma'am," Layla said.

She closed the door, then zipped up her bag. "Ready for a road trip to perform for a super-rich dude?"

"Yes, ma'am!" I put on my biggest fake smile. "See that?" I pointed to my cheeks. "That's cheer."

"No, that's disturbing. Don't do that. Let's go."

CHAPTER 30

The returning court members were assigned to one of the Mansion's luxury busses - complete with leather seats, carpeted flooring and even a rumored snack bar and lounge area at the back of the bus. But the New Members were assigned to an older model, with tightly packed seats in clumps of three, discolored plastic walls and large windows that lacked any kind of shade or tint. My heart pounded when Eric announced that our seats on the New Members' bus were assigned in alphabetical order by season in sections of three, which meant Marigold, McCray and Novak would all be sitting together. My heart pounded even harder when I watched Ari pause before taking his seat on the window. "I don't think I can handle the window seat. Darden, can I switch with you?"

Darden and Ari switched seats so when I sat down, I was right next to Ari. If my heart had been pounding before, then it switched to nearly breaking free of my rib cage. I pulled out my book and Ari skimmed through a Mondarian tourist magazine from the seat pouch while tapping his heels against the floor. The three of us were silent as the bus rolled forward, but when we hugged a curve on a mountain slope, Ari's body went rigid. "That was too fast. This driver needs to slow down. Don't you think he needs to slow down?"

His head swiveled from me to Darden, to the row of court

members behind us, which didn't make it clear who he intended to answer his question.

Ari clutched the armrests, hitting my arm. "Sorry," he said as he wiped his palms on the top of his legs. He grumbled something about the bus driver, then leaned his head forward to look out Darden's window. "Oh, wow. Oh, wow. Look at that. Clouds. We're as high as the clouds." Ari closed his eyes and leaned his head back.

I stared out Darden's window, mesmerized by the snowcapped peaks and grey clouds the clung to them. The bus bumped over something and a strong hand gripped mine.

"Sorry." Ari tucked his hands under his armpits and shut his eyes.

I fought the urge to cry. Had we been on the bus before Christmas, Ari wouldn't have removed his hand from mine like my skin was deadly to the touch.

But then I heard something unimaginable—the drummer began to sing.

"*I'm a man of Mondaria, strong as can be...*" Ari paused as the driver took another sharp turn, then continued with a louder voice. "*No money or big fancy Mansion for me. Up in the branches, I'm as high as the king. Don't tell the queen, I'm drunk in a tree! No don't tell the queen, I'm drunk in a tree!*" He opened an eye to look at me.

"Well done, Mr. Novak," I said with a laugh.

Darden groaned. "I think it's best to leave the singing to Miss Marigold, friend."

Ari rubbed his forehead. "My dad sings that song when he's in a good mood." He turned his head. "So, have you told him yet?"

"Told who what?" I asked, unable to meet Ari's eyes.

"Told Reese that you like him."

I caught Darden's raised eyebrows behind Ari's head.

"Oh. Um, no. Not yet."

Ari shifted in his seat. "Maybe tonight's the night. After our show. You can tell him at Sugar High."

"What's Sugar High?" I asked.

"The place we're all going after our show for the Earl. It's a nightclub with a trapeze," Ari said.

"Oh." I nodded like I knew what a trapeze was as the bus driver stopped for clearance at our destination's security gate.

Ari let out an exhale. "We didn't die."

Darden slapped his friend on the back. "And what better way to celebrate conquering death than performing for the Earl of Moon Valley?"

THE PERFORMANCE for the Earl and his family was shorter than our bus ride to the northernmost point of Mondaria. We weren't even invited to stay for dinner and ate boxed meals on a bus as we traveled from the Earl's estate to *Sugar High.*

We entered an old aviation hangar that had been transformed into a nightclub with a trapeze. Darden explained the trapeze to me, but I couldn't grasp the concept until I watched the flying people inside the club. Three long nets formed a ceiling above our heads as people occasionally fell into them in a roar of laughter.

"What I love about this club, is that all the guys have to wear tight pants and no shirts if they want to do the trapeze," shouted Raya over the loud music.

"And they have a room dedicated to making-out!" Jasmine pointed to a room with a blue neon sign above the door that said *SUGAR CRASH.* She and Raya handed some money to a server with a tray of small glasses, then downed the liquid and headed to the dance floor.

"Why would Maestro allow us to come here?" I shouted at Darden.

"Look behind you."

I turned to see clouded glass doors with a neon sign above them that glowed the words *SUGAR RUSH.*

"They have a one-of-a-kind liquor here made with their high-intensity sugar."

"So that's what's in those drinks?" I nodded to the server with the tray.

"Yeah, but it's just the sugar mixed with water, no alcohol. The theory is that the sugar is so concentrated, it makes you brave."

"That ridiculous. If anything, the sugar is absorbed through the bloodstream as—"

I watched in shock as Darden handed the server money and downed a glass of sugar water. "What are you doing?"

"Living." He headed to the clothes-changing station for the trapeze which sat under the largest neon sign that read *SUGAR HIGH*.

Layla had somehow already made it to the top of the trapeze ladder in her nude bodysuit and waved down to me. I waved back, then grabbed a glass of plain water without sugar and lingered by the DJ's table.

"Just as a reminder for everyone joining us, we haven't had any takers for the Sky Dive Challenge! If you think you can do a catch without a net, then you'll win your very own 'I cheated death at Sugar High' t-shirt and coupons for a free appetizer! Not to mention, bragging rights!" The DJ switched off his mic. "Are you part of the King's 100?" he shouted to me.

I nodded. "Why would anyone ever do the Sky Dive?"

"For the t-shirt and coupons! And...because it's not actually that life-threatening."

"What do you mean?"

"Well, I work here a lot so I watch people swinging back and forth all the time. The ones who fall into the net either do it on purpose or they're not communicating with their own partner. But the ones who use the instructors as partners get it almost every time."

The DJ shouted something into the microphone as I ran some math in my head and observed the activity of trapeze lines above me. My observations and quick calculations matched the DJ's hypothesis. I was about to shout another question to him when I spotted Heather and Ari on the dance floor. Something was off about Ari and I hadn't noticed it before on the bus, but Ari wore a plain black collared shirt.

It had to be one of the shirts Heather gave him for Christmas.

Because of the loud music, Heather's mouth nearly touched Ari's ear as she spoke to him.

I saw Reese nearby and marched straight to him. He danced with me for a couple minutes, then asked if I wanted to go to the Sugar Crash Room with him. I nodded and clung to his arm as he led me away from the dance floor.

This is good. I'm selling my crush on Reese to Ari.

The Sugar Crash Room was lined with white couches and chairs tucked between sectioned walls under dim lighting. And like Jasmine and Raya had said, there were couples kissing on nearly every couch. Unlike the chest-pounding music of the trapeze area, the Sugar Crash room remained quiet with soft music playing in the background.

My heart started to beat wildly. Did Reese want to kiss me? Was Layla right? Could I solve all of our problems by kissing Reese?

Reese leaned into me and lifted an arm, so I leaned into him too and puckered my lips.

"Woah, what are you doing?" Reese looked at me with raised brows as he held a cup of water in his hand.

I looked behind me to see a small table with a water pitcher and cups.

"I thought you knew I liked Layla?" he asked.

"Yeah, I know that," I said, suddenly wanting to disappear into the white cushions of our couch.

"Then...why did you try to kiss me?" asked Reese with a confused look.

"Um...I don't know...I think I had too many sugar waters."

"Yeah, that stuff is nasty. It's definitely not helping my stomach." Reese swallowed some water and upon closer observation, I spotted beads of sweat at Reese's temples. He shivered and his face was pale even under the dim lighting.

"You're sick!" I said a little too loudly, proud of my conclusion. "That's why you wanted me to talk to you in the Sugar Crash Room."

Reese winced. "Let's hope not. I have my duet with Layla tomorrow. And apparently you and I now have a kiss together," he said with a pained smiled.

"I'm sorry about Layla, Reese. She's just...being stubborn."

"No, I get it. I just wish I knew what guy did this to her."

"Why?"

"To see why he's so hard to get over. Maybe punch him in the face, too."

I didn't have the heart to tell Reese that punching Layla's ex would mean punching his kingdom's own prince, landing him in jail and on all the media channels in The Lands. "I hope you feel better, Reese. And I'm sorry for acting crazy."

Reese smiled through heavy eyelids. "It's okay. Like I said, I have that effect on—" Reese clutched his stomach and tore away from our couch. I stood to follow him but he entered the men's bathroom. I lingered on the couch for a few minutes, then headed back out to the trapeze area.

Laughter turned my head to see Ari shirtless and Heather in one of the skin-tight nude bodysuits. Ari had two handprints on his chest where Heather marked her hands in yellow paint that glowed under the luminescence of the UV lighting. Heather pulled them closer and closer together and then she whispered something in his ear. She laced her fingers in his and led him toward the Sugar Crash Room.

I sprinted to the DJ's table and shouted my request.

"Attention Sugar High party people! We have our first Sky Diver for the night! I have—"

The DJ held the mic to my mouth. "Paris?"

"Paris from the King's 100 is going to Sky Dive!" The DJ played some ominous music, and the club erupted in cheers. The DJ told me to head to the clothes-changing station where a young girl handed me my outfit. I changed and waited at the ladder for my instructor when a rough voice sounded behind me.

"Paris, what are you doing?"

I turned to see Ari's angry face.

I found it to be a satisfying reaction to my newfound bravery. "I'm letting go, remember?" I dipped my finger in some orange paint and drew long, curvy lines down each arm.

"I didn't mean kill yourself! You don't have to do this."

"I know I don't have to. I *want* to."

"But people have *died* doing this!" Ari grabbed my wrist before I could dip my finger in a bowl of pink paint.

I yanked free of his hold. "Then it was nice knowing you, Ari Novak."

A muscular man met me at the ladder. "Okay, Sky Diver. I'm ready for you."

I followed my instructor up the tall ladder and refused to look down at the diminishing floor or angry black-haired boy below me.

"Paris!" Layla waved to me once I reached the top of the ladder from the next platform over. "You're actually doing the Sky Dive? You're crazy! Don't die! I love you!" Then she leapt from her platform and swung back and forth a couple times on the trapeze bar before letting go and falling into the net below in a fit of giggles.

My instructor, Karl, walked me through the steps of the catch— holding on to the fly bar on the swing forward, hooking my knees on the swing back, then reaching for him on the release on his cue of 'hup.' "Are you sure you're ready to do this?" he asked. "Most people try it a couple times over the net first."

I stared at the floor far, far below me. I could still see Ari with Heather at his side. "No. I'm ready."

The odds were in my favor. They had to be. Otherwise, I would be committing suicide just to prevent Ari from kissing Heather in the Sugar Crash Room.

Karl patted my back. "Okay, Sky Diver, meet you on the other side."

Another Sugar High employee stood with me on the platform as we waited for Karl to take his position on the catch bar.

Hold forward. Hook knees back. Release on 'hup.'

Breathe. Focus. Breathe.

The employee and I watched as Karl mounted the catch bar. She pressed a button and the net below lowered and moved under Layla's net. The DJ shouted something to pump up the crowd. My heart threatened to leave my body before I forced it into a deadly stunt.

"Don't worry," said the employee. "There's an invisible net to catch you if you fall."

Hold forward. Hook knees back. Release on 'hup.'

Breathe. Focus. Breathe.

Invisible net.

Karl signaled with his hand. The employee next to me nodded and lifted her arm. "Okay, Sky Diver. Time to fly." She handed me the fly bar.

Hold forward. Hook knees back. Release on 'hup.'

Breathe. Focus. Breathe.

Invisible net.

Let go.

CHAPTER
31

The first thing I noticed when Karl tossed me into a pit of foam on the other side was an overwhelming feeling of peace. I wanted to do the trapeze again and experience the sensation of flying all over again. But when I climbed down the ladder, adrenaline flooded my veins from the celebration of the crowd. I accepted my t-shirt and coupons as if I had been named queen of the planet.

"You didn't mention the invisible net," I shouted to the DJ.

"Invisible net? Who told you that?" he shouted back.

Then my stomach twisted at the realization that the employee lied to me for a final boost of confidence. There was no invisible net—there was only me, flying over a crowd of people.

The court shouted my name and a couple boys lifted me on their shoulders and tossed me into the air. Heat engulfed me with the crowd of bodies and adrenaline continued to run wild in my veins. Everyone was happy for me, except for one person. I left my celebration to grab a glass of plain water from the table beside Ari. "Aren't you going to congratulate me?"

"No Paris, I'm not going to congratulate you. That was the stupidest thing I've ever seen. You could have died!"

I chugged the water and slammed the glass down on the table. "So what? It's not like you would have cared, with how wrapped up in Heather you've been." I turned away. "Honestly, Ari, I've heard of rebounds, but—"

Ari spun me around and pulled me against his chest, closing the distance between us. His heated bare chest pressed against the thin layer of my leotard, allowing me to feel the intense rise and fall of his chest against mine, paired with the reverberation of our beating hearts. His lips brushed against mine as he held me so intensely close. The light tease of his lips sent a surge of desire through me that I could barely contain. I wanted to feel the crash of his mouth against mine and savor the taste of his tongue. I wanted to let go and give myself completely to Ari, but I restrained my desire with the few remaining brain cells that held true to logic. Even though I was experiencing a delirious high from my death-defying trick, it still wasn't enough for me to forget that I was the Capalon Princess.

"Ari?"

We stepped apart to see Heather staring at us.

The DJ's voice boomed over the speakers. "If you're a member of the King's 100, it's time to go!"

Heather's eyes welled with tears and she disappeared inside the crowd of exiting court members.

Darden appeared as Heather darted off. "Come on seat-mates, we gotta get going or the bus will leave without us." He waited for a beat. "Did the sugar water put you two in a catatonic state?"

Ari and I finally moved and dressed ourselves without speaking one word to each other. It wasn't until we boarded the bus that I heard Ari talk. "I'm okay to take my window seat back, Darden."

Knowing that Ari hadn't suddenly overcome a fear of being driven off the side of a mountain, I angrily reached for my book. But reading a *Drake and Daniella* novel wasn't an ideal choice when anytime I saw the word *lips*, I would be reminded of the sensation of Ari's lips brushing against mine. The word *hands* took me back to how he held me so close—like we were performing our own death-defying trick.

I glanced over to see Ari's head resting against the window with his eyes closed and mouth partially open.

"That guy can sleep anywhere," Darden said.

I returned my attention to my book as if Ari's partially open mouth didn't stir up a craving so intense I had to press my fingernail into my thumb to fight it.

Darden closed his brand-new notebook and folded his hands. "You know my magic requires me to be extremely observant, right?"

"Are you talking to me?" I asked, not bothering to soften the edge in my voice.

Instead of responding to my question, Darden continued. "And you don't have to be me to know what's going on. But because I *am* me and your friend, I think you're making a mistake."

"I appreciate your eagerness to discuss my mistakes, but I'm not really in the mood," I said, not taking my eyes off my book.

Darden leaned his head back against the headrest as if he was ending the conversation but he continued speaking. "My mom has an obsession with birds. Her favorite one is the bird of the kingdom."

"Good for her. So patriotic."

"Do you know what our kingdom used to call the bird before the Ancient Data was recovered?"

I didn't answer and kept my eyes focused on my book, hoping Darden would just get to the point and leave me in peace.

"Black-winged-red-bird. She told me some Mondarians were so connected to the name, that they protested its real, given name. People would put signs in their yard; 'save the black-winged-red-bird!' They had rallies and marches. It was ridiculous, all for the name of a bird. If you ask me, *scarlet tanager* is a much cooler name and easier to say."

Darden pulled my book down and met my eyes. "But it doesn't matter what you call it because it's the same beautiful bird either way. And if you talked to a certain friend of mine and told him the truth, I think he would see it that way too."

"Weren't you the one who told me it's better to hide behind the truth?"

He nodded. "I see how I might be contradicting myself, but I think it's different for you and..." he looked over at Ari, whose mouth was wide open.

I shook my head. "No, it can't happen. And that's the way it's going to be."

"But—"

"Enough, Darden. One more word and I swear I'll drive this bus off the mountain myself."

"Yes, ma'am." Darden closed his eyes.

I turned my head and wiped my cheeks.

"I can hear your tears, Miss Marigold."

I shook my head. "Darden...how did you know so early on—that night at Grape Stomp?"

He took a deep breath and then a long exhale. "The same way I know when a trick has worked." Then he opened his eyes to look at me. "Whenever you were around, he looked at you like you were pure magic."

Darden handed me a clean handkerchief from his pocket.

"And did I look at him the same way?"

"No. You looked like a girl who was starved of a certain kind of love and found the one person who could give it to you, but you refused to do anything rational about it."

"Wow. I don't get a pretty little metaphor?"

"No, ma'am."

"You know you could take a note from your earlier bird story. The queen of hearts might be willing to trade her king in for a new suit."

Darden adjusted his glasses. "Ah, now who's mastering the metaphors? I'm comfortable where I am. But you, clearly, are not."

"I'm doing the right thing, Darden. I don't want to hear any more about it, okay? You should think about other things like where your notebook wandered off to."

"You're right, Miss Marigold. I'm done talking now."

"Thank you."

Darden leaned into me. "But just remember that you almost killed yourself for the attention of a boy, not the person you came here for. If you were to ask me, I'd say your priorities have shifted."

I HARDLY REMEMBERED WALKING up the stairs to our room and collapsing on the bed. I think Agnes stopped by our room to ask if we had seen Little Bernie again, but what I distinctly remember is the sound of Heather's biting voice just as I drifted off to sleep.

"I thought you and Ari were just friends."

Peeling my eyes open, I found Heather standing at the foot of my bed.

"We are, Heather." My thumb and index finger squeezed the bridge of my nose.

"Then why were you trying to kiss him?"

Wind pounded against our window as I failed to produce a reasonable explanation.

She crossed her arms. "I know what you're doing."

"Trying to sleep?"

"Now that you've been rejected by both Darden and Reese, you want to move on to the next court man and steal him away from me."

I sat up. "That's not—"

"You're jealous. You might not have liked Ari before but you do now because you see that he likes me and you can't stand it."

"Heather, please just listen, I—"

"Ari hardly has any free time and whenever I get a chance to see him, you just happen to show up."

Layla returned from the bathroom and shot me a confused look behind Heather.

I scooted to the edge of the bed. "Heather, if you would listen to me, I can—"

"You just need to back off, Paris, because Ari doesn't like you—he likes *me*."

Anger flooded my veins, and I squeezed my fists. "Okay, you're right. Ari doesn't have any free time. You know why? Because the only time he has to spare is early in the morning and up till a few days ago, he's been spending that time with *me*. And I wasn't trying to kiss him—*he* was the one trying to kiss *me*. He's not interested in you but you can't seem to get that through your dense, blonde head."

Heather clenched her jaw. "I thought you were a nice girl, Paris, but I guess your bitch of a roommate has rubbed off on you."

Layla proudly nodded.

My fingers dug into the edge of my bed. "You lied to Ari about me behind my back after I went to the maestro's office and *fought* for you. If I'm a bitch, then you were a bitch first."

Heather reached for the closest thing to her, which happened to be Ari's moose, and hurled it at the wall behind my head. To avoid injury, I bent forward, only to see Little Bernie tear out from under my bed. In his nervous escape, he took a strap of my bag with him and flung my hidden Capalon coins all over the floor.

I watched in horror as Heather picked up and examined a coin. "Why do you have Capalon coins in your room?"

I stood frozen, not knowing what to say. My eyes darted to Layla and her face reflected the same fear in mine.

Layla picked up a coin. "One of the Thirds hazed us and left a sock full of fake Capalon coins around our door handle."

"These don't feel fake," Heather said.

Layla faced Heather. "And how would you know? Wait... Heather, are you Capalon?"

Heather dropped the coin. "What? No!"

"If you don't mind, we need to get to bed," Layla said, opening the door for Heather. "We have this little thing called the New Year's Eve Ball tomorrow. And the bitchy court ladies need the most sleep."

Layla slammed the door behind Heather. "I thought I told you to get rid of these things." She bent down to help me gather the coins and put them back in the bag.

"I can't just throw them in the trash! Somebody will inevitably find them and then it will be a Mansion-wide Capalon-hunt. I'm leaving in two days, anyway."

"What do you mean you're leaving? You never said anything about leaving."

"I'm not doing anyone any good by being here, Layla."

She handed me the coins. "Why *are* you here?"

I exhaled as I shoved the bag back under my bed. "I came to Mondaria to find somebody."

"And?"

"And they're here, but they don't exactly want to be found or they can't be found because somebody's holding them captive. But I said I'd be back home in time for my match ceremony whether I found my...the *person* or not."

Layla blinked as if everything I had just said bored her. "Did he really try to kiss you?"

I sighed and moved on to the moose debris, swallowing my anger toward Heather with the touch of each piece. "Yeah, and I wanted to kiss him so badly. But you even said yourself that love isn't worth the pain."

Layla plopped on my bed. "Look, I know I said that, but maybe I'm wrong. You've made it this far without being caught, so isn't it worth a try to tell him who you are?"

I tried to speak, but my throat swelled. I shook my head, unable to fight the tears.

Layla moved down to the floor where I sat. "I know I might be bitter about love right now, but I at least had the chance to feel what it's like to love someone and have them love me back, even if it was for a short time. Before you leave this kingdom, you might as well take the chance." She stood to get me a tissue. "As Heather pointed out, I might be a bitch, but I still like to believe that sometimes things happen for a reason."

I laughed and blew my nose. "Thank you, Layla. I'm so lucky you were assigned to be my roommate."

"Hey, don't do that. You're not leaving yet. I'm not good at goodbyes and we are *not* saying goodbye right now. And it turns out my prediction about you was right."

"What prediction?"

"I said you would become a wild woman with bite. And after the events of tonight, you've blown my prediction out of the water!"

I groaned and buried my face in my hands. "Mondarians are so complicated."

Layla wrapped her arms around me. "Yes. And it takes one to know one. Congratulations, Paris. You're officially Mondarian."

CHAPTER 32

I headed to the maestro's office after breakfast the next morning to tell him the Winter Showcase would be my final show with the court, whether the king kept me for the following season or not. But when I approached Maestro's office, Captain Murphy stood in his doorway.

"Captain Murphy, what gives me the disgusting pleasure of seeing your face in my office?" asked the maestro.

"A Records Room key has been missing for a few weeks and I wanted to see if you know anything about it."

Oops. I needed to add 'return Records Room key' to my list of things to do before leaving Mondaria.

"Oh, you lost something and you're blaming it on me, how nice of you," Maestro said.

The captain sighed. "I'm just doing my job, Bernie. This is an important matter."

"If it's an important matter, then you should focus on your group of dimwits you call 'guards' and not me so I can do *my* job."

"So, you haven't been in the Records Room recently?"

"No, I have better things to do than play in the Records Room. Now please remove your sweaty body from my office before your stench settles into the carpeting."

I heard the captain shift his weight. "A guard spotted you coming down the hallway of the Records Room early this morning. So, I'll ask one more time, do you know anything about the missing key?"

"No. And I'll tell *you* one more time that your guards are lying sacks of—"

"Maestro!"

Both their heads turned as I stepped into the maestro's doorway. "You left this in the Rehearsal Room this morning." I handed him a copy of sheet music I dug out of my bag. "Thank you again for agreeing to meet me so early."

"He was with you this morning?" asked the captain.

I nodded. "Yes, sir. Maestro was helping me with my solo. I'm so nervous to perform it in front of the king for our Winter Showcase."

Captain Murphy looked from me to Maestro and sucked in a deep breath through his wide nostrils. "You're not off the hook until I find that key."

The maestro and I stood in silence until we watched the door click behind the captain. The sheet music I handed over came flying back at me. "Take your music and get out."

"I was just helping—"

"You didn't need to help with anything. Now go."

I took a deep breath. "I'm leaving after the Showcase. You can tell everyone the king put me on his dismissal list."

Maestro bent his head down over some notes and shooed me away with his hand.

I sighed. "Happy New Year, Maestro." I turned to leave.

"Miss Marigold."

I stopped as the air seemed to thicken. Maestro's face softened just enough for me to think he held words of gratitude in his head. "Close the door when you leave."

"Yes, sir." I closed the door and headed to the Ladies' Dressing Room to get ready for my final ballroom show at the Mansion, but when I pulled out my chair, a lavender rose urged me to read its message.

Go to the hallway of the East Courtyard thirty minutes before the start of the New Year's Eve Ball. It's time for us to meet.

I completed my hair and make-up in record time. I didn't even take the time to soak in the details of our New Year's Eve gown. Layla said something about it looking like a shattered mirror. My brain could only process that it was a silver dress with a low, exposed back that required an extra set of hands on the zipper. After Genevieve zipped me up, I bent down to pull out the photograph Maestro gave me from my bag. I folded the photo and stuffed it in the hidden pocket of the dress. I wanted my mother to see the photo of herself when she was so young. I put the rose in the bag, but removed the message, clutching it tightly in my fist.

I didn't know what would happen when I saw my mother. Would she immediately try to take me away to Capalon? Try to convince me to join some sort of revolution? Or...what if she was bait for some grandiose plan for the king to capture me?

I grabbed Paris Marigold's ID and put it my dress pocket too, then flung my arms around Layla.

"Woah there princess, you okay?"

"Um...yeah. Happy New Year." I looked around the room but didn't see Genevieve. "When Genevieve gets back, will you tell her I said Happy New Year too?"

"Sure...where are you going, Paris?"

"Nowhere. I'll be right back."

"You better. Don't forget our deal."

I must have looked at her with a blank expression.

"I need to avoid kissing my duet partner because..."

"Bad things will happen. Right. Deal. I'll be right back, Layla. Goodbye."

She waved goodbye to me through the mirror and I turned to head out the door, but my heart fluttered with fear.

What if my mother takes me away from the Mansion and I don't get to say goodbye to Ari?

I took a step forward, then another.

It would be for the best.

I came to Mondaria to find my mother, not a drummer.

CHAPTER
33

I paced the hallway next to the East Courtyard. What would I say
to my mother when I saw her? Was it safe to acknowledge that I
knew her in case somebody saw us together?

I heard footsteps approach, but the face didn't match the one I
had in mind. "Darden, you need to leave. I'm meeting somebody
here."

"Well, *I'm* meeting Genevieve here."

"I thought you weren't going to tell her who you were?"

"After our conversation last night, I changed my mind. You need
to go. The note I left her told her to me here."

"What note?"

"The notes I've been leaving her in the dressing room."

A weight pressed against my chest as electric currents sparked
my brain. "The ones attached to the lavender roses?"

"Yeah..."

"Darden, you've been leaving those notes at *my* chair! I switched
seats with Gen at the beginning of the season because of Layla.
Agnes probably never updated the seating chart. And the roses...why
would you leave her the Queen of Capalon?"

"Queen of Capalon? Lavender roses are symbolic for love at first sight. I got the idea for the notes after your showed me the one from the Harvest Ball."

The messages of the notes resurfaced in my mind. "Genevieve has a solo?"

"Yeah, she has a quick dance routine with a disappearing candle while the rest of us are resetting backstage."

I shook my head and lifted his final note to his face. "This isn't your handwriting."

"Yes, it is." He nodded and lowered my hand. "It takes me forever to write that well, but it's me." He laughed. "I'm actually relieved. I've been a mess since I wrote that last note. Actually, I'm not ready to tell her. I was just feeling oddly brave this morning." He met my eyes. "But Paris, if you're the one who's been getting my notes, then who did you think you were meeting?"

The photograph burned inside my dress pocket. "I thought...I thought..." I couldn't breathe as the weight on my chest grew heavier and I realized how clearly the notes pointed to Darden.

"Paris, are you okay?"

"I'm fine. I just need..." I darted away from Darden and ran outside into the courtyard, tearing his final note to shreds and tossing the pieces into a frozen fountain. My palms pressed against the rough edge of the fountain, letting the heat from my body radiate against the cement. Sucking in deep breaths, I fought to calm the fire that roared in my rib cage.

Evelyn was right; the belief my mother would still be alive was foolish. Capalons didn't belong in Mondaria. Unfolding the photo from my pocket, my mother's gentle eyes met mine. I wanted to scream at the woman in the picture. Why couldn't she have left her dead body behind like my father? If we had buried her body, I would never have set foot in Mondaria and believed in something as childish as a secret admirer's note left for the wrong person. The only Paris Marigold would have been the smiling girl from the identification card I found in the creek. I never would have befriended kids who were my enemies. And I never would have fallen for a boy who loved a girl I could never be.

My shaking fingers started to tear the corner of the photo, when my mother's eyes found me again and something Layla said weighted my sorrow even heavier.

You always come back for the people you love.

My mother didn't stop going to the Annual Lands Assembly because my father didn't want her there—she stopped going because *she* wanted to stay home with my sister. She never went anywhere with him after we were born because she didn't want nursery drones raising us—*she* wanted to raise us.

And if she were truly still alive, she would have already been back in Capalon. She wouldn't have made use of her time devising a plan to overthrow Mondaria and prove her love to me—she would have been fighting to get back to my sister and me because *'you always go back to the people you love.'*

I sucked in a breath to fight the threatening tears when footsteps fell on the gravel path behind me. "Darden, I said leave me—" but then the scent of lavender, peppermint and lemon tickled my nostrils. I held my breath, clinging to one final ounce of hope as I turned.

"Good evening," Queen Marisol said as she eyed the photo in my hand.

I failed to curtsy or offer her a formal address.

She stepped forward to pass me on the path but I stopped her with a question, which bordered on a verbal attack. "Have you always worn that mix of oils?"

She turned her face, just enough to speak to me through her periphery. "One year at The Lands Assembly, I was pregnant at the same time as our enemy queen. She saw I wasn't feeling well and offered me a vial of oil. I had my herbalist recreate it and have been wearing it ever since." She let out a soft laugh. "I've never told that story to anyone."

My father hated my mother's fascination with herbs and scents. He hated anything that only had anecdotal evidence, rather than concrete scientific facts. But for me, her oils gave life to an otherwise stale and sterile world. Being close to the queen, my nostrils determined that the scent was slightly off—too much lemon. An imposter scent that I wasn't able to previously detect.

Accepting that there was no longer a case for my mother to be alive, my brain lit up with logic. "You recognized me from my solo performance in the auditorium. Then you told Maestro who I was, and he came up with the idea to say he saw me in the photo. But why the secrecy? Why didn't you just tell the king?"

She pursed her lips and for a beat I thought she might walk away but she turned to face me. "She was my kingdom's enemy. But she was kind to me and...I felt I owed her a favor."

Our eyes locked and I should have thanked her but my throat felt swollen with anger. I didn't want to hear any more about my dead mother or my stupidity for believing she was still alive.

As if sensing my uneasiness, she nodded. "Happy New Year." She continued on to the entrance of the Ballroom Wing, when the door to the hallway opened behind me.

"Paris! We're lining up!" shouted Layla.

I tucked my mother's picture back in my pocket and followed Layla up the stairs to the dressing room. I took a final look at myself in the mirror. After posing as a Mondarian for nearly three months, I had nothing to show but a sparkling gown and brown hair.

"You okay?" asked Layla.

I nodded.

She hugged me and wished me a good show. "Shopping trip to the Village tomorrow?" She whispered, "Last one before you leave?"

"Yes," I said with a weak smile. But I wouldn't be going to the Village. And I wouldn't be performing in the Winter Showcase. New Year's Eve would be my final night in Mondaria and my final time to perform as a singer on the King's 100.

CHAPTER 34

I entered the Stardust Ballroom for the final time, focusing on the small details I would never experience again—the hum of a hundred conversations happening all at once, the taste of sugared berries mixed with a buttered crust and the way my arm hairs tingled when the drummers symbolically pounded on the door for the king's entrance.

I closed my eyes, not wanting to find Ari among the drummers. I planned to leave the court like a card in a magic trick—my only purpose having been to fool my spectators and go back into my original deck where I belonged.

The stage lacked the king's head table that normally sat atop the stage. Instead, the king and queen sat at a round table with a few hand-picked VIPs, giving room for the King's 100 to perform for their New Year's guests. The drummers took their positions below the front of the stage as the magicians performed their New Year's Eve set on stage. I acted surprised by their choreographed finale of flaming hands. Reese and Layla climbed the stairs to sing their duet, which served as the other singers' cue to leave our tables and make our way to the stage. When their duet ended, I met Reese center stage to take my spot for the traditional countdown and kiss before the final song of the night.

I stepped closer to Reese, prepared to 'solve all my problems with a kiss' as Layla had said, only to feel him peel away and disappear off the stage. Out of the corner of my eye, I saw him retch into a potted evergreen.

I stood on stage front and center, looking like a smiling idiot without a partner. The maestro's eyes narrowed on me as he shouted some curse words in my direction, causing the couples on either side of me to break their stance and look at me. His head disappeared from my periphery and I decided I would applaud when the kiss was cued, hoping it would look like a planned move. But then the couple to my left stepped back as a court man walked between them to stand next to me.

I felt my fake smile fade.

Of all the court men Maestro Leto could have chosen from, he picked the one person I had been trying to *not* kiss since setting foot in Mondaria.

Ari.

CHAPTER 35

A ri looked at me with wide eyes and he asked me something but my attention had to refocus on Maestro. We stared at the back of the maestro's head as he addressed the audience and cued the drumroll. The countdown began when Maestro turned to face the singers. "Hold her hands, Ari!" he shouted.

Ari grabbed my hands after he looked at the couple next to us, mimicking their stance. My heart rate increased with every count.

"Five, four, three, two, one, Happy New Year!"

The couples beside us pulled each other into a choreographed kiss as the audience raised their champagne flutes to the stage. I looked at Ari, neither of us moving a muscle.

Maestro shouted through a smile. "Kiss her, dammit! Kiss her!"

Ari looked down at Maestro, then back at me, wrestling with his next move. He dropped my hands and placed his palms on my waist. He closed the distance between us, so I felt the heat of his body through his tuxedo. His fingertips tensed against my dress as his eyes darted back and forth, searching for answers on my frozen face.

No, I pleaded. *Please don't make me kiss you when all I want to do is leave this kingdom and forget you.*

But then he sealed his decision by pressing his lips to mine.

I closed my eyes, shutting out the light of the room and drinking in the taste of Ari's lips. Feeling lighter than air, I curled my fingers around the smooth satin of his lapel, anchoring myself to his body. I was suspended in time, where midnight was the only hour. The curtain within me opened fully, replacing my dark, crimson blood with liquid gold.

Ari gently removed his lips from mine to look at me with a soft gaze and a parted mouth. The magicians released silver foil confetti, cloaking us in our own private sanctuary. The rhythm of our breathing dampened the sounds of the outside world as we stared into each other's eyes.

Then Maestro shouted something, causing Ari to step back and dissolve our sanctuary. The sounds of clinking glasses and laughter hit my ears as my hands floated in front of me, desperate for their warm resting place to return.

I took my position for our final song, standing still and holding my court smile like a poised statue. Tears dotted my cheeks, and I imagined the light danced off the moisture, making my face sparkle. I mouthed the words to the song, but I thought something completely different; an admission of the unthinkable and wanting it so deeply that giving up my life in Capalon felt like the easiest decision I would ever make.

I wanted nothing more than to be with Ari Novak, the black-haired drummer from Badger River.

Maybe I had known all along that the second I tasted his lips I would be hooked and never able to leave him. And maybe I didn't find my mother, but I found something else alive within me that I would have never found in Capalon. I battled with a constant intersect of logic and emotion, but with my curtain open, I no longer had to avoid combining both worlds.

"For auld lang syne, my dear, for auld lang syne—"

I can never go back to Capalon.

"We'll take a cup of kindness yet, for auld lang syne."

I can never go back because I'm undeniably in love with a Mondarian.

CHAPTER 36

King Orson gave his final remarks to the audience and when Maestro cued our exit, I followed the singers offstage as Mansion employees handed us one-size-fits-all jackets. We moved outside into the cold where we were to hand cups of hot chocolate to guests as they filed onto the terrace to watch the fireworks display.

I found Ari handing off steaming cups to two elderly guests. He picked another cup off the long table beside him then met my eyes, taking me back to the first day I met him when he was a stranger from my enemy kingdom and I was a princess in hiding.

A firework exploded in the distance, signaling the start of the show. The crowd and other court members watched the following hiss, crack, and boom in awe, while Ari's brown eyes failed to tear from my gaze.

I stepped forward, ignoring a guest's question about the dairy content of the hot chocolate.

Ari extended a cup to me. "Hot chocolate? It's no Dan's but I'm not supposed to—"

"I have to tell you something," I shouted over the next boom.

Ari's joyful face turned serious as he processed my expression and set the cup back on the table. I signaled for him to follow me down a narrow set of steps at the back of the terrace. The steps led to a path encased in tall hedges and spat us out into a gravel circle, where a gigantic statue of a bronze moose stood in the center.

"Look at that," Ari said, smiling up at the statue. "We finally found the moose." He turned to me, expecting to see my shared joy for our accidental discovery. "Hey, what's wrong, Paris?"

Breathe. Focus. Breathe.

No.

Just breathe.

Let go. Let go. Let go.

I clenched my fists and stared into his concerned eyes. "I know I've been pushing you away, and I wanted to say...I'm so sorry." I reached for his hands, no longer able to fight the urge to touch him. "The truth is...I lied when I said you were just my friend. I want so much more than your friendship because...I've developed romantic feelings for you, Ari."

Ari's eyes searched for truth on my face. "So, you're not into Reese?"

I shook my head. "Only you. It's always been you."

"I knew it," he said with his sun-bursting smile that warmed my soul. He dropped my hands to place his fingers at the base of my neck and rest his thumbs against my temples, pulling me closer. My hands clung to the open zipper of his coat and I considered the option to not tell him the truth of my identity—to let the moment of our closeness last for the entirety of the fireworks display and beyond. Lean in for one more kiss and forget the chilling reality that hid behind a few simple words.

But the curtain had opened and could no longer hide things like lies or tears.

He brushed my cheeks with his calloused thumbs. "Why the tears for such a happy occasion?"

My breathing hitched. "Because of what I'm about to tell you."

His brows creased hard lines across his forehead. "What is it?"

I reached up for his hands, bringing them down between us. "Ari, I meant it when I said I've never felt more myself when I'm with you.

And I know I want nothing else but to be with you, but...I also want to be honest. Which is why I need to tell you who I really am."

I winced as three loud booms exploded in the black sky.

Ari kept his focus on me.

I shut my eyes.

Just breathe.

My eyes flashed open. "I'm not Paris Marigold and I'm not from Mondaria."

He cocked his head to the side.

Let go.

I forced out my words. "I'm Piper Parish, Princess of Capalon."

Ari's grip on my hands loosened. "I don't understand."

I released his hands and let my coat fall to the ground, ignoring the biting chill of the winter air across my skin. "Chip, state my identification on speaker." I extended my wrist toward Ari.

"The subject before you is Princess Piper Parish, sister to Queen Evelyn, the current ruler of the kingdom of Capalon."

Ari's eyes popped at the sight of my blue, glowing wrist. He took a step back. "You're the Capalon princess? But how..."

"I came here to find my mother after receiving a note back at our Compound that said she was living in the Mondarian king's Mansion. But I know now that she's not alive, and I was a fool for believing that note in the first place. My plan was to leave tonight, but after kissing you, I—"

"You've been lying to me this whole time?"

"Only my identity, Ari. Everything I feel for you is real. I—"

"You're Capalon. And you're the princess." He turned and ran his hands through his black hair. "I don't believe this."

I reached for his arm. "We can still be together, I just—"

"We're enemies," he said, jerking away from my touch. "And you're the princess. Paris, I mean, *Piper*, you can't be here. They'll find out. And they'll...they'll throw you in prison. Or kill you! You... you have to leave."

I shook my head, wanting his words to be different—wanting so badly for him to change his mind and ask me to stay. I reached my fingers out to touch him. "Ari...please, I—"

"You lied to me!" He took another step back. "You're no different from Tasha or my dad. You need to leave. Now." Under the silver light of the moon, his soft eyes were dark, nearly matching his threatening look from my nightmares. He turned his back to me and spoke so softly that I could barely hear him over the fireworks but just loud enough to kill my soul. "You have to go. We can never be anything more than enemies."

My head spun.

I needed to leave.

I pushed my way through the tall hedges concealing the moose statue and headed to the public transportation stop at the bottom of the hill.

"Paris! Where are you going?" Layla's voice shouted behind me. She sprinted down the wide set of stairs of the terrace that blocked the hidden moose.

I couldn't respond, couldn't repeat the painful words Ari had just spoken and relive the pain all over again. I hit the call button on the kiosk.

"An auto-taxi is...*one quarter* of a mile away. Would you like me to call it for you?"

"Yes, dammit! Get me out of here!" I shouted, hitting the call button even harder.

"You're leaving now?" asked Layla. "I thought—"

"I don't belong here, Layla. I'm leaving because..."

Because my mother was dead, and I was an idiot for believing she was alive. Because the boy I loved rejected me. Because he said we could never be anything more than enemies. And because I knew he was right.

"Miss Marigold, don't leave." Darden sprinted toward us. "Is this about Ari? Just give him some time. I'm sure—"

"No!" Anger filled every inch of my body with heat so strong, I felt like I could melt a frozen lake. "This is your fault," I said, turning to point a finger at Darden. "How could you fill my head with false hope?" I moved my finger to Layla. "It's your fault too. You said yourself that love isn't worth the pain and you both...you both told me to tell him. And...and now he hates me!"

"Miss Marigold, if you could just—"

"My name is *Piper*, Darden. Piper Parish, *Princess* of Capalon."

Darden's eyes widened.

Layla's mouth dropped. "The princess?"

"Yeah, didn't see that one coming, did you? Or maybe you did since you've been calling me 'princess' from the beginning. How ironic, right?"

Darden took a step forward. "*Piper*, maybe Miss Tanvi and I thought you and Ari were the exception and we thought, well we hoped that—"

I shook my head. "No. I know why you both did it." I paced back and forth, waiting for the taxi. "Deep down, you know that we're enemies and you both wanted to hurt me. I can never be with Ari. And I should have never come here. It was a mistake. My sister was right. Coming here was a waste of time." I lifted my arms and shouted up at the sky. "I never even got to see it snow!"

The auto-taxi's tires crunched over the gravel behind me. "I'm getting matched in two days on my *real* birthday and I couldn't be happier! There's a reason why Capalons don't believe in romantic love and *this* is why. All I've been able to think about since I've been here is Ari. How would Capalon be the greatest kingdom in The Lands if we had something like romantic love occupying our minds all the time? It's pathetic!"

Layla took a step forward. "If that's what you want to believe, then fine. We're enemies. You don't deserve to be with Ari and you don't deserve to be our friend!"

I climbed inside the taxi.

"Have a nice life, princess." Before Darden could add anything to Layla's sentiments, she slammed the door closed.

"What is your destination?" asked the voice from the console.

"Capalon," I said, sinking down in the seat.

"Entrance to Capalon is prohibited. I can drop you off at the nearest auto-taxi station."

"Fine!"

The vehicle lurched forward, and I ignored the finale of fireworks bursting behind me as my tears turned to sobs. I cried for Ari, I cried for my mother, I cried for my friends and I cried for myself.

Tasting the forbidden evils of love in all its forms only led to suffering. The pain of my stupidity weighed on me like a pile of boulders. I kept my eyes shut tight until I could no longer see the glow of fireworks through my eyelids.

When my wet sobs turned to dry, trembling breaths, I peeled my eyes open to see only darkness inside the vehicle.

This is where I belong. In darkness, away from the light of false hope.

I sat up as relief numbed my body.

I didn't *have* to feel pain.

In Capalon, love was an illusion of the mind. Citizens of Capalon were required to turn off their emotions.

"Chip, talk me down."

The interior of the auto-taxi filled with blue light as Chip steadied my breathing.

My heartbeat settled into a slow, melodic rhythm with a newfound appreciation for my kingdom. Capalons avoided distraction for the success of innovation.

And I would no longer be distracted.

I would no longer be a failure.

"Chip, put me back online."

There was only one version of myself worth living—Piper Parish, Princess of Capalon.

CHAPTER
37

"Princess, you have two unheard messages. Would you like me to play them for you?" Chip asked.

I sighed. "Okay."

"Go on," said my sister's voice.

Sniffing covered the mouth of my sister's receiver. "Hello, Princess Piper," said a little boy's voice. "My name is Walter Breason, son of George and Joanna Breason of the Engineering Ward. I...I'm the one who wrote you the false message about your mother. I was in the Meeting Hall kitchen with my classmate. We were consuming ice berries. We had too many and the forbidden amount of sugar infiltrated our minds. It was my idea to leave you the note. My...my decision was spurred by rumors of your strange beliefs about your mother. I'm so very remorseful."

"And how do you plan to correct your distracted behavior?" my sister asked.

"With eight hours of self-discipline in Focus."

"End of message. Play next message?" Chip asked.

I sighed. "Yes."

My mother's voice hit my eardrums, causing lightning to strike down my spine. "Gavin, you seem distracted this evening."

"I'm just concentrating on the points I want to bring up to...wait, that's odd."

"What is it?"

"The temperature gauge. I think it's spiking."

"I'll check the coolant tank." I heard a faint click from my mother's restraint belt. "It's probably just—"

An explosion screamed through the feed, followed by the sickening sound of metal twisting around metal and a roaring fire.

"Chip, how long is this message?" I asked in horror.

"Eleven minutes," Chip's voice said under the continual sound of the fire.

"End message! End it! Now!" For the three months I was absent, my sister felt the most beneficial audios to share were the admission of the writer of my secret message and a recording of my parents' deaths. I should have been furious for her vicious act but it was the way of a Capalon's thinking—sharing the hard facts to support a hypothesis.

Without listening to the rest of the audio, I knew why she let it continue for eleven minutes. Because there would be no other sounds for eleven minutes until the rescue vehicles arrived. It was hard evidence—the evidence she hoped would finally settle my mind about my mother.

Two auto-taxis approached mine and one passed to take the lead. As it passed, I saw the familiar face of the female Capalon patrol officer from the Village. Going back online made me visible to anyone tracking my Bio-System. When we arrived at the auto-taxi rest stop, the two officers instructed me not to leave my vehicle through Chip. After running a health and weapons diagnostic, one of our smaller speedcraft models landed in a grassy field on the opposite side of the LVR. They marched me to the aircraft and after we landed in Capalon, I was led straight to my sister's office.

Before stepping inside, I glimpsed myself in the reflective metal door—wearing the glittering silver performance gown and my new brown hair curled into an updo that allowed only a few loose strands to escape. Streaks of black mascara covered my cheeks and my bright red lipstick smudged over my lip and onto my chin. I looked like a sad joke or the epitome of a Capalon's image of a Mondarian.

The door opened to reveal my sister sitting at her desk in a long charcoal evening robe. She looked me up and down with a stone-cold expression and waited for the door to shut behind me before she spoke. "Chip, switch Piper back to auto-operation and reset her search restrictions."

Chip's voice responded to my sister through my wrist. "Yes, Your Majesty."

Evelyn cleared her throat. "Welcome back, sister. Was your trip a success?"

I clenched my jaw and kept my focus on the back of her monitors.

"I had to tell our inquiring citizens that you left for some confidential research on water energy down in Whitefalls. Thankfully, nobody questioned your intentions. And even though you found a way to set your Bio-System to manual, we can still find a ping from you within a ten-mile radius. We just weren't able to pin down your exact location—another technical error we need to improve." She tapped her fingers on the desk. "A patrol officer was arrested during your search. I haven't heard if they've executed him yet. Look at me, Piper."

My eyes didn't move.

She slammed her hands against her desk. "Look at your queen!"

Heart racing, I forced my eyes to meet hers. They were my mother's eyes, surrounded by my father's bone structure. Keeping her glare on my face, she pulled something out of her pocket—the white card with the secret message about our mother bounced to the edge of the desk.

"I did what you suggested and had some tests run on the paper. It's a new stock paper the primary school is using for drafting exercises. You received my audios?"

"Yes. Both of them," I forced out in a low voice.

She nodded with approval. "What is your interpretation of the audios and your illegal trip to Mondaria on the subject of Mother's life?"

"Mother is dead, Evelyn. You were right. Can I please just go to my room now?"

Her knuckles turned white against the desk. "You have *no* idea what kind of danger you put yourself and your kingdom in by entering Mondaria. Did you make it inside the king's Mansion?"

I swallowed. "No."

"What have you been doing for the past three months?"

I pulled my shoulders back and straightened my neck. "I found work as a server in a cafe using a Mondarian girl's ID I found in the creek. I never set foot in the Mansion."

She pursed her lips. "Your appearance says otherwise. Or do Mondarian servers wear ball gowns when they're giving their customers artery-clogging foods?"

I inhaled to steady my heart as the lie formed in my head. "I was attending a costume party for a Mondarian holiday when I felt homesick and—"

"Home *sick*? Are you ill? Your scans came back normal."

I bit my lip. "No, um...I felt a longing for the kingdom of my birth and finally listened to your audios. That's when I ended my search and came back."

Evelyn nodded, but a hint of suspicion lingered behind her eyes. "What happened to your hair?"

"It was a protective measure by my own doing."

"Did you tell anyone who you were?"

Darden and Layla figured out who I was on their own. The queen put the pieces together herself and told Maestro. But I had only told one person—a fact that I wanted to forget. "No. I kept to myself and nobody questioned me. Now may I please go to my room?"

My sister crossed her arms. "I think I deserve an apology, Piper."

"I'm sorry for putting the kingdom in danger."

She took a deep breath. "That's it, then? You're back home and ready for your match?"

"Yes. I won't be searching for Mother any further. And I..." air caught in my throat, "and I look forward to meeting my match and preparing for our ceremony."

Evelyn nodded. "I'll have a lunch arranged for the three of us tomorrow. You'll need to be returned to your birth-hair color before any of our citizens lay eyes upon you. Dottie, download the chemical compound for blonde hair dye and forward to the grooming droid."

Evelyn dismissed me, so I bent my head and turned for my room.

"Piper?"

I paused.

"I'm satisfied with your safe return."

I didn't respond to my queen and headed to my room for an uncomfortable, restless sleep in my windowless bedroom.

CHAPTER 38

I awoke to the sound of metal tapping metal. The grooming droid waited outside my door until I answered. "Good morning, Princess. It's time for the reinstatement of birth-color for your hair."

"What about breakfast?" I asked the tall, oval-shaped droid.

"Her Majesty thought a morning fast would benefit your mind."

"Of course, she would think that," I mumbled as I pulled on a grey sweater and matching grey pants.

Near the end of the droid's hair-dying process, I was eager to meet my match for the simple reason of finally being able to eat. I reviewed his details on the projected image above my wrist as the droid brushed out my hair. His name only appeared as 'Highest Placement' followed by every grade, test score, research project and debate speech. The details failed to include a physical description or interests other than research topics.

Our lunch took place in a windowless dining room smaller than my bedroom. I wore my traditional royal Capalon garb—grey pants and a grey high-necked blazer with the kingdom's insignia over the heart. I waited alone at the cold, grey table until Evelyn entered with my match.

He stood about an inch under my height with red hair, green eyes and a spray of freckles on his cheeks. He was attractive in a way that I think Layla would have described as 'boyish.'

But there was no more Layla and no more reason to talk about boys with other girls. I punched my thumbnails into my forefingers at the reminder of my terrible last words to Layla.

"Your Highness," my match said, addressing me. "It's an honor to have received this position."

I pushed away thoughts of Layla and smiled at the reference to his union to me being considered a position. I then shoved a barley and kale cube in my mouth and ignored my sister's glare. It was *her* fault I had been starved all morning.

Evelyn cleared her throat. "Piper, this is Gregory Harp. Gregory is from the Science Ward. Do you have any questions for Gregory?" she asked with angry eyes.

I sucked a rogue piece of kale off my tooth before speaking. "Um, Gregory...what's your favorite drink?"

"Peppermint tea. And yours?"

"Hot chocolate," I said without hesitation.

Both my sister's and Gregory's eyes widened.

I licked my lips. "I mean peppermint tea too. It was a joke."

Gregory smiled and my sister squeezed her hands around her cup of tea, as if it were my neck.

"I enjoy humor at acceptable times of the day too," Gregory said. "In fact, something humorous occurred in my father's lab the other day and he shared his experience with my family over dinner. May I share his experience with you, Princess?"

"Yes, sir."

The spoon my sister held in her teacup fell against the saucer.

Capalon Royalty never addressed others as 'sir' or 'ma'am.'

"You have to excuse my sister's mood, Gregory," Evelyn said. "She's choosing to be far too humorous for this occasion. But please, continue your story."

Gregory continued to tell a dull story about a beaker breaking in his father's lab while I asked the service droid for at least three more kale cubes and a spoon of salt, if there was any salt available in the entire kingdom.

"Accept," whispered my sister as she took an incoming call in her ear.

I politely offered my attention to Gregory as he droned on about his father and wished the service droid would have brought my food first before searching Capalon for the salt.

Then two words out of my sister's mouth killed any ounce of attention I had mustered for Gregory. "A drummer?"

CHAPTER 39

E velyn turned her head to the side and covered her mouth but I could still hear her. "How long?"

"Chip, open patrol channel," I said between heavy beats of my heart.

The officer's voice played in my ear with the most beautiful sound of a steady drum cadence in the background. "He says he won't stop playing until he can speak with the princess."

I sprang up, knocking my chair to the floor. "This is Princess Piper. Let me speak to him."

"Override," said my sister.

"No!" I shouted. "Patrol, turn on direct communication so I can talk to him."

"Piper, we're in the middle of something." She tilted her head toward a pale-faced Gregory. "And you said you didn't tell anyone who you were," she said in a sharp whisper that Gregory could clearly hear.

But there was only one boy I would ever care for and he was at the gate of my kingdom. "Just let me hear what he has to say. Please."

"Directive?" asked the patrol officer.

My eyes pleaded with Evelyn. "Please, Evie. Maybe he has some sort of message for us. Just let me hear what he has to say."

She sighed. "Allow for one-way audio from subject."

There was some muffled talking on the channel, followed by the silence of the drum. "I speak into your wrist?" asked Ari's voice.

My hands flew to my mouth as I held my breath, not wanting to miss a single word from Ari.

"Piper, if you can hear me, I just wanted to...well, I wanted to say I'm sorry. I said you were the same as my dad and Tasha but you're not. You actually told me the truth before I had to find it out on my own." He sighed. "And I don't care who you are. I was doomed the first time I saw you and you called me an ignoramus," he said with a laugh.

Salty tears fell onto my tongue as my smile stretched to its capacity.

"The truth is, I've never felt more myself when I'm with you, too. Piper, I—"

"Cut channel to the princess," said my sister.

"No!"

"Patrol, please escort the subject back to his kingdom." Evelyn's eyes narrowed on mine and her chest rose with heavy breaths. "You... developed romantic feelings for a *Mondarian?*"

Gregory cleared his throat. "I would like to dismiss myself from what sounds like a confidential conversation."

Neither my sister nor I said a word as Gregory left the tiny dining room.

I dismissed myself too, taking the skybridge back to our Compound.

Evelyn followed at my heels. "How could you, Piper? They're our enemies. And to imagine romantic love on top of it, I—"

"I didn't imagine anything," I snapped as I picked up my pace. "I love him. And he loves me."

Ari loves me.

Not Paris Marigold, but *me.* I could have sprouted wings and flown myself out of Capalon with the level of joy coursing through me.

Evelyn scoffed. "Those people are not even close to the same caliber of human beings that we are."

"Why? Just because we're more scientific? I can't even imagine being happy in a match with that...that *stiff*!" I said throwing my hands in the air.

"We're smarter than them, Piper. They're dull-minded and idiotic!"

I shook my head. "No. They're highly intelligent but just in a different way."

"They've brainwashed you."

I ignored her comment and kept walking. "When I was at the Mansion, I—"

"You said you never set foot in the king's Mansion."

"I lied. I lived there for three months."

"But how—"

"I auditioned to be a singer of the King's 100." I paused at the door of my bedroom and turned to face my sister. "I lived with the other court members in dormitories and I made friends, Evie. Yes, they're different, but they're...*human*. They feel things and talk about it—express it through art, laughter, crying...kissing. Do you know what they call us? Stiffs. Because we're more robotic than human. Mother might be dead, but I'm alive, and I want to live my life by *my* terms. This kingdom won't care if I'm gone. Tell them I ended my life. Tell them I died in Whitefalls. Or tell them I died the same way Mother and Father did."

"You're speaking malicious words, Piper. You must stop this."

But I couldn't stop. "And I know you don't believe in love but you have to know about Xavier. He can't give you an heir when he's not even attracted to you!"

I heard the sound of Evelyn's palm against my cheek before the pain set in, stinging the entire right side of my face.

I refused to give her the satisfaction of settling the pain with my hand, holding it at my side. "I'm leaving, Evelyn. Tell the kingdom whatever you want, but I don't belong here." I stepped inside my room after commanding Chip to open my door.

Evelyn spoke to me from my doorway. "If you go back to Mondaria, you'll be my enemy. And if they find out who you are, they'll kill you and I won't stop them."

My pulse spiked. "I would rather die happy as your enemy, then live one more day in this prison!" I opened my arms to show off my windowless room to her, then took a deep breath. "For being the smartest, most powerful ruler in The Lands, you could change things, Evie. Change the match law. Change relations with Mondaria. You could be happy, too, and allow yourself to fall in love."

I reached for the picture tucked inside the pocket of my New Year's Eve dress, which hung inside my closet. "Look." I handed the picture to my sister. "This photo is what finally convinced me that Mother wasn't alive—not your audios. She stopped going to the Annual Assembly because she didn't want to leave you. And if she really were still alive, I know in my heart she would be back by now. Because you always go back to the people you love and she *loved* us, Evie." A breath hitched in my throat. "I think that's why I left. It's been three years since I've felt loved by anyone. The closest thing I had to it was a piece of tech in my arm. But I found it again from my friends at the Mansion and...from Ari."

Evelyn examined the photo, and another photograph sparked my memory. "Evie, something made you happy at the last Assembly."

Her head snapped up from the photo in her hand.

I took a step toward my sister. "I saw the photograph. I just need you to imagine whatever joy you felt at that dinner and multiply it by infinity and that's how it feels to be in love."

Her face paled more than I thought was possible as she handed the photo back to me.

I stepped toward my closet when I heard a click at the door. "No..." I jumped to the other side of the room to ask Chip to open the door but it was too late. "Evelyn?"

She spoke to me from the other side. "I think you just need some time in Focus, Piper. For however long it takes."

"Evie, don't do this. Please, please don't do this."

I pressed my ear against the door to hear her footsteps walk away. "Evelyn! Come back here! Let me out!" I pounded on the door first with my hands and then with my feet but nobody came to my reprieve. "Chip, call Evelyn."

"Direct communication to the queen has been cut from your system."

"No! Evie!" I screamed for my sister repeatedly but the door remained shut.

Bruises formed on my knuckles, my voice went hoarse and exhaustion grew heavy on my shoulders. I slid down the metal door to the cold cement floor. "Please," I whispered in a desperate loop. "Open the door. Please. Open the door." Hours passed, but I didn't allow the relief of sleep to take me away from the reality of my despair. "I want to go back," I said with what was left of my voice. "I want to tell him I love him."

Time continued to pass as sleep encouraged me to forfeit my fight to stay awake. Speaking was the only thing keeping me awake but eventually even my own words gave up on me. "No," I rasped. "I... Ari..." I could no longer fight the weight of my eyelids. I gave in. Sleep and my sister won their battle over me.

Then the door opened.

CHAPTER
40

Fluorescent light poured in from the hallway, backlighting the figure in the doorway. My fatigued eyes took a minute to communicate the identity of my visitor to my brain. I addressed him from my spot on the floor. "Xavier?" I coughed out.

He stepped into my room and closed the door before taking a seat on the floor next to me. "I might have overheard your discussion with Evelyn," he said. "Did you really fall in love with a Mondarian?"

I nodded.

"That's forbidden in more ways than one and is deserving of punishment."

I shivered, unsure of Xavier's intentions for his visit.

He sighed. "But if you deserve punishment, so does your king. And I would say being matched with your sister is the harshest form of punishment I could imagine. Don't get me wrong, Evelyn is my queen and I would die for her. But it's her sorrow for *what* I'm unable to give her that feels like a punishment." Xavier placed his feet on the floor and wrapped his arms around his legs, mirroring my position. The image reflected the confidence of a young boy, rather than a powerful king. "When my family found out I had the highest score on our Placement Exams, they were elated. Couldn't believe that their son was going to be matched to the queen. There is no higher honor for a Capalon citizen. But that night, I couldn't sleep. And over the following months leading up to our match ceremony, I couldn't sleep. My parents knew my...*preference*, but like the rest of our kingdom, it didn't matter to them. Sexual attraction is arbitrary. I even told Evelyn the first day I met her and encouraged her to choose the next match on the list but she shut me down. She said my genes were needed for the future of Capalon. Then on our match night, nothing happened. And nothing has continued to happen. She has me on medication but it's only giving me headaches." Xavier let out an exhale and touched his head. "I guess what I'm trying to say, Piper, is if you're really in love—even if he's our enemy—I think somebody in this Compound should be happy...for however long it lasts." He stood up and offered his hand.

I took it and forced my weak legs to support my weight.

"I know what I'm doing is wrong. And perhaps I'll finally anger Evelyn enough to send me back to my Ward. You just have to promise me you won't die. I think that would be bad for both of us."

I smiled and flung my arms around his neck. "Thank you," I whispered.

His arms hovered in the air for a beat before hugging me back. He reached for my wrist when we stepped apart. "Chip, switch to manual-drive for the princess and take her off-line," he said.

"King Xavier, doing so requires—"

"Permission granted by King Xavier Emmanuel Demetrios of Capalon," said the King of Capalon with a proud smile.

"Voice override approved. Princess Piper is now on manual-drive and off-line," Chip said.

Joy flooded my veins, followed by the heavy weight of dread on my shoulders. "I don't have a way to get out of Capalon. The gate's been fixed."

A mischievous grin appeared on Xavier's face. "Well, I just happen to be in need of somebody to test my new hover pod prototype. It's undetectable to our own radar. And being the king, I don't have to get permission from anyone to use it. But I suggest we go before I turn into a *good* Capalon king."

I grabbed my dress, thankful to see Paris Marigold's ID still resting in a pocket, then stood beside Xavier as he opened the door. He paused before crossing the threshold.

"And Piper?" he said with a sad smile. "I know it may be hard to see, but your sister does care for you. And if love is real, then she's just loving you the way a Capalon should love you."

XAVIER OPERATED the hover pod remotely, landing me behind the auto-taxi station on the LVR. I had spent the entirety of the court's off-day in Capalon and estimated I would arrive at the Mansion just as the Winter Showcase was beginning for their late morning show time. I changed into the silver crystal New Year's Eve dress and did the best I could with my hair as the auto-taxi took me to the king's Mansion. I would stand out like a sore thumb on the stage against the standard black performance dress of the other court members, but I had no other option with the time remaining. I had to not only make it to the Mansion on time, but perform well enough for the king to ask me to return for the next season. And when it was all over, I had to see Ari.

After showing Paris Marigold's ID to the guard at the service entrance, I entered the black backstage of the Polaris Auditorium. My ears were instantly hit with the sound of the drums, sending my heart into a series of wild beats.

A cold hand gripped my arm. "Paris, your hair is blonde again!" Genevieve said with wide eyes. "Is that where you've been? In the Village getting your hair done?" Her hand flew to her heart. "I've been so worried about you. I thought maybe...well, I was so scared..." Her chest heaved, and she took a couple deep breaths. Her eyes were stern. "You should have asked me to come with you! Why are you wearing your New Year's Eve dress? Did Maestro tell you to wear that? Oh, and you don't have any make-up." A tube of lipstick appeared in her hand and before I could protest, she glided it over my lips.

Why did Genevieve look so traumatized by my short absence? "Thank you, Genevieve. You're a good friend," I said with an appreciative smile.

The orchestra picked up after the drummers' final cadence, signaling the singers' cue to take the stage. I sang my solo like my life depended on it and ignored Maestro's angry comments about my dress. But my heart rate quickened when I remembered I needed to tell the maestro my change of plans. Assuming the king would invite me back for the following season, Maestro would need to know that I wasn't planning on leaving the court after all.

While the magicians performed, I hoped Ari would find me backstage and wrap his arms around me but he waited in the hall with the other drummers to make his entrance for the finale.

A pair of short arms *did* encircle me and we cried in silence together, holding onto each other and whispering "I'm sorry." Layla wiped my mascara away from under my eyes and I did the same for her before we took the stage for the final number.

When the show ended, Maestro instructed us to hold our places on stage and relax. I could do anything *but* relax. My fingers twitched, aching to see Ari and touch his face. The house lights came on, illuminating the auditorium and a pair of brown eyes smiling at me from the back of the auditorium. A cloak of calm rested on my shoulders. I was back in the Mansion. I would be reunited with Ari and that's all that mattered.

The floor of the orchestra pit rose to ground level so the musicians could leave while the king gave Maestro his feedback. I moved my head anytime a musician blocked my view of Ari.

A voice boomed from the box above stage-right. "The girl in the silver dress. What's your name, dear?"

It pained me to remove my eyes from Ari but I tilted my chin up to the king's box. "Paris Marigold, Your Majesty."

Was the king going to kick me out for wearing a different dress? The thought of being escorted off the stage before I even had a chance to talk to Ari twisted my stomach.

"Paris Marigold," said the king. "Lovely name and lovely voice. Bernie, showcase this girl more. Her voice—it's vulnerable and untrained—a different feel from some of these other powerhouse voices. I like them all the same but it's nice to have variety. Also, the magician who—"

A commotion at the back of the auditorium stole the king's attention. Captain Murphy and three of his guards marched down the center aisle, pushing past the exiting musicians.

"Captain Murphy, can't you see we're in the middle of something here?" asked the king.

"I apologize, Your Majesty, but I've come with a warrant to arrest one of your court members."

An icy chill ran down my spine, freezing every organ in my body.

Maestro lied.

He turned me in, despite our deal.

But before the maestro turned to address the captain, his eyes met mine with a reassuring softness that helped thaw my lungs. "Captain Murphy, are you really interrupting our Winter Showcase to ease your boredom?"

The captain ignored the maestro's words and addressed the king up in his box. "Your Majesty, we received a tip from one of your court members about a girl holding Capalon currency in her room."

Heather's body stiffened beside me.

"And with the recent Capalon we took into custody, we had to take the claim with serious attention." Nervous whispering spilled across the stage as the captain retrieved something from his pocket. "When we checked the girl's room, we found the Capalon currency and the missing key to our Records Room. After running a profile check on Paris Marigold, we were sent a picture of the *real* Paris Marigold with a signed letter from her parents." He held up a picture of the girl with brown hair, brown skin and brown eyes.

Court members gasped and backed away from me, making me more exposed on stage. A few of the remaining musicians in the auditorium sprinted to the exits, while others stayed to watch the drama unfold.

The captain addressed me from the other side of the orchestra pit. "Paris Marigold, whoever you really are, you're under arrest for espionage from the enemy kingdom of Capalon." My eyes jumped to Maestro for a silent plea for help. The guards climbed the stairs to the stage.

"This is ridiculous, Captain Murphy. Paris is from Green Heights and has the ID to prove it." Maestro turned to look up at the king. "Your Majesty, are you really allowing this to happen?"

As Maestro continued to try to fight for me, my brain searched for options. Down stage to my left, stood Darden. He found my eyes, then disappeared backstage. I hoped he was leaving to get a handful of smoke bombs. Genevieve looked at me as if I had just transformed into a ferocious bear. Behind me, I found Layla trying to mouth something but I couldn't make it out. I looked to my right to see the king peering over the box at the commotion between his maestro and his captain and just below him, stood Ari. He had removed his snare and left his position at the back of the auditorium.

Our eyes locked, and I took a step in his direction.

Then the entire auditorium went black.

Somebody pulled me by the elbow as the captain shouted to lock all the exits. I lost a shoe as court members darted and cried in the confusion.

"Go through the service exit," whispered Darden. He pushed me backstage and left before I could thank him. Nobody blocked my exit.

I was free to go.

But go where? Back to Capalon? Apologize to my sister *again* and commit to a loveless match? Perhaps after the confusion died down, Maestro would convince the captain and King Orson that it was an embarrassing misunderstanding and I would stay on the court as Paris Marigold.

But Paris Marigold was an illusion.

Darden felt love was most alive hidden under layers of illusion. Layla felt love was too painful and best avoided. But knowing that I loved Ari, and that he loved me, I wanted nothing but him. And I wanted him to have *all* of me—not an illusion or an avoided risk. And above all, I wanted the freedom to love. I wanted to be the real me and I wanted Ari to love the real me, even if all we would ever have was a missed opportunity.

I stepped away from the service exit and entered the chaos of the auditorium. Nobody noticed as I stepped up the hot microphone. "Everybody stop," I said into the mic. But chaos ensued.

"Chip, activate alarm." I held my wrist above my head as a loud alarm filled the auditorium with the rapid flash of blue light. The house lights flipped on and the sound of my alarm was replaced by silence. "It's true," I said into the microphone. "I'm from Capalon. In fact..." I found Ari at the edge of the orchestra pit and took a deep breath. "I'm...Piper Renée Parish, Princess of Capalon and sister to Queen Evelyn."

The whispers of disgust stung like a swarm of angry bees. I stepped closer to the microphone and spoke louder to be heard over the hum of disapproval. "I know that what I've done is illegal and I'll be punished by imprisonment or...by death," I choked out, "but Your Majesty," I tilted my head up to his box, "I renounce my title and my kingdom."

The auditorium responded in a shock of silence.

"I came here thinking my mother was still alive, and that I would bring her back to Capalon. But it turns out that I found something greater than I could have ever imagined—I found joy. Friendship. Love. All things that have been absent from my life until now." I took the mic out of the mic stand and rested my knees on the edge of the stage. "And that's why I kneel before you and ask you to please take me into your kingdom as a Mondarian citizen. I know you'll want me off the court and as far away from you as possible. I'll live on the border in the woods if that's what it takes. But, Your Majesty, I will forever pledge you as my king and do whatever you wish to be able to stay in this kingdom, where love truly exists."

My position on the stage made it is easy for the captain to slap a pair of cold handcuffs over my wrists. He muttered a standard line of arrest as I held the king's gaze. But the king dropped his head, signaling his answer.

Panic surged through my body as the captain pushed me through the King's 100-turned-angry-mob.

"Piper!" I heard Ari's voice behind me but no matter how hard I tried to fight I couldn't turn my body under the grip of the captain.

My shoulder dipped as Genevieve flung her arms around my neck. "You're not my enemy, you're my friend. I love you, I love you." She covered my face with tears and kisses.

The captain pushed me past her to see Layla leaning over the pocked-faced guard's arm. "Let her go!" she shouted. "Paris! The king is a demon, I'm so sorry!" She tried to push her way forward, but the guard pushed her back, knocking her to the ground. Reese appeared behind her and helped her to her feet before sending a fist into the guard's jaw. The guard stumbled backward, falling in front of me and the captain.

Then a green wall of smoke billowed up around us but Captain Murphy held me closer, his fingernails digging into my skin.

"Piper!" Ari's voice carried through to me despite the commotion from the smoke bomb. He was close.

"Ari!" I shouted. I blinked, wanting the smoke to clear so I could see him.

The captain adjusted his grip on me as he reached for something at his side. The sound of a gun cocking sent shivers down my spine.

As the smoke cleared, the captain extended his arm and turned us together in a slow spin. "If anyone else gets in my way, shouts in my face or sets off a magic bomb, I swear I will shoot you."

The auditorium fell silent and a wide path opened before us. The captain pushed me forward as another body stepped onto our path but I didn't have a chance to see who it was because the captain's gun fired, sending me to the ground with closed eyes and deaf ears. In those few seconds on the ground, everything that generated life within me came to a cold stop. There could only be one person willing to step in front of the captain. And if he died because of me, I was already dead before my eyes could will themselves to open.

CHAPTER 41

Ringing filled my ears, followed by muffled voices. The first person I saw when my eyes opened was King Orson, with his head tilted up to the ceiling. I followed his eyes to a fresh bullet hole smoking inside the intricate woodwork. I was slumped on the floor but a warm hand stroked my arm. I turned my head and Ari's brown eyes met mine. He asked me something but the only thing I could hear was the fervent beating of my own heart, choosing to be alive.

The captain clicked something on his gun and shoved it back into its holster. "I apologize, Your Majesty, I—"

"You couldn't hear me over all the commotion, so I came to you." The king approached me, lifting my chin up with his fingers. "Princess of Capalon," he said, examining my face. "You are my enemy. But you're also a magnificent performer. To avoid the boring trial, I'm making my decision now. You will be Mondarian and you'll hold the title of Head Lady of the Court. We'll announce it to The Lands and they will see that Mondaria has won over the daughter of their enemy. And if you fail me...well, I suppose I'll let Captain Murphy here shoot you. Do we have a deal?"

I moved my jaw in the king's firm grip. "Yes, Your Majesty."

"Good," he said as he released my face. "Captain Murphy, take her in for interrogation. Round up her closest comrades for questioning as well, so we can confirm we have no more Capalons living inside our walls."

✱

AFTER HOURS OF INTERROGATION, I was escorted to the Royal Wing of the Mansion. With my new title of Lady of the Court, the king thought it best that I have my own room, a seat at his table for every future event and even a custom-made tiara. His intentions were clear—I was to be a spectacle and a symbol of Mondaria's power over Capalon.

My new room was about five times the size of my dorm room. An enormous four-post bed sat as the centerpiece, adorned in shades of white, cream and gold. Mansion staff moved all of my belongings from my dorm room into my new walk-in closet. I ran my fingers across the few pieces of clothing I owned, landing on a shirt I hadn't seen since my first day in Mondaria. Eager to get out of my dress, I changed into my pair of jeans and Ari's red and black flannel shirt he gave me in Dan's. I rolled his long sleeves up to my elbows, revealing the bandage on my left wrist.

I mourned the loss of Chip but it was a necessary action to proclaim my allegiance to Mondaria. I cried throughout the procedure—not because of the pain, but because Chip assisted the clinician through his own removal. Placing a hand on my bandage, I moved to the bed, where a folded card waited for me to read it:

Lady Piper—

Congratulations on your new title! Here's a gift to offer my sincerest welcome into our kingdom. I wanted to let you know that this doesn't change anything about our agreement. I could have picked anyone to fill Mr. Olsen's spot on stage, so you're welcome! In fact, please share this mix with Mr. Novak. I hear he enjoys a good cup of hot chocolate. Happy New Year!

-Maestro Bernard Leto

I picked up the generic bag of hot chocolate mix and tossed it into the waste bin. It sickened me to think I had the maestro to thank for my kiss with Ari. What would have happened if we never kissed? Would I be matched with Gregory Harp and comfortable in my old life in Capalon? I moved to the window which sat ground level with the West Courtyard and yelped when a face appeared.

"Are you alright, Lady Piper?" My assigned room attendant looked up from placing a stack of laundered towels in my private bathroom. "Yes, just stubbed my toe. I'm exhausted. I need to rest."

She scurried to the bed to draw back the covers.

"I can do it myself. I just need some time alone."

She curtsied and exited the room. I locked the door before sprinting to the window and pushing it open. Ari climbed through and I shut the window and the drapes.

When I turned around, I expected him to take in the luxury of the king's private guest room but his eyes took in only me. His lips formed a straight line.

I repeated his words from our last night together on New Year's Eve. "Why the frown for such a happy occasion?"

Ari stepped forward and turned my wrist with a stronger grip than I expected. His eyes lingered on my bandage. "This isn't what I had hoped for you." He dropped my hand, looked around the room, then settled his focus back on me. "You're the king's prisoner."

I shook my head with a half-smile. "This definitely isn't prison. There's a window. And I'm still on the court. And..." I wanted to say *I get to be with you*, but something in Ari's demeanor made me question my certainty about his feelings. Had he changed his mind? I tucked a strand of blonde hair behind my ear.

Had he only loved me as the brunette, Paris Marigold?

Ari chewed on his bottom lip. "You're about to be the most talked-about person in Mondaria and probably The Lands."

"But I just want to talk to *you*," I said, taking a step closer.

He pulled something out of his back pocket. "This fell off your foot in the auditorium." Ari handed me a glittering silver high-heeled shoe.

"Thanks." I took the shoe and ran my fingers over the rough stones set in the fabric. "You came here just to give me my shoe back?"

Ari shoved his hands in his pockets. "Piper, I walked, ran, hunted down an auto-taxi and played my snare for over an hour to talk to you from the outside of your kingdom. I didn't come here *just* to give you your shoe back." He rubbed the back of his neck. "I'm so sorry about what I said on New Year's Eve. I—"

"You don't have to apologize again. I understand."

He pulled his hands out of his pockets. "What you said to me after the New Year's show...do you still feel that way?"

I nodded and took another step forward. "And what you said on the patrol feed...about being doomed from the first time you saw me?"

He smiled and placed his hands on my waist. "Yes. There was supposed to be more, but I was rudely cut off by the Queen of Capalon. I shouldn't be too mad at her, though, since I'm in love with her little sister," he said, looking into my eyes. "And when she hears that you're officially a Mondarian, she's really going to—"

I dropped the shoe, pulled the collar of Ari's flannel shirt and pressed my lips against his. His response was tentative at first, but then certain with firm hands on my back and a crashing mouth against mine. He carefully parted my lips and the taste of his tongue sent me into a delirious frenzy. My arms wrapped around the back of his neck as I pressed my entire body into him. Without releasing his mouth from mine, Ari hoisted me up and wrapped my legs around his waist. He took a few steps, then gently laid me down on the four-post bed as he hovered above me. His hand slid under the back of my shirt, sending my body into a pleasing arch. My hands explored the firmness of his abdominal muscles, causing Ari to moan something in my mouth. I reached up to caress the soft hairs at the base of his neck as his mouth moved down my neck in a trail of kisses. My body and mind buzzed with euphoria.

This.

This is all I want.

He lifted his mouth from my skin. "I was supposed to bring you back to the Lounge tonight for a surprise, but I think I want you all to myself." He placed a soft kiss on the side of my neck. "Plus, it's only a fair trade—a shoe for a shirt, right?"

I pulled his face back on top of mine but my interest was piqued. "It's not a surprise flogging by the King's 100, is it?" I asked between kisses.

He fell beside me on the bed and propped his head up with his fist. "No, everyone but those of us being interrogated were dismissed for the weekend." His fingertips brushed a few strands of hair off my face. "Wow," he said, with a grin that could have melted me into a puddle.

"What?" I asked, already missing the taste of his mouth.

"You are so beautiful."

I traced a finger around his top lip, resting it on his scar. And then the events from the auditorium flooded my mind.

"What's wrong?" Ari asked, watching my eyes swell with water.

I took a rattled breath. "For a second, I thought the captain shot you and you died. It was like losing my parents all over again but a different kind of pain. Like a new spot in my heart opened up just for you, only to be taken away. I never want to have that feeling again. And I know Mondarians have rules about dating and milestones, but...I love you, Ari Novak. I love you so much."

He wiped the tears off my cheeks. "Hey, it's okay. I'm here. I'm not going anywhere." He smiled and kissed my forehead. "And I love you too, Paris Marigold...Princess Piper...Lady—"

"Just Piper is fine." I laughed through two final tears.

"I love you too, *Piper*." Ari pulled me into him for a deep kiss, then rested a warm palm on my stomach. "Is there anything else I should know about you? You don't really like hot chocolate?"

I positioned my face so close to his, that our noses nearly touched. "I performed a death-defying stunt so you wouldn't kiss Heather."

"You thought I wanted to kiss her?"

"I wasn't sure!"

His fingers played with my hair. "That doesn't count. Tell me something I don't know."

"Okay." I chewed on my bottom lip. "I performed that stunt without any sugar water."

"You mean you're just naturally that crazy?"

I nodded. "And there's one other thing."

Ari's brows raised.

"Today is my real birthday."

He grinned. "Then I'm happy to be the first one to say happy," he kissed my neck, "birthday." Ari planted a kiss in the dip of my clavicle, then lifted his head up. "Wait, how old are you?"

"Seventeen."

"And here I thought I was with an older woman." He punctuated his felicitations by picking me up off the bed and spinning me in a circle. After setting me on my feet, he pulled me into one more deep kiss. "We better get going," he said in my ear. "They'll wonder what's taking so long."

Ari helped me out the window to slowly wind our way through the courtyard, stopping to kiss occasionally in a shadow. I squealed with delight as I watched a fat snowflake land on Ari's black brow. Soon, hundreds of snowflakes fell all around us. I opened my arms and tilted my head back, welcoming the cold flecks of joy to land on my face. When we finally entered the Lounge, one of the six hearths roared with a bright yellow fire but the room was absent of court members.

"They're out back," Ari said, leading me with laced fingers.

When we stepped outside, Darden, Layla, Reese and Genevieve shouted "Happy Birthday!"

Ari's arms wrapped around me from behind and he planted a kiss on my temple. "Surprise," he whispered in my ear.

"We didn't forget you told us your real birthday is today," Darden said. "Happy birthday, Piper Parish."

Ari released me so I could give Darden and my other friends hugs. Reese and Layla handed out pieces of cake and I didn't fail to notice their shared smiles and polite chatter.

After telling my comrades the whole story of my journey to Mondaria, the group dispersed into separate conversations.

Layla placed her arm over my shoulders. "So, friends again?"

I pressed the side of my head against hers and nodded.

She removed her arm, but I stayed close to whisper, "You're talking to Reese."

She smiled. "And that's all it is—talking. But I'm guessing you and Ari were just doing more than that."

I blushed and couldn't stop the smile from stretching across my face.

She shook her head. "Oh no, Genevieve is going to—"

"Eeeek!" Genevieve squeezed her arms around my waist. "You and Ari are such a cute couple!"

Layla rolled her eyes but kept her smile.

"Thanks, Gen," I said returning a one-armed hug. "And thank you for what you said back in the auditorium. That was really kind of you."

She looked at Layla. "Can I have a second alone with Paris?"

"Piper. Her name is *Piper*." Layla shot a glare at Genevieve before heading to the group of boys.

Genevieve removed something from her coat pocket and slid it into my hand.

"Darden's notebook? But how—"

She shushed me and guided my hand into my coat pocket, hiding the notebook from anyone's view. "Heather planned to talk to the captain about the coins she found in your room and I tried to stop her. I knew who you were, but I didn't want you to get hurt. I promise, Paris, you have to believe me." Tears formed at the corner of Genevieve's eyes. "It was such a relief seeing you backstage for the Showcase because I thought you had been captured!"

"It's okay, Gen. I believe you."

"What Heather did was just awful," she said with balled fists.

I shrugged. "It was bound to happen, eventually. Heather just sped up the process." Ari caught my eyes while Reese told a story. The back of my neck tingled as our eyes locked. "I'm actually thankful for how it all worked out."

Genevieve picked up her cake plate and took a bite. "Yeah, well, her backstabbing makes it that much easier since the king dismissed her from the court."

I gasped. "What?"

Genevieve nodded. "The king turned in his dismissal list and she was the only one on it. She was kicked out while the rest of the court packed up to go home." She sighed. "So, I'm down a best friend *and* a roommate."

"I'm so sorry, Genevieve. But...what about *Darden*?" I asked in a whisper.

Genevieve sucked frosting off her fork as she gathered her thoughts, then let out an exhale. "I want you to know I didn't steal his notebook. He dropped it after sectionals one day and I just...didn't give it back to him. The trick he did for me was truly amazing. And the things he wrote about me...nobody has ever said kinder words. Not even Robert."

My heart jumped with excitement for Darden. "Genevieve, are you saying that you have feelings for—"

"What I'm saying is that I'm confused. Darden's only said maybe three words to me the whole time I've known him and I find out he's the one behind the most romantic illusion I've ever seen? I don't want to make any sort of decision that would hurt Robert...or break the heart of the boy who brought Paris to life for me," she said with a smile. "So, please don't tell him I'm the one who had it, okay?"

I nodded and hugged Genevieve, just as Darden approached.

Genevieve offered a quick smile to Darden, then scurried away to talk to Ari.

"Princess of Capalon," Darden said with a nod.

"That's me...well, *was* me."

He crossed his arms. "I'm disappointed in myself for not picking up on that detail."

I laughed. "I guess I'm a better magician than I thought. I can even make objects reappear."

His eyes widened. "Where did you find this?"

I handed him his notebook. "Backstage. You were right. Nobody read it. Otherwise I would have been arrested."

Darden rubbed his forehead and let out a long exhale. "I can't tell you how glad I am you found this."

I lowered my voice. "Still not ready to reveal yourself to the queen of hearts?"

He shook his head. "No. I've been thinking about that and she *is* taken. So, maybe there's somebody else out there who's meant for The Magnificent McCray."

"Oh, is that what we're calling you now?"

"Yeah, I figured if you get a title, I do too."

I nudged him with my elbow just as guitar chords cut through the cold air.

"Attention all Capalon Princesses-turned-Mondarian-royal-figureheads!" shouted Reese, sending a wave of laughter through our small group. "Piper, since the reason you came here in the first place was because of your mother, we thought we would share one of our Mondarian traditions with you."

Reese retrieved a tall paper lantern from under the cake table. "We have a remembrance festival every year when Mondarians light lanterns and send them into the sky, in remembrance of lost loved ones. Before we let them go, we write a message."

"Would you like to write anything before we release it?" asked Genevieve, holding up a marker.

I nodded and stepped forward to take the marker from Genevieve's hand. Before I wrote my message, I turned to face the group. "Thank you. This all means so much to me. Before I left Capalon, I was taught to think death had no meaning—that it was just an end to a life. But in a way, I believe that my mother's death gave breath to a new life—the one I have now, here with all of you."

I turned back around and the words flowed without much thinking at all:

Your love for me was the real secret message.

I found my way back into Ari's arms as Darden and Reese lit the lantern. I leaned into Ari's warm body and allowed the tears to flow freely as we all watched the glowing paper bag rise into the black sky. It drifted slowly, illuminating the nearby falling snowflakes, just as my mother had illuminated the lives of those she loved most.

Ari's lips pressed against the back of my neck.

I took a deep breath and finally, I let go.

EPILOGUE

The six of us talked into the early hours of the morning, watching the snow form a thick white blanket on the ground from inside the Lounge. One by one, our small group retreated back to their rooms, leaving Ari and me as the two who refused to leave, sharing a couch in front of one of the six hearths. Ari's arms served as my warm covers as the fire died off and the even rise and fall of his chest lulled me into a peaceful sleep.

I awoke to the sensation of Ari's fingers stroking my hair. "You should probably get back to your room before the chambermaid claims you've been kidnapped," he murmured in my ear.

I turned to sit face-to-face on the couch. "But I *was* kidnapped. And I don't want to leave my captor." I placed my hand on Ari's lightly stubbled jaw and pulled him into a kiss. He moaned in my mouth, which only made me kiss him harder.

"Lady Piper," he said between two deep kisses. "I don't want you to piss off the king and then this whole...*wonderful* arrangement is off."

I traced the outline of his lips with my finger. "Fine. But you're walking me back. And that's an order."

"Yes, ma'am." Ari smiled and kissed me one final time before we peeled ourselves from our warm cocoon on the couch. We walked hand in hand down the hall until we heard the voices of a couple of guards at the entrance of the Royal Wing.

Ari pulled me into a hug and I inhaled his scent. "See you tonight," he said.

I reluctantly released myself from his embrace and turned down the hall. I had just reached my door when the Mansion's alarm sounded.

My first instinct was to ask to Chip to connect me to the patrol channel, but that was no longer an option. I headed back to where I left Ari when a guard stopped me. "Lady Piper, you'll need to come with me."

"What's going on?" I asked as he tugged my arm. "I'm not going to run away, so I'd appreciate it if you'd release me."

The guard released my arm but picked up his pace. "Everyone else is being directed to their lockdown locations but you've been instructed to meet her in the lobby."

"Meet who?"

But before the guard could answer my question, I saw her—my sister, standing in the lobby of the Mansion with King Orson and a full set of his guards. Evelyn wore the standard Capalon high collared traveling coat and her eyes were bloodshot. She stood as if somebody carved her out of the side of a mountain.

"Your Majesty, what's going on?" Formally addressing my new king sparked a twitch under my sister's eye.

King Orson smiled and rocked back on his heels. "Evelyn wishes to speak to you and me." His eyes narrowed on my sister. "You do know that our mandate allows me to execute you right here in the lobby of my Mansion?" The king gave a nod to a nearby guard who positioned his gun behind my sister's head.

I froze with terror and Evelyn only swallowed. "Yes. But my Patrol is listening from a hovercraft above your precious Mansion and if you so much as pinch my skin, they'll drop a weapon that will kill every single person in here, myself and my sister included."

A vein in the king's forehead bulged. "You're breaking our treaty!"

"And you're holding my sister and one of my patrol officers captive." Evelyn took a step toward me.

"Don't think about touching her," said the king. "She's no longer your citizen."

The guard behind her cocked his gun, sending my stomach into a hundred twisted knots.

"And what makes you think your precious patrol officer is still alive?"

My sister's brows knitted together. "Because you would have boasted about your execution of him across all the media channels in The Lands."

King's Orson's neck reddened.

Evelyn folded her hands in front of her. "Orson Anders, I want to make a deal for my patrol officer's and sister's return."

"And what might that be?"

"I—"

A belch echoed in the tall dome of the lobby. Prince Corbin leaned over the railing of the second level, shirtless and with mussed hair. He looked at my sister with his signature amused expression. "What's the stiff doing here?"

"It's not your concern, Corbin," said the king. But the prince ignored his father and made his way down the curved staircase to our grouping.

Evelyn cleared her throat. "As I was saying, I wish to take my sister back in exchange for a Capalon product."

"And why would you want to do that?" asked the king.

Evelyn met my eyes. "Because you come back for the people you love." Her eyes bounced back to the king. "And you'll release my patrol officer without harm."

The king crossed his arms as he pondered my sister's request.

Corbin wedged his way between me and Evelyn, allowing his exposed skin to touch her coat. "You've come all the way here for your little sister? How sweet. It's not also a reason to see me again, is it?"

Again? I had never known Evelyn to interact with anyone in the Mondarian Royal Family aside from sitting in the same room with the king and queen at the Annual Assembly.

Evelyn's composure wavered, and she took a small step away

from Corbin's half-naked body. "I'd appreciate if you'd listen to your father and dismiss yourself from this confidential meeting, Corbin Anders."

He nodded. "Fine, I'll go." Then he whispered in a low voice, intended only for Evelyn but just loud enough for me to hear. "But remember last time we were together, I was dismissing *you* from *me.*"

Evelyn's pale face blushed, the rose hue running all the way to the tips of her ears. If a stranger observed her, they would think she was livid with Corbin's presence and suggestive words.

But I knew my sister. I had been the cause of her highest level of anger, witnessing her balled fists, creased brows and rigid back numerous times—but never once did her face change color.

"And welcome to the kingdom, Lady Piper." Prince Corbin lifted my hand to his lips and wrapped my fingers around something cylindrical and cold. His eyes held onto mine, and for a brief moment, seriousness wiped the smugness clean from his face. "We know how to throw a good party." He winked before he released my hand and headed back to the staircase.

The king's baritone voice filled the lobby. "I don't want any of your products, Evelyn. My kingdom has survived this long without them. What I do want, is your presence at my next dinner where Lady Piper will attend as my youngest son's guest. You'll admit your sister's defiance of her kingdom and you'll attend as Corbin's guest."

I was to attend a Mansion dinner as Prince Taran's guest? *Layla's* Taran?

"I'll do no such thing," Evelyn said. "I refuse to admit anything on behalf of my sister and I'm a matched woman to King Xavier Demetrios. I will not allow you to make a mockery of the Queen and Princess of Capalon at your event." Her fists tightened into those familiar balls.

"You no longer have a princess!" shouted the king, his voice nearly knocking me to the ground. "She is *my* citizen and Head Lady of *my* court. I can swear to only go as far as to introduce you at the dinner, but how I choose to present Lady Piper is my choice. If you go through with the event, then we can discuss your sister's return, but only then."

Evelyn's spine went rigid. "I request the protection of my Patrol at the event."

"No."

"You have your whole house full of armed guards and I will have nothing. It doesn't seem like a fair deal to me, Orson."

King Orson's nostrils flared. "You can have *one* Patrol guard escort you. But if you do anything during my dinner, other than sit and eat, I'll make sure that you never see your sister again."

If glares could kill, both Evelyn and King Orson would have collapsed on the marble floor. The silence was disrupted by somebody clearing their throat above us.

"I think you've made our new dinner guests feel very welcome, Pop," said Corbin, leaning over the railing. "Don't let my little brother bore you to sleep, Lady Piper. And see you again soon, *Evelyn*."

My sister ignored the prince and focused her attention on me. "I'll do whatever it takes to bring you back home." Then she was escorted out of the Mansion, leaving me in a state of shock.

I walked into a vacant hallway, then opened my palm to see an indigo glass bottle.

"What is that?" asked Ari, emerging from the shadows of the hallway.

I unscrewed the cap and inhaled—the scent instantly relaxed my muscles. Not an imposter, but the real, original recipe. "The last memory of my mother."

And the one thing that held my sister and me together—she hadn't destroyed it after all.

But if what they said was true about Prince Corbin's affinity for magic, his unannounced stance by my sister was no mistake. He lifted the vial from her as a planned move. She would have known the king wouldn't allow her to get close enough to me, so somehow, she had communicated to Corbin before entering the Mansion.

"Ari," I whispered, "I think Prince Corbin is secretly working for my sister."

"Wow, that's crazy," Ari said, running a hand through his black hair.

"No, the crazy thing is..." I could barely speak the words, not truly believing them myself. But the image of Evelyn's face in the last Assembly photo resurfaced as I put the pieces together about not what, but *who* had given her red cheeks and the urge to laugh.

There was a reason I couldn't locate the king in the last photo— because someone else represented the kingdom in his place. I stopped and looked at Ari as a rush of adrenaline swept through my veins. "I think my sister has feelings for Prince Corbin."

ACKNOWLEDGMENTS

First, I'd like to thank YOU, the reader, for giving the King's 100 a try! I hope you lost yourself in Piper's story for at least a moment to escape the real world — this is what reading does for me and what I hoped the King's 100 would do for my readers. I'd like to thank the team at Immortal Works Press for giving this story a home and turning a long Google doc into a real, gorgeous book. BIG thanks to my acquisitions editor, Rachel Huffmire, for being the first stranger to tell me that she 'melted' after reading a scene from the manuscript. Not everyone is as lucky to have an award-winning author as their mentor and friend. Thank you to John Olsen, editor extraordinaire, who is probably cringing while reading this acknowledgments section — you are a magician and Darden McCray would be very impressed with your work. Since becoming a published author, I've jumped into the world of social media, so thank you to all my followers and especially to my 'Court Members' who have helped to share book covers and release information — many many hearts and prayer-hand emojis to you all. Thanks to Camille Millar for my lovely website header and to Morgan Frank for bringing Ari and Piper to life through your stunning artwork. Shout out to my fellow #Roaring20sdebut authors — you are all so talented and I'm honored to be in this debut year with you. Thank you to all my mom friends for helping me stay sane through hard times being a mom and a writer — the isolation is too much for even Queen Elsa to handle at times. Thank you to the best Roundtable critique group a girl could ask for — Mary Kate Varnau, Danny Coleman, Gracia Gillund, Joe Cameron and Tony. You deserve all the hot chocolate and Dan's pastries Mondaria can offer. Thank you, Malina, for being a forever friend and inspiration — one of us became a police officer and the other writes YA novels, so we're obviously like the same person. ;) Thank you to my 'sisters-in-song,' who still sing with me and keep me young at heart when the time allows. Thank you to my in-laws, parents and family members for jumping in to help with childcare so I could write. Thank you to my big sister for reading her first YA romance and not hating it. I'd like to thank my parents for supporting my interest in singing in sequins and traveling to high school show choir competitions, college performances and community choir concerts. I'm not on Broadway, but my experience in various performance groups is what inspired this book, so you never know where your interests will take you! Thank you to anyone who offered their encouragement during my time writing this book — a positive word can go a long way for a doubtful writer/new mom. And finally, thank you to my number one fan/best critique partner/father of my children and favorite black-haired drummer, Tony. We are my favorite friends-to-lovers trope.

<3 Karin

ABOUT THE AUTHOR

 Karin earned her bachelor's degree in Hospitality and Tourism Management from Purdue University and served as an event planner for two Big 10 universities and various non-profits for over eight years before becoming a stay-at-home-mom. She enjoys chocolate-covered peanuts, uninterrupted sleep and singing with other people. Karin lives in Ohio with her husband, daughter, cat and dog.

This has been an
Immortal Production

CPSIA information can be obtained
at www.ICGtesting.com
Printed in the USA
LVHW031437210221
679584LV00009B/597